EDENHOPE

EDENHOPE

FRANCIS JOHN SIMCOCK

YOUCAXTON PUBLICATIONS

OXFORD & SHREWSBURY

Contents

PART ONE

ONE

Return: *Stephen*

I did not dream of a return to Edenhope, last night or any other. But it was starting to read *Rebecca,* again, and that evocative first line, that sent me back there, after a near-lifetime of avoiding it. Not that the house is or was anything like Daphne du Maurier's Manderley. It is not "grand" like the abandoned mansion she once discovered and from which her imagination carved the central features of her novel. There is no curving staircase down which an anxious young wife descends to wreak havoc with her husband's already-doomed peace of mind; nor, being a hundred miles from the sea, a beach where the doom was engendered; not even a sweeping driveway. Edenhope was the absolute opposite; a gloomy labrynth of low-ceilinged rooms and passages. But during the time I was there, and in my memory and imagination since, it seemed to exercise a power of its own, over the minds and actions of the people fated to inhabit it. Even the rambling garden, well kept as it was, and the farm buildings and barns seemed to share the atmosphere. Perhaps it was all my imagination. Perhaps it was the people, not the house. Perhaps it was those awful events, that ruined all our lives as we then knew them, and could not do other than drive me away, and, at that time, never want to see it again.

It was fifty years – half a century – since I had been inside, or set eyes on it, except at a distance fleetingly, when I drove up, on a pleasant September afternoon, warm enough to wear only a light sweater with the top of the car down. I saw no other vehicle, nor indeed any other person, after leaving the main highway and taking to the two miles of single track road climbing through beautiful woods of ash, beech and oak, descending briefly and climbing again to the tiny hamlet – six other houses – marked as Edenhope on the ordnance map. I had to pass the cottages as I neared the house itself, and cars standing outside indicated that at least three were occupied. They had been expanded, most doubled in size from the years when they housed farmhands and their families. The other three had been renovated and extended, but on a more modest scale. The one I knew best, from childhood years, was one of those.

I parked on the wide grass verge opposite the house, no more than thirty yards from the front door, and got out to look over the wooden double gates. There was only a small part of the garden on this side – the biggest part ran round the end and on to the back, between the house and the buildings. What I could see looked bedraggled and run down. Grass on the once-immaculate lawns was a foot high, tangled and brown. The rambling roses were still there, climbing over two trees that I could see, but a pergola that had supported others was leaning drunkenly, held up only by the climbers themselves and the wild vegetation invading the whole area. The drive, which ran from the gates and round to the back of the house, with an arm branching to the right along the front, was half obliterated by grass and weeds.

The house itself, seen from this point, did not appear to be in bad repair. The whole length of the slate roof looked sound, as did the stone wall, and the porch, small but resembling a church entrance in having seats each side; and "our" front door. Paint was peeling, from all the windows I could see, and some of the frames seemed to be rotting, but there was no glass missing from any of the six-sided panes.

I walked through the gates, along the drive and round the house. It was a similar story everywhere. There was a back drive, in rather better shape than the one at the front, leaving the road a hundred yards further on and serving the farm buildings and the rear of the house. I tried several of the doors in the buildings. Some were locked or jammed but others opened to reveal musty emptyness apart from the odd crumbled bale of hay or straw, a sack or two, in one two pairs of overalls hanging on nails and almost smothered in dust. In another, a rat scuttled through a wooden partition. There was an archway which had also served as an engine-house and led to the rick-yard, where there was evidence of the most recent occupation, in the form of a large open cattle shed, with concrete block walls about five feet high and an asbestos sheet roof; and two bays of the double dutch barn were full of hay and straw. The barns were still standing on their steel columns, but one or two corrugated iron sheets from their roofs were lying on the ground, adding to the air of dereliction. The only occupant of the barn was an ancient combine harvester that did not look as though it had been moved for a score of years. I wondered if I knew whoever had driven it there.

The cattle yard was empty but there was some evidence that it had been occupied. I walked beyond it and looked down the sloping fields. They appeared, from what I could see, to be farmed and cared for, hedges cut, other fences in stockproof order. Some distance away I could see sheep. Beyond, I could see across a wide valley to the Clee Hills, one of the views that always had me catching my throat whenever I returned to Shropshire.

I returned to the car via the other end of the house, the manorial end as it had been, and looked through two or three of the big windows. There was still some furniture, some of it sheeted over. I did not attempt to peer through *that* window, even now I just could not bear to witness the scene, but went on through the garden, or rather gardens. There must have been more than an acre, all in the same abandoned state. Rabbits bolted before my approach. But there was still plenty of evidence of the toil and care that had once produced those roses, clematis, hollyhocks and a myriad other blooms and, in one part, the vegetables that had helped feed a dozen inhabitants. Not loving care, though. Little had been done with love, in and around Edenhope.

A woman of near my own age was walking up the road past the cottages, stopping to put a golden retriever on a lead as she reached me.

"Hello," she said. She seemed a nice lady.

"Good afternoon. A lovely day."

"Yes. And you're making the best of it, in that beautiful car."

"I don't often get the chance to have the top down."

"Come far?"

"Not very far, today."

She looked at me, asking the question. I knew what it was, but did not answer.

"You've been looking round the farm. It's in a state, isn't it?"

"To tell the truth, it's not as bad as I thought it might be. Nobody's been living there for a dozen years or so, have they?"

"Not since we've been here, and that's ten years next month." And she put words to the question.

"Are you thinking of buying it, perhaps?"

When I again did not answer, but looked once more at the house, she added: "I'm sorry, to seem so... nosy... but all of us up here wish something could be done with it. It's not right for a place like that to stay empty for so long. Even if it was split up..."

"No."

"Have you been here before? Sorry, being nosy again."

"A long time ago."

She was embarrassed. No doubt she had heard something of what had happened, and connected me with it. "I'm sorry. I shouldn't pry," she said.

"It's alright. I only wanted to see what it was all like nowadays. Do you like it up here?"

"Oh, yes. I think we all do. We wish something could be done with *that,* though."

"Has everyone here bought the houses they live in?"

"Yes, we were the latest, ten years ago. We did a lot to it. It hadn't even got a bathroom."

She seemed such a nice lady, I could happily have gone on talking to her. But it might have led to questions that raised ghosts better left undisturbed. I said goodbye and drove away.

TWO

Arrival

Stephen was seven and Elspeth three years younger when they and their mother first arrived at Edenhope, in a taxi from the little station at Maestonbury, on a miserable, damp day at the end of September, 1937. They would have walked, as they walked many times afterwards, but for the amount of luggage Rachael had kept with her because she would not trust it to the mercies of the removal men.

They got there an hour and a half before the furniture and her husband, who was travelling with it, and who had kept the key because he thought he would be there first. It meant they could not get into the cottage. They were tired and hungry, a cold drizzle was falling and Elspeth would not stop crying. Rachael decided to walk to the farm to see if there was a spare key.

The three, already bedraggled, went round to what seemed to be the back door of the house and she knocked. No-one answered. She looked further along the house, saw another door, and knocked again. This time a girl, the kitchen maid she learned later, answered. Rachael explained who she was and asked if there was a spare key. The girl left them standing outside and shouted to someone else: "It's the new bailiff's missus. 'Er canna get into the cottage an' 'er's askin' if there's another key." The response was another voice asking "How should I know?" and an older woman appeared, dressed like the girl in a wrap-round pinafore.

"'Anna you got a key, then?" Rachael explained again. The woman said: "Well, that inna very good management, is it. What do you think I can do about it?"

"Well, we thought perhaps there was a spare, somewhere. We need to get in so we can get a fire going and a bit of food, if we can. We don't know how long the men will be."

The woman said: "Well, there's no spare key here. If there is, it'll be in the master's study and I darena go rootin' in there. An' 'er's away an' it's the maid's day off."

Rachael, although put out by what seemed to be an unhelpful reception which made her uninclined to ask for any favours, could not leave the children out in the rain for she did not know how long. She asked: "Is there somewhere we could shelter until my husband comes with the furniture?"

"Well, I suppose you could stop in 'ere a bit. I'll bring a couple o' chairs out o' the kitchen. I darena ask you any further. If 'er come back there'd be 'ell to pay."

"Here" was a cold, cheerless back entrance lobby about ten feet square, with wellington boots and other outdoor footwear along one side of a blue brick floor, various items of clothing hung from pegs. The modern farmer's wife would no doubt call it the dirty boot room. The woman and the girl each brought a wooden chair, and she said: "I'm sorry I canna take you into the kitchen, but 'er played merry 'ell the last time an' you never know when er'll come back. I suppose you wouldna say no to a cup o' tea, though. We're just goin' to 'ave ours, so one more won't matter."

"Thank you very much, Mrs...?" She had seen the woman's wedding ring.

"Marchett. Violet. You'll be livin' close to us. My Ted's the wagoner." She left them, returning moments later with tea, a cup and saucer for Rachael and small mugs for the children, and milk and sugar.

She said: "If I'd 'ad the key with me you could 'a gone to my 'ouse for a bit. But we leave it there so Ted an' Geoffrey – that's our lad – can get in for their dinner when I'm 'ere."

Rachael thanked her, and she returned to the kitchen and work, whatever it was. They drank the tea, and she gave the children some of the biscuits she had stowed in her bag, at the same time keeping an ear open for any sign of the lorry with the furniture. Elspeth stopped crying. Her mother kept watching the weather, and when it stopped raining she decided to get back to the cottage and wait there. She shouted through the door leading into the house: "Hello, Mrs Marchett" and the girl appeared. Rachael told her what she was doing, thanked her for the tea, and set off. Stephen was glad to get away. He did not like the place.

Before they reached the cottage, they heard the lorry climbing up the lane. It stopped outside and Edgar climbed out.

"Have you been here long?" he asked. She told him.

"We didna manage that very well, did we," he said. "I thought we'd be here about the same time."

"Never mind, love. We're here now. Open up and I'll see what I can do about a fire and some food."

The cottage's kitchen-cum-living room felt as cold and dank as the lobby at the big house, but Rachael was grateful that it had been left clean. Edgar, the lorry's owner-driver, and his young mate immediately set about bringing in the kitchen furniture, which had been loaded last so was the first to come off. In the meantime Rachael had found paper, sticks and coal from small amounts left in an outhouse, and lit a fire in the small open range. Soon they unearthed a primus stove, methylated spirit and paraffin to boil a kettle and make tea.

"There's a tea chest with bread and things at the back of the wagon," she told him. "If you'll bring that in I'll get us all something to eat while you carry on unloading. You won't have to hang about, or we'll be in the dark. Bring the lamps in as soon as you can."

Frank, the driver, joked to his mate: "I can see who wears the britches in this house."

§

Frank was right, although only up to a point. Edgar Topham was a good practical farmer as far as stockmanship and knowledge of cultivation was concerned, but the leader in family matters, and indeed business, was his wife, even though she was eight years younger. It was a great pity that he only married her when his financial fortunes were already almost beyond repair even with the help of her energy and resourcefulness.

He inherited the tenancy of the 160-acre Eaton Home Farm, on the border of Staffordshire and Cheshire, on which he had been brought up, when his own father died near the end of the 1920s and he was already 32 years old, and unmarried. He was a popular figure in the village, a good footballer nearing professional standard, secretary of the men's institute, and a proficient shot who enjoyed the occasional day out with the guns, when he was invited by the landlord. An easy and natural charm, and his sporting abilities, meant he got on with most, men as well as women, and although he had never been a great reader, he was intelligent and au fait with current affairs. And he was good looking with grey eyes that twinkled readily, and an abundance of dark, silky hair. Balancing all these features however was another – he had at that stage little drive or business initiative, probably as a result of never having had to develop any.

His father also bequeathed to him a housekeeper, Mrs Brownlow, a lady of his own years who local people always suspected of really being Mrs Topham in every way that mattered. Edgar always maintained that there was nothing of the sort between them, but his father left the lady all he had, apart from what was in the bank for running the farm, which was not much, it soon became obvious. Also, she and Edgar never got on, why those who knew them both never quite understood, but the result was that within a year she had departed to live with a daughter and he was left on his own apart from a young live-in worker and a middle-aged lady, wife of his other employee, who came in daily to clean and prepare his and the men's midday meal.

His elder sister Ida, married to a prosperous farmer and cattle breeder ten miles away in Cheshire, suggested this was no way for her brother to live. She saw him as perfectly marriageable, in fact there had been two occasions when he had been "going out" with young ladies, either of whom, in her opinion, would have made him a fully acceptable wife. Aunt Ida did not know for sure, she told Stephen many years later, but she strongly suspected that their father had vetoed both of them, probably because he thought they were from families not good enough for his son.

Stephen never knew his grandfather, but Edgar had a framed photograph of him and his grandmother, which hung on the stairs in their Edenhope homes. He had a severely-cut white beard and gave the impression of having never smiled in his life. His wife, who died years before, looked a pleasant lady, in a long black dress, and a Mona Lisa-ish half smile on her face which Stephen always interpreted as a look of patient resignation. The picture stayed with him all his life, and although it suffered through being relegated to one loft or another, he was able to get a good copy made when that kind of memory started to become important.

His Aunt Ida was again his source of information for what happened next. She told him, amongst other things, one day when she suspected she did not have unlimited time on earth, after one of their talks about his mother.

"I told your dad I knew what had happened over those two girls," she said. "I told him he shouldn't have given in the way he did and he should start going out again so he'd meet more people – I meant young women. But I didn't reckon on it happening the way it did.

"I didn't go with your uncle on cattle-showing trips very often, but one was at Ashbourne, about two years after your grandad died, which would be a twelvemonth or so after old Mrs Brownlow left. He was dropping me off at Eaton while he went to the show. We went to the back door and I opened it and shouted for your dad. I didn't expect to find him in the house, and I thought it was probably too early for Mrs Broad to be there – it was only half-past nine. But you could have knocked me down with a feather when this young woman came out of the kitchen, and asked if I was looking for Mr Topham. I said I was his sister, Mrs Maginness, and before I could ask who *she* was she said 'Oh, good morning, ma'am. I'm Rachael. I've come to be Mr Topham's housekeeper. P'raps you didn't know about me. I've only been here a week.' It was your mother, of course. Your uncle was as taken aback as I was. Your mum was a bonny lass, looked about nineteen, although of course she was actually twenty-three or four, I think, at that time. She didn't look at all the sort to be housekeeper to a youngish man, though. Anyway, your uncle said he'd have to leave me, he'd see me about five o'clock, and I was left with your mum for most of the day. We got on well from the start, but more than that I could see she'd got a bit of something about her. She couldn't stop to talk to me much, she'd got a lot to do, but I helped her a bit and in between she told me about herself, how she'd been left on her own when the grandparents you never knew were killed in the crash with the train, and she'd been put in a home – more like a workhouse, it sounded – and then put out to service when she was fourteen, as a laundrymaid at Eaton Hall, and ended up as a parlourmaid there. I don't know exactly how she came to the job with your father. She just said she'd been told he wanted a housekeeper and she went to see him, but I think there must have been a bit more to it than that. But when him and the men came in for their dinner I soon saw there was every chance she'd end up as a lot more than housekeeper. An' I wondered what your grandad would have made of that!

"Anyhow, I liked her, as I said, and I got your uncle to bring me over as often as he could so I could see how things were progressing. He was my little brother, after all. My first impression, that she was a young woman with a lot of character and common sense, never left me. She'd brought a few books with her, good ones, no trash, and I picked up enough from talking to her to see she'd read them. There was *Pilgrims Progress,* and *A Tale of Two Cities,* and books of poetry, and *Jane Eyre,* and *Pride and Prejudice* that I remember especially, and one about Marco Polo, and a big book called *History of England.* Oh, and a book of John Wesley's preachings. Not that she was especially religious, but she wanted to know what great writers and thinkers thought and said, she told me once. I also saw *Black Beauty* and those books by that American woman – *Little Women* was one, wasn't it – on her shelf, and they all added up to my idea of the sort of girl she was.

"She'd been there about eight or nine months when she told me she was going to have a baby, and she and your dad were going to be married, and they were, very quietly, in Eaton Church, with me and your uncle and the girls the only other folk there, although Mrs

Broad and the men came for the meal, afterwards. The baby – that was you of course – was born four or five months later.

"Oh, Stephen, I wish your dad had met her ten years before, although she'd have been too young to be married then. I'm sure she'd have managed to keep the farm steady, and things might have turned out very different. As it was, I think it had gone too far already.

"You see, your grandad left all his money to that woman. Every time there was a bit to spare in the bank he put it into his investments, which went to her. There wasn't that much, but what there was would have made things a lot easier for your dad. As it was, all he got was the stock and the implements. There wasn't even enough for the wages and the housekeeping, never mind the rent, until the milk cheque went in, and it meant he started out in the red, although the estate were very good, I believe, and let him have time.

"Your mum soon caught on to what the situation was, and came up with ideas for making a bit extra. She got him to buy a couple of Jersey cows so she could have the cream from the milk to make into butter without the dairy complaining that the milk sent there was below standard. Then she went and stood the market at Leek with the butter and eggs, and used the money for housekeeping so your dad didn't have to give her so much. She'd saved a few pounds from her own wages at The Hall and she went to a pig breeder and bought two Wessex Saddleback sows so the litters could be sold for breeding. And she learned to milk, to take the place of one of the milkers who left.

"Really they should have got on well, and prospered. But when you were about two, she had a miscarriage, which knocked her about, and then went down with pneumonia which stopped her doing anything for months, and meant they had to have help in the house. Then that awful Johnes Disease. That was the killer. We never knew where it came from, your dad hadn't bought any new cows since he took over. But they lost five or six in a year. The dairy tests showed infected milk and they had to have all the cows tested, and slaughter half a dozen more. They'd no option but to give up. Your grandad wanted shooting, leaving it all to that woman. No, I don't mean that really.

But he should have put his own flesh and blood first. If your dad could have had half of what went to her it would have seen him through that bad time, I reckon.

"You might ask 'couldn't you and Uncle Arthur help at all?' "…. Stephen interupted: "I wouldn't ask that, Aunt Ida"…. But she continued: "Well, we should have. The thing we ought to have done, at the beginning, was offer your dad a long term loan to make up for the capital he didn't get from your grandfather. But we didn't know he needed it until it was too late. And I don't think he'd have taken it. That was one of his problems. He didn't have an eye for business. Rachael – your mum – would have seen it as a sensible business idea, but she was too proud to think of asking us. We did help when you moved to Hooley Bank. Not with money directly, but we did a lot of things that saved them money, like transporting the animals, and your uncle slipped a couple of good in-calf heifers in with your dad's own stock.

"It didn't work though. Thirty acres of hill land and ten cows wasn't a living. Your mum had complications when Elspeth was born and she was no good for anything for weeks. Your dad was working all the hours God sent and a lot he didn't, especially after he took that forestry job. The farm, such as it was, barely held its own, moneywise. When your mum got better she helped do the milking and the outside work. But they couldn't go on like that. Your dad was getting up before five to do the milking, then walking two miles to his work, then starting again when he got home. And it wasn't as though he was a youngster, after all, although he'd always been fit and strong."

Ida, who had been reeling it all off quite steadily, stopped as though she had come to something she did not want to talk about. Stephen wanted to know, though. At seven years old, he had known nothing about the money side, except that there was not much of it. His friends at school, to which he had to walk nearly two miles, with neighbours' slightly older children, who often had pocket money and bought sweets at the village shop, but he never had even a few coppers. But now, all those years later, he wanted to know, desperately, how they came to end up as they did. After a few moments' silence, he had to ask.

"So what happened? I mean, I know we went to Shropshire, to Edenhope. But why there? Nearly a hundred miles away?"

His aunt said: "I'm sorry, Stephen. I wish it hadn't happened. I really do wish it hadn't happened. It was our fault. We were trying to help, but I wish we'd kept away and left your mum and dad to sink or swim on their own. It couldn't have been worse. And they'd have pulled through, together."

The old lady turned her head away, and went quiet. But after a few moments she started to talk again.

"Your uncle was selling some cattle to the man at Edenhope, Unston. He'd never met him – being a member of parliament and quite a landowner, he was a bit outside our circles. It was through Tom Pierce, who had some other business dealings with Mr Unston, and got to know he wanted to start dairying at his home farm, where he lived when he wasn't in London. Tom told him your uncle would be the man to supply him with enough good cows to get his dairying going, and Unston came up to see us and look at the farm and the stock.

"Your uncle didn't like him, especially the way he spoke to his chauffeur, and looked down his nose at everything round him, but he had to do business with a lot he didn't like, so he just got on with it. The man was after twenty cows, as many as we'd sell in six months, usually, more than your uncle liked to let go at once, and probably more to come, so he couldn't afford to worry about whether he liked him or not. And he hardly quibbled over the price, only insisted that it should include delivering them to Edenhope, which amounted to a good big quibble, really. It cost quite a lot, even in those days, to transport twenty cows seventy miles. And he didn't want them for another few weeks because he was getting rid of his bailiff and he'd no dairyman yet. Arthur said that was the expression he used – 'getting rid.' The man knew nothing about dairying so he was getting rid of him.

"We should have seen it as a warning, Stephen. It should have shown us the sort of man he was. But instead your uncle thought he saw a way to p'raps help your mum and dad. He asked Unston whether he wanted a new bailiff, and when he said he did, but hadn't been able to find anybody locally who knew about dairying, Arthur told him he knew somebody who'd fill the bill. Mr Unston I suppose could see that your uncle knew what he was doing and the outcome was that he said that while he was in the area he'd go and see your dad. I can just imagine what the neighbours thought when they saw this posh car drive up at Hooley Bank. Or what the chauffeur thought about where he was driving to, for that matter.

"Your dad wasn't there. He was working in the forest, so Unston only saw your mum, and little Elspeth. I don't know for sure what happened that day, but I'm certain as I can be it was then he decided. It was your mum he wanted. I'm sorry to be saying such things to you, Stephen, and I could be wrong. P'raps it was later that those kind of thoughts came into his mind. It was years before... But I don't think so. I think I was proved right. And he wouldn't have more or less told her the job would be your dad's if he wanted it, and asked her to get him to go down to Edenhope and see him, expenses paid, when he'd never even met him, if something like that hadn't been the case. I wish she'd told him what he could do with his expenses. And his job."

THREE

Skeletons

A unt Ida, always close to her brother's family, even when she only saw them infrequently, was the source of most of Stephen's knowledge of what happened over the next few years at Edenhope. He witnessed much at first hand, but he was too young to grasp the real significance of events as they unfolded in the family's first years there.

Although Edgar had never been in paid employment before, apart from the forestry work he had done when he and Rachael were at Hooley Bank, the financial anxieties they had suffered in recent years had made them ready to accept the situation of no longer being their own bosses in return for a regular income. The cottage at Edenhope was much smaller than the Eaton farmhouse but as big as Hooley Bank and more comfortable. They did not miss electricity because they had never had it, likewise a hot water system, but cold water was on tap, piped from the farm's borehole supply, which had not been the case at Hooley where it had to be pumped, by hand, from an outside well. Mr Unston had promised a bathroom, and electricity would be with them in two years, although it was in fact delayed by the war and did not arrive until 1946, a circumstance used by Unston as an excuse for holding back on the cottage improvements.

Edgar by no means fell in love with his prospective employer at their only meeting before he actually moved to Edenhope. He did not like the way he called him "Topham" even on first acquaintance. And he clearly expected obseqiousness, although on that occasion he stopped short of actually insisting on being called "sir." On the plus side however Unston made much of the importance he attached to the job. Edgar would be much more manager of the farm than the old bailiff, because he, Unston, now spent most of his time in London. In fact, without getting down from the high horse he always mounted when talking to subordinates, Jasper gave the impression that he wanted Edgar to take the position. He asked – told would be a more accurate description of the invitation – the potential employee to join him for lunch, where the two of them were waited on by a good-looking, young-middle-aged woman in a black dress, who Unston seemed to speak to familiarly but was clearly not his wife, Edgar thought. And where he explained what had brought him to the idea of a dairy herd.

"My wife wants to have some Jerseys," he said. "She thinks they're pretty. But they tell me they don't make any money."

Afterwards a worker was summoned to take them round most of the farm's four hundred acres on a trailer towed by its only tractor at that date. Harvest was coming to an end and the binder, as the reaping machine was called, was cutting the last field, drawn by two of the farm's eight horses. Unston introduced him to the driver, Mrs Marchett's husband Ted, and told him this was "Mr Topham, who I hope will be coming to manage the farm for me." In another field, wheat was being carted and stacked under the direction of a man who had been made temporary foreman.

It was a Wednesday when the Tophams arrived at Edenhope. Mr Unston had told Edgar to take the first few days getting to know all the dozen workers and have a good look round the farm's 400 acres then meet him on Saturday for the first of their regular weekend briefings, as Unston called them. He also had to eye over the dairy that was under construction, and the conversion of some of the buildings to make them suitable for milk cows, with pipes to carry the vacuum needed for the milking machines, and an engine and pump to create the vacuum. This part of the work was new to Edgar, but the firm supplying the equipment sent a technician who lodged in the Unston Arms at Maestonbury. The cows supplied by his brother-in-law Arthur would arrive a month later.

It did not take Edgar long to discover that his first doubts about his employer's personality were well founded. Freed from the financial anxieties which had beset him at Eaton, the new bailiff quickly got to grips with the running of a large farm, and after a few weeks, Unston left it very much to him. Indeed he had little option, because he was away a great deal. But the man's intrinsic colours, never hidden unless their concealment was required by some particular ulterior motive, almost immediately began to show in their personal dealings. He would not tolerate dissent, even on quite minor matters. He had once told James Wadham, Edgar's predecessor: "If I say black's white, Wadham, black's white." He did not go quite so far with Topham, for there *was* an ulterior motive in his case. But his manner was always domineering, and if any of his idiosyncracies came under threat by anything Edgar did on the farm, he would be distinctly unpleasant.

One such instance came the following spring, after the establishment of the dairy, when Edgar started a system of splitting two of the nearer grass fields into small paddocks so that the cows only grazed them for a few days before being moved on, giving the sward a chance to recover. He had read of the idea, the forerunner of the later system of strip grazing using electric fences, in one of the farming journals and put it to Unston who told him, almost disinterestedly. "I don't like the sound of it, Topham. But you can give it a try."

Jasper was away for the next four weeks, however, and when he came back four paddocks had been fenced and the cows were grazing the third. Unston immediately embarked on a tour of inspection. Edgar did not know he had returned and was at home having his lunch – it was a Saturday – when a young servant girl from the house knocked on the door and told him: "The master wants yer – 'mediately, he said. E's in his study." Rachael said: "Finish your dinner, love. He can wait that long." Edgar obeyed to the extent of clearing his plate but said he did not want any pudding and went off to the house and Unston's study, their usual meeting place, only to be told the master was not there – he was outside. He went to the dairy first, thinking that was the most likely place to find him, inspecting progress, but he was not there either. He then tried the gardens, and the small front fields where were grazing the half dozen Jersey cows demanded by Mrs Unston, with the same result, before turning to the new paddocks which were next to the rick yard.

"Where the hell have you been, Topham? I told the girl I wanted to see you immediately," Unston rapped at him.

"Sorry, sir, she said you were in the study. I've been looking for you."

"You might have known I was looking at this bloody mess, man. What did you think you were doing? Get those fences down immediately. They must be gone when I come back again on Friday."

"You did say I could try them, sir."

"Don't argue with me, Topham. And don't ever let me see such an ugly mess again. All that barbed wire! Where'd you get it from?"

"Most of it was already here, in the yard; and the posts. I had to get a bit of new stuff."

"Send it back. And if they won't have it, I shall take it out of your pay. I never saw such a mess. Whatever were you thinking of?"

Sighing inwardly, for he had explained the principle of paddock grazing when he had put the project to Unston in the first place, Edgar said: "I thought it was a better way of making use of the grass. We could probably keep the cows on two thirds of the grass they'd need otherwise."

"You're talking rubbish, Topham. And anyway, I don't like it and I won't have it."

"The paddocks are only the same size as the little one at the front where the Jerseys are, sir."

"Do as you're told and get rid of them, Topham. I don't like them. Now, come indoors and we'll go through what else has been going on."

The incident was typical of the man. Although he allowed Edgar to run the farm without too much interference, in aspects of the management that really mattered, he habitually gave an impression of being degrees above him and insisting on being regarded as such. He was not only saying "I am a superior being," nineteenth century style, but implying that even if Edgar's knowledge and intellect was as good as or better than his own, that was irrelevant. "I am superior to you in all the things that matter and you must always, always, accept that what I say is right" was not only a grown-up version of a school bully's playground tactics, it was the way upper class snobbery manifested itself in those individuals who, like Unston, thought it was their due and their right. Edgar, targeted as he had been by the slings and arrows of financial misfortune, and never having found within himself an ability to launch a meaningful counter-attack, could only deal with the bully like a hedgehog deals with a tormentor. He rolled himself up in the skin of what really mattered to him – doing a good job in farming terms and being grateful that his wife and family could now be well fed and clothed. To himself, and occasionally to Rachael, he would laugh quietly at some of Unston's ridiculous utterances. Putting up with his employer's hectoring manner was a price worth paying, he concluded. Life as a tenant farmer had been by no means free of restrictions and impositions from above. He could do nothing but watch when the hunt ran roughshod through his crops; he was not allowed to use barbed wire for fear of injury to the horses; and was forbidden to sell hay when he had a surplus. And he and his family were now better off financially than at any time since he and Rachael married. He could not personally like his employer, but as he found he was left largely alone in terms of running the farm, by the end of his first year at Edenhope he had come to the conclusion that life all round was better than it had been for years.

Rachael was also content to accept her bread as it was now buttered. The first few months at Edenhope occupied her fully in making the cottage into a pleasant home. Though smaller, it was as good in practically every respect as Eaton, and better than Hooley Bank. There had been no piped hot water system at either, and not even cold water at Hooley. A nightly bath for the children had to be given in a mini-tub on a special little deal table, made by Edgar, in front of the kitchen fire, with water heated in a kettle and a large pan. Bathing for herself and her husband could only be weekly, in one of the bigger tin baths seen hanging on cottage walls in those days, also in front of the fire with water heated in the washing copper in the outhouse; with a flannel-down at other times, unless Edgar had been involved in some especially dirty operations.

The sale of their stock, and equipment, had left them with a few hundred pounds but she and Edgar, on her initiative, had decided it should stay in the bank, intact, earning a little interest, and their spending should be kept within the bounds of his wages, paid weekly in cash. But as soon as she had a little spare, she would take off to

Ludstone or Cravenbury, walking the two miles to the station or bus stop, carrying or leading Elspeth after leaving a cold lunch on the table for Edgar. She always went on one market day or the other, for that was where she could find the best bargains in curtain material, or hearth rugs, or clothes for them all. Food was bought, in those days, from the butcher's, baker's and grocery vans which called weekly. Often she would also bring a volume or two from a second hand book stall. Occasionally a toy for Elspeth or Stephen. And once, oh joy of joys, a little-used Meccano set.

(Years later, Stephen told his own sons, he remembered a master at his school amusing the boys with a probably justifiable rant about the advertising industry's attempts to brainwash potential customers: "Meccano," the teacher scoffed. "'Buy your son a Meccano set and make him an engineer!' Bah! You're more likely to make your son into an engineer if you give him a kick in the pants." Old Tommy Jeffrey's scepticism might have been well based, in principle. But Stephen was sure that his own lifelong fascination with engineering and science stemmed at least partly from that little construction set, presented with such loving delight by his mother. Although perhaps there was also something in the genes, for Edgar always liked making things.)

Home comforts dealt with, Rachael began to be ready to direct some of her energies towards fresh fields She was only 32, and although the struggles at Eaton and Hooley Bank had exhausted her, by the time Stephen was halfway through his ninth year, and Elspeth was at school, she was starting to want something more to do besides running her home, full time job though that was, in 1938 when washing machines, vacuum cleaners, electric irons and cookers were no more than items on most countrywomens'wish list; tumble dryers were only on the cusp of invention, and microwaves more than a world war away.

§

When Aunt Ida told Stephen that she thought there was "a bit more to it" than Rachael simply hearing Edgar was looking for a housekeeper, she was right. There was.

She was born in 1906, as English womanhood, even in the lower brackets of society, was beginning to break free from the shackles – often welcome, loving shackles but shackles nevertheless – of previous eras. The suffragettes were getting into their stride. Her mother, somewhat inaptly named Victoria after the then queen, was an example of the new feminity; a partner to her husband in almost every sense of the word.

They made an enterprising young couple, and before Rachael was born were showing it by starting to make and sell bicycles, expanding the enterprise to motorcycles, and even venturing into the infant motor industry.

"This is where the future is," Josh told his wife, who was equally ready to get her hands dirty with oil and grease and apply an active brain to the business end of the work. She kept it going when her husband joined the army at the start of 1917, anticipating the call-up he knew was inevitable as conscription was brought in late in the war.

His mechanical skills were seized on by the army, he never saw a front line, and he returned to civvy street unscathed and ready to take up the reins of the business, which Rachael was looking forward to joining as she left school. But then came the disaster that changed her life completely.

Her father had bought a motor, to sell again, and he and Victoria were taking the car on a trial run. It was mid-January in the severe winter of early 1919. There had been rain followed by a sharp frost, and the road was like a skating rink – there was no gritting or salting in 1919. Travelling faster than he should, Josh braked as he approached a level crossing, crashed straight through the gates and into the path of a train. Both he and his wife died. Rachael was at school, and learned of the accident when she was called to the headmaster's office to find a policeman waiting.

She coped with the disaster in a way that impressed all around her. But there were no relatives that they or she knew of, and even then, not many years after children of her age would have been working in mills, or on the land, even down the mines, churches, schools and charities could not countenance the thought of allowing her to live alone. Also, it soon became clear that there was little money available to buy her necessities, after her father's debts had all been settled. She was shuffled from house to house while teachers, parsons and genuinely concerned others decided what should happen to her.

In the end, an independent local orphanage agreed to find a place for her, on the understanding that she should help with "housework" outside school hours – no doubt the origin of Aunt Ida's description of the place as "more like a workhouse." The work was also justified as "industrial training," supposedly to fit her for domestic service, to which she was duly allocated as she reached the age of fourteen. She became a laundrymaid at Eaton Hall, residence of the local squirearchy, which helped fund the orphanage.

Rachael was not desperately unhappy at Eaton Hall. She was ready to work and had a disposition that enabled her to get on with people, including the other servants, the master and mistress and their son and daughters. After a year, she became kitchen maid, within two years more a housemaid and by the time she was twenty-one, a parlourmaid with her own tiny attic room. Which was when she came to meet Edgar Topham, at a "harvest home" gathering of estate tenants. He was then in his early thirties and had recently succeeded to the tenancy of what had been the estate's home farm, and was already struggling to make ends meet. But they were immediately attracted to each other, and were looking forward to meeting again at the Hall's Christmastime party dance for tenants and servants, by when Edgar had taken steps to find out a little more about her – not difficult, for everyone remembered the crash which had left her an orphan.

Spare time was in short supply for both, but they made the most of what there was, and within a year, at the various "socials" and other local events which Rachael attended as often as she could get away, were seeking each other out, quite deliberately, although they pretended otherwise.

There was an element of truth in her telling Ida that she'd "heard" Edgar wanted a housekeeper. She had indeed heard it – from Edgar himself. Little white lies of that kind were surely forgiveable when she was deeply in love with him, as she remained all her tragedy-marred life. And he with her.

§

One aspect of the working of Edenhope unkown to the Tophams was what was meant by Violet Marchett's reference to "'Er" on the day of the their arrival. Rachael's first assumption was that it must be the lady of the house, Mrs Unston, although she would not have thought that such a personage would have stooped to playing "merry 'ell" just because the wife of the farm's most important employee was taken into a kitchen and given a cup of tea on a cold, miserable day. It was not a point which cost Rachael any sleep, but she and Edgar always discussed his weekly meetings with his boss, and an inevitable question after a few weeks was: "Have you seen his wife yet?"

"No," Edgar said. "I just go into his study from the passage and he's told me to go in an' wait for him, if he's not there."

He would not have dreamed of asking any of the farm men for information on their employer's private life, and such comments as he overheard, usually veiled when he was around, brought little enlightenment. Until one day, a few weeks into his employment, he went into the office, stood waiting, and was surprised when instead of Unston there appeared a tall, rather gaunt-looking woman, dressed in unglamorous and not particularly well-fitting tweed skirt and jumper.

"You must be Mr Topham," she said. "I'm sorry we haven't met before. Can I help you? My husband isn't here."

Edgar explained that he usually met Mr Unston at this time on Saturdays.

"I don't think he'll be here at all this weekend. Is there anything urgent?"

"No, I don't think so, ma'am. Not from my end, anyway."

"How are you liking it here?"

"I'm liking it very much, thank you," Edgar said.

"And your wife? Does she like these Shropshire hills?"

"Oh, yes. It's not so very different from where we were. A few more hedges and no stone walls, perhaps, and more arable land."

"Good. I must walk up and meet her."

Edgar was agreeably surprised by Mrs Unston's manner and apparent affability, although also surprised that she had not appeared to him or Rachael before. But as he was about to make a suitable response, the inner door opened and another woman appeared, somewhat younger and dressed in a mauve frock, her hair tied back severely, and with a look on an otherwise good-looking face that he would later describe as something between a smirk and a sneer.

"Yes, Mrs Lartin?"Griselda asked. "Did you want me?"

"No, Mrs Unston," the woman said. "I just needed to look at this book." And she picked up a small ledger-type volume from the desk.

"I expect you've met Mr Topham, the farm manager," Mrs Unston said.

"No," Mrs Lartin replied. "But I've heard about him. How do you do?" But never made a move to shake his hand and said it almost as she walked out through the door.

"Mrs Lartin's the housekeeper here," Griselda said.

There was a pause. Edgar had the impression that she would have liked to have added something. But she only asked: "What do you think of my Jerseys?"

"Well, they bump up the butterfat a bit," he said. This was in the days when high butterfat content in milk was important.

She laughed. "They're only a fad. But you have to admit they look pretty."

He smiled back. "They're alright, ma'am, no trouble. And if you want any cream from them, it'll be easy to arrange. I don't suppose there are any skim pans in the house here but I think my wife's still got one or two."

"Thank you," she said. "I don't suppose... I'll tell Mrs Lartin." Edgar wished he had never mentioned cream.

That evening, he told Rachael about meeting the two.

"I think she's alright," he said, appropos Mrs Unston. "But I didn't like that other one."

"I think that was who Violet Marchett was talking about when she said "Er" was away. I don't think she likes her either."

"You know, I reckon there's something a bit odd going on there," Edgar said. "P'raps I'm wrong, but I got the impression they hated each other."

§

It was some time before Edgar and Rachael were able to put any flesh on the bones of the skeleton he had discovered. And then it was she who did it, discovered a situation, through becoming acquainted with her female neighbours, that she would have thought unbelievable.

Over the next few weeks, she made a point of trying to get to know them, all wives of men who worked on the farm, plus the gardener and his son. She had called on all six within days of her first arrival, but that was a perfunctory matter of courtesy, which she thought was important because she had heard from Ida that the former bailiff, a well thought of local man, had left in an unpleasant atmosphere, summarily dismissed by Unston. She thought Edgar, and therefore herself, might be regarded with disfavour by the workforce and their families. Now she made efforts to get to know them more thoroughly, for example by telling them she was going to town and asking if there was anything she could get for them. One, who had been particularly intimate with the old bailiff's wife, gave her something of a chilly reception, at first, which she accepted as understandable. Violet Marchett was at "the house" most of her time so Rachael did not see much of her. The gardener's wife also worked part-time there. The remaining one was Marion Richards, wife of the head shepherd. She also worked two days a week at Edenhope, doing the laundry – washing and ironing – so had much inside knowledge of what went on in the house. Rachael did not mean to use their growing friendship to pry, although after Edgar had told her about meeting Mrs Unston and the housekeeper, and suggesting there was "something a bit odd" going on, she was quite keen on learning more. Eventually she found Marion ready to unburden herself of what she knew about the Edenhope House inhabitants.

It came out first when Rachael found her washing two of the house's sheets, at her own home, on a Wednesday. The Edenhope laundry was done on the traditional wash day, Monday, and the ironing next day, and Marion was allowed do her own washing with it.

"I thought you did your washing at the house, with theirs," Rachael said.

"These aren't mine." And after a short pause: "They're that woman's."

"Who – Mrs Unston's?"

"No – at least, I suppose they are 'ers. But I don't mean 'er. I mean that Lartin woman."

"The housekeeper?"

Mrs Richards looked at her.

"Housekeeper?" She laughed. "Yes, that's what 'er calls 'erself."

"That's what Mrs Unston called her when she introduced her to my husband."

"Well, I suppose that's what 'er is then."

Rachael would have liked to ask more, but refrained.

"How come you're having to wash house sheets here, Marion?"

"Er said they werna clean, an' I mun do 'em again, 'ere."

"Weren't they – clean, I mean?"

"They were when I ironed 'em – spotless. But 'er saw 'em hangin' on the airer, and there were dirty marks on 'em. Violet told me they'd been made by 'er dog, comin' in wet and rubbin' against 'em, but of course madam wouldn't 'ave 'ad that, even if Vi 'ad dared tell 'er. So I just fetched 'em 'ome."

"Does that kind of thing happen very often?"

"It's never happened to me before, over the washin'. But 'er leads Violet and the others an awful dance, finds fault with 'em all the time."

"So it's not a happy household?"

"I reckon you could say that," Marion said ironically. She put the second sheet through the wringer, into a basket, and said: "Well, it's no good thinkin' o' puttin' it on the line today. Will you have a cup o' tea?"

They sat at the kitchen table, Elspeth stroking the cat. When

Marion had poured, she said: "You don't know how things are, then, over there?"

Rachael was about to repeat Edgar's comment, that he thought things seemed "a bit odd," but thought better of it, and simply said: "No, but we haven't been here long, have we? Edgar's only met Mrs Unston once, but he rather liked her."

"Oh, she's alright. A bit dotty, p'raps. But she inna there much, lately. Gets herself out o' the way, I suppose, an' the girls. Must be terrible for 'er. I think if I'd a husband like that, I'd shoot 'im."

"Like what?"

"Oh, always got to 'ave some woman or other on the go. And so domineerin'. I expect your – Mr Topham's – found that out."

"Are you saying Mrs Lartin – the housekeeper, is Mr Unston's mistress?"

"Well, I wouldna call her that. Sounds too respectable. I'd call 'er 'is fancy woman. Or 'is tart – live-in variety."

"How long have things been like that, then?"

"Oh, about three years. Since before he got into parliament. 'Er an' 'er husband were stewards at the Conservative Club at Ludstone, which was where Squire spent all 'is time in them days. 'E wasna much good, from all I've gathered – the husband I mean – he was knockin' off the barmaid – so I suppose you couldna blame 'er for lookin' round a bit." She broke off.

"Look, I shouldna be talkin' to you like this. You wunna let it go any further, will you?"

"I can tell Edgar, can't I? I didn't tell you, but he'd guessed there was something – oh, a bit odd, he called it."

"He'd find out sooner or later, anyway. It's no secret. Folks down in Maeston know about it, I know. I just mean, you wunna let on it was me told yer, will yer?"

"Of course not. And I shall tell Edgar not to let on he knows anything. But how did she come to be living here, as housekeeper?"

"Well, Jim Wadham's missus was cook, but 'er had to give up when 'er got ill. I don't rightly know what it was, but anyway 'er couldn't work any more. Er's still alive, but 'er canna do much, they say. They live at The Junction. I don't know what Jim's doin'. Anyway, the master walks into the kitchen one day an' tells Violet Marchett an' the girl, who's parlourmaid now, as he's engaged a new cook-housekeeper, as'll live in the house an' be in charge of all the runnin' of it."

"I thought perhaps Mrs Marchett was the cook. So what is she, then?"

"Oh, she's cook alright, in all but name and money. And she's a good one. Used to be cook at old Colonel Hamilton's before 'er married Ted. She starts at eleven o'clock an' goes 'ome at six, after 'er's got the dinner ready for me lady, seven days a week, an' the master when 'e's at 'ome. I don't know 'ow 'er sticks it."

FOUR

Jasper Unston; and Griselda

Jasper Unston was latest in the line of a landowning family which owed the foundation of most of its wealth to friendship with another Shropshire squire, Robert Clive, in the second half of the eighteenth century. Profits from the family's resulting share in trading through the East India Company were so great that the Unstons were able to expand their modest estate in the south of the county until they owned nearly ten thousand acres. However, as happened with so many aristocrats or people who thought of themselves as such, much of the wealth was then frittered away through poor management of the properties including reliance on inefficient or even corrupt agents and stewards, excesses in personal lifestyles and finally by taxes such as death duties. All three factors featured in the case of the Unston estate and when Jasper succeeded to it only four farms were left, including Edenhope. One of his forebears built a mansion at Brandwood, two miles away, but in the 1870s it was burnt down in a fire believed to have been started by an arsonist with a grievance against the family, although nothing was ever proved. The owner, Jasper's grandfather, strapped for cash, decided against rebuilding and instead used as much of the stone and brick that could be rescued to expand the farmhouse at Edenhope, a house built in the style of the Welsh longhouse – one room deep, two low-ceilinged rooms high and up to half a dozen in length.

It might have been a good idea, if this particular Unston had employed an architect to make a decent job of the expansion. But he thought he could manage without such a luxury, merely employing jobbing builders and his own workmen. The result was a rambling hotch-potch with, it always seemed to Stephen when he got to know it, as many passages as rooms, and, eventually, three different flights of stairs, none of which connected with each other. There was no hot water system worthy of the name, and no thought was given to the working of the house from the point of view of the servants who had to carry food and anything else needed by "the family" through what seemed like miles of corridor. Squire Unston did however create the acre-plus garden and employed a man and a boy to make it something of a local showpiece.

After his infant days, Jasper spent little time there, until some years after the first world war. His mother was a socialite who refused to live at Edenhope for more than a few weeks at a time. He was sent to boarding school at the age of seven after a succession of nannies failed to find anything attractive or tractable about him, and at least one had left rather than succumb to the attentions of his father. At his first school, a local establishment for girls which took boys up to the age of nine, he was seen as something of a cry-baby and tale-teller. At his next, where he was supposed to be prepared for public school at the age of 12, he turned into a clever bully, facilitated by being big for his age. Academically, he was middle of the road, and he could hold his own in sports. In the holidays, he was allowed to run wild, easily escaping the supervision of his sisters' nursemaids and later governesses who were given nominal charge of him. His father's approach was straightforward: "Let him rough it a bit – it'll make a man of him." What he really meant was he did not care what happened to Jasper or his daughters as long as they were kept out of his way and did not interfere with his own activities, including his philanderings, which were still being carried on by the time Jasper went to Radston School.

Radston might have proved a turning point. His housemaster was an enlightened and caring Welshman who believed there was no such thing as a really bad boy and through a combination of discipline and understanding contrived to rescue a number of potential failures and wrong-doers from the results of their own shortcomings. He spotted Unston early in his first year, when he found the boy blatantly "cribbing" from another pupil who earlier in the day he had put through the mill of arm-twisting and other tortures beloved of schoolboy bullies. Teachers at Jasper's earlier schools had either ignored such practices or were too lazy to do anything about them.

This one, who could have punished him with a beating, instead gave him "lines" in the form of copying out an interesting though moral boys' short story but took him to his own study to do it, and afterwards discussed the story with him.

This approach, repeated several times in the ensuing terms, was having an effect, Mr Jenkins believed. He detected signs of the boy showing interest in things other than himself. But as Jasper came to the end of his first year, the master departed to take up a headship, and his successor did not have anything like the same feelings for the pupils in his care, simply believing in a regime of punishment and reward, routinely and rigorously enforced. The character which had shown signs of strengthening under Jenkins responded to the new housemaster's approach by taking these different essentials on board, and by the end of the next four years, and his Radston education, he had become what he remained through the rest of his life – a selfish bully, mentally if not physically, one of whose core beliefs was that those below him should be kept in their place.

He left Radston in 1913, nineteen years old and with all the attributes of a Flashman, assuming he would go to Oxford or Cambridge and enjoy three years of rollicking freedom. But his father, by then feeling more financial embarrassment, said he must start to earn a living. "You can go in the army," he told him. "They tell me there's going to be a war before long so you'll be able to get on a bit."

Jasper was not enamoured of the prospect, except with the glamour of an officer's uniform, but accepted a commission in the Kings Shropshire Light Infantry. As the war began he was a second lieutenant and had made a start on a lifetime of encounters with different members of the opposite sex, seducing one girl and using the contents of his wallet to secure the favours of others.

The autumn of 1914 found him in the initial retreat before the Germans, in Belgium and France, but by the winter he was one of the hundreds of thousands of soldiers in three allied armies embedded in the trench-bound deadlock that was to last for most of the rest of the grisly, often mishandled conflict. At first, he was not unpopular with his fellow officers and the men. He did not shirk danger, led abortive attacks which saw infantrymen slaughtered in droves, and was wounded twice, neither time seriously and needing only treatment at the advanced dressing stations. But in another few months the colours that had made him disliked at school showed through in the horrific conditions of hardship of months in the trenches. By then a full lieutenant, and second in command of a platoon, most of his fellow officers disliked him, although army esprit de corps prevented their showing it; but the men grew to loathe him, for his petty impositions, especially on the weaker individuals among them – the hallmark of the true bully. One little private, aged 19, was a particular target. It had to be admitted, by other men, NCOs and officers that the lad was bit of a sniveller who was afraid of his own shadow. But the last thing such a youth needed was to be continually shouted at and put on charges for near-imaginary offences, most often by Unston, whose treatment of the boy was noted with disfavour by fellow officers, even those among them who thought of the tommies as inferior beings.

Eventually he became so disliked and distrusted that his colonel decided to get rid of him. In 1917 he was promoted to captain and sent to a staff job in Paris, where between visits to brothels and cafes he carried out adjutant-type duties, and shuffled papers until the end of the war. As a regular officer, he was able to hang on in the army until 1920, when he was demobilised, and returned to Edenhope. His father got him a job as a junior steward on the big estate of a distant relative of his wife, in far away Lincolnshire. That he managed to hold the job down as long as he did – four years – was due only to the fact that it was a grace and favour appointment, for he was overbearing and disliked almost from the start, bullying any employee over whom he had authority, or thought he had. His boss, a Boer War army veteran, complained about him to the estate's aristocratic owner, but was told he would have to make the best of things, because it was a family matter. But it was only a matter of time before his besetting sin – an inability to keep his hands off any girl or woman he fancied as sexual prey – took him into territory from which even those connections could not rescue him. First there was a big-breasted, wide-hipped, loose-mouthed local girl known in her neighbourhood as the village bike, who kept him happy for best part of a year, until she became pregnant. She named him as the culprit, and her father confronted Jasper with the accusation, but he simply blustered and bluffed and threatened the man with dismissal, a measure he had no power to implement, but he got away with it. Everyone knew the child's father could have been any one of half a dozen, anyway. Others followed, but his undoing came when he tried it on with his chief's daughter, a child of 15, and her father caught him in the preliminaries of seduction. No connections could save him that time, and he was forced to return to Edenhope in disgrace.

Unston senior, nearing his seventieth birthday, realised that there was no chance of finding him another position, and told him he would have to stay home, and help him run farm and estate.

He had never thought much of his son's ability or willingness to work, and had a fair idea of his profligate inclinations and activities. They were after all only an echo of his own in younger days. But he tried to keep his heir's nose to the grindstone, even telling him, when Jasper complained of one of the farmhands going sick, to "get your coat off and take his place, man." He wriggled out of that one but confined his work to nothing more arduous than riding round the farm and the three others making up the estate, exercising his bullying propensities, making no friends and bringing comments from the hands, to each other, such as "I can see we'm goin' to 'ave a bloody good time when the old man goes." Increasingly, he contrived for his "duties" to take him to Ludstone, where he soon became a member of the Conservative Club and a recruit to its card-playing and drinking set.

His mother had a private income of her own on which, despite apparently being little more than a society butterfly with brains to match, she had refused to allow her husband to get his hands. For years, she spent much of her time in London and eventually departed permanently for the city, with her two daughters who hated the thought of being cooped up in what they saw as "a miserable hole of a house in those bloody hills;" and pursued their own ends which included marrying City businessmen. Jasper saw little of any of them, and nothing of their money, through the rest of his life.

The home farm was well-enough managed, mainly because the bailiff, James Wadham, was a hard-working practical farmer with a good knowledge of cattle, sheep and crops. Jasper did not like him, mainly because Wadham would argue points when he thought he was right, and at one time he tried to get the man sacked and replaced. But Unston senior would not have it.

"He's a good man, Jasper," he said. "You won't find anyone with a better working knowledge of this kind of farming. Ask Lummas, or Pritchard." Lummas and Pritchard were two of the estate's tenants.

But the estate as a whole was only tottering along, financially. Although Robert Unston was not the kind of hectoring master and landlord that his son was on the way to becoming, he was not a good enough manager to make sure the income kept ahead of his personal expenses, which were helped by an appetite for whisky, the demands of his son, and the expenses of daughters to whose high life their mother insisted on his contributing. However, he had enough family pride to want to stop the Edenhope estate disintegrating completely on his death, and when a neighbouring estate was bought by a rich Yorkshireman, and he and Jasper were invited to shooting parties there, he thought he saw a way to not only prevent it, but to enhance its value and safeguard its future.

"Jasper," he said over the port on one of the rare occasions they were dining together: "What do you think is going to happen to this lot when I leave you?" Waving his arms to indicate the house and surrounding acres.

"What do you mean? Your will says it'll come to me, doesn't it?"

"So it does, apart from some of the cash – and there's not much of that, I can tell you – which'll have to go to the girls. But do you know what it'll mean to you?"

"I don't know what you're getting at."

"I mean, how do you think you're going to pay these death duties that bloody Lloyd George saddled us with? Eh?"

Jasper said nothing. He and his father had so little discourse. The issue had never before come up.

"Well, I'll tell you. You'll have to sell one of the farms. That's what'll happen. And one farm probably won't be enough, even with the cottages. And then where will it leave you? That'll clip your wings, won't it?"

Jasper still remained silent.

"You know what you've got to do, don't you, boy?" Still no reply.

"You've got to get married. And it's got to be a gal with money – a lot of money – who won't do what your mother's done and keep it all to herself."

Yet again, Jasper said nothing. Until: "Where are we – I – going to find someone like that? I certainly don't know of anyone."

"Yes you do."

"Who?"

"Bradwell's daughter – Griselda."

This time Jasper leapt to life.

"Father, you must be joking!"

"Why?"

"She's as ugly as sin. And she must be nearly 50."

"She's thirty-nine, not much older than you. And she's heir to at least one million, as well as those farms. Yes, I know she's no oil-painting – that'll make her easier to get. You've got to realise which side your bread's buttered, Jasper. You've got to come down to earth."

More advice followed, involving good tunes, old fiddles and the impossibility of judging a book by its cover. Next time they were invited to shoot at Withymoor, Jasper surprised Griselda by seeking her out for conversation when the guns returned to the house for refreshment.

§

Griselda Bradwell had never known happiness of more than the most superficial kind, at any time in her last twenty years. Her father was a mill-owner with a canny feel for the kind of investment that, alongside huge profits made from supplying army uniforms in the War, made him a millionaire at a time when a quarter of that wealth would have labelled him super-rich, if the term had then been invented. He had found his own happiness in marrying the daughter of a miner, to his father's intense displeasure, before going off to fight in the Boer War, also against his father's wishes and leaving behind his wife and small son and daughter.

Safely back at home, he pleased his father by buckling down to helping run the mill and making a considerable success of it, through a period which Griselda, for many years, thought of as her halcyon days. She and her mother, an intelligent and self-taught woman who read widely and was much respected in their town, spent most of their time together. Her mother taught her to read, write and do basic arithmetic, as she had her son, before he was sent away to school. When her father returned, around her eighth birthday, he insisted that she should have more formal tuition, and they engaged an older lady who had been a governess and who came in daily to teach her Latin, French, geometry, basic science and even some music and painting.

This was still in the halcyon period, which Miss Hardaker augmented and became a treasured friend of both mother and daughter, and of the son, when he was at home. But it came to an end when the good lady died, at the age of seventy-five, and Mrs Bradwell followed soon after, in 1910 when Griselda was 17. A year later, on the advice of his own sister, who had married away from her family's wool-spinning, cloth-making background into the ranks of polite society, her father sent her away to a finishing school in Switzerland; where she was thoroughly miserable and, among the daughters of aristocrats and society high-flyers, never learned anything that was of use to the daughter of a Yorkshire mill-owner, and granddaughter of a coalminer.

When she returned, the "war to end war" was not far away. As it opened her brother joined the army, against their father's wishes, and died in one of the first German attacks, in Flanders. Griselda was left as her father's only family help and support. She wanted to do something to aid the war effort, but was persuaded to stay and "keep house," which she did with reasonable efficiency but without any flair for the features that make a house, even a rich house, into a loving and welcoming home; and which might have lifted her father out of the depressed obsession with wealth acquisition in which the loss of his wife and son seemed to have left him. It was not a happy time. Griselda was not by nature a bright and outgoing creature; such effervescence and interest in art, music, literature and the outside world that she had evinced in younger days, through her mother and the governess, had been mostly negated by their deaths and the two years in Switzerland, where it should have been enhanced and encouraged. And the fact that she was unattractive physically, gawky and with no great sense of dress or deportment did not help. Even the remnants of her grandparents' family, who had moved on from their mining background to become shopkeepers and small businessfolk, thought of her and sometimes referred to her as "poor Griselda," in spite of her superior position and wealth. Plain women are not necessarily unattractive, but they must have that extra something, like a sparkling personality, or an intellect that demands attention, to make them appeal, not just to men, but to anyone. Sadly, Griselda had neither of these. She was not unintelligent, by any means, as anyone who took the trouble to try to engage her interest would have found. But her father, even before the deaths of his wife and son, was reclusive by nature, and never dreamed of having dinner parties or any other kind of gathering at his home, which would at least have created a circle that might have nurtured more social skills in his daughter, and encouraged development of a livelier personality. So that she met few young or even not-so-young women; and young men of her own age, a few of whom she came across through her father's business, were usually looking for pretty faces and attractive figures as the starting point for acquaintance, and even her father's wealth did not make up for her lack of both. She became, frankly, a dull young and then not-so-young woman.

Potential for improvement came when, in 1930, her father bought a small estate in far away Shropshire, and they moved there. The estate had been offered him by a business acquaintance whose wife refused to live in the back of beyond, and Mr Bradwell, pecuniary instincts to the fore, as ever, thought it must be a good investment. Besides, it was good to be the first member of his family to own land, in any amount. Griselda could not avoid taking the lead in shaping the new home, in a farmhouse somewhat smaller than the Yorkshire near-mansion, and the effort lifted her somewhat. But she was, after all, 38 years old, no young man had ever shown any interest in her, she had no consuming passion, she could not even cook very well, and she was, she had to admit whenever she saw herself in a mirror, quite definitely and decidely plain. Few of either sex came calling at Withymoor Hall except a few business acquaintances of her father, offered the chance of a few days shooting in the beautiful South Shropshire countryside, and who occasionally brought their wives and families with them. But none left enthusing to each other on the charm or vivacity of the daughter of the house.

However, pride in ownership of an estate had brought something of a modification in Mr Bradwell's approach to social life, and when neighbours made a point of calling, he received them more warmly that had been his wont, and soon invited them to join the shooting parties. The Withymoor farms linked up with the Unston land, Robert Unston accepted the invitation, and when he found that Griselda was unmarried, likely to remain so, and the heir to the Bradwell million or perhaps even millions, his financial eyes glistened and his pecuniary ears expanded; bringing the conversation with his son already recorded, and an eventual acceptance by Jasper of his father's arguments, albeit without any resulting joy in what passed with him for a heart.

FIVE

A Kind of Marriage

Jasper was, to a degree, popular at the local Conservative club, where he was being thought of as a possible parliamentary candidate, which in that area at that time – and since, mostly – meant a safe route to parliament. The club was the centre of Tory activity in the area, and prevailing thought there around 1930 was "thank God we saw off the general strikers and got rid of that terrible Labour government." The general election of 1931 brought a sweeping victory for the Conservatives but because of the financial crisis following the American stock market crash the so-called national government formed by Labour's Ramsay MacDonald continued in office.

In a decade we now know as a period of dismal and disastrous futility, at home and abroad, culminating in six years of worldwide conflict, the horrors of Hiroshima and Nagasaki and a dreary and pointless "cold war," one of the few politicians who could possibly have pointed a way through the mire was relegated to obscurity. At least, he held no office. But Winston Churchill, persistently urging the country to arm against the danger of war, always a passionate supporter of the British Empire, and just as passionate a hater of left wing socialism, became the hero of the Ludstone Con Club. Its hard-riding, hard-drinking core forgot, if they ever knew, that Churchill had been reviled by Tories in the first years of the century when, following in the footsteps of his father, Lord Randolph Churchill, he had enthusiastically joined with David Lloyd George in carrying through social reforms which were to transform British society through the new century. The club's members noted only Churchill's calls to re-arm and his condemnations of the extreme left. And when they heard Jasper Unston talking big, strong and very British, they saw him as a local copy of their hero. And he had been an heroic fighter in the war, hadn't he, and was a member of an old county family.

The sitting member, a well-liked and inoffensive individual but suspected by some of having liberal leanings, was over 80 and eager to retire. Club companions found Unston would be happy to stand and started to sound out the constituency association, which invited him to a one-man hustings, where he made an impression with his talk of hanging on to the empire and standing no nonsense from this man Adolf Hitler who was just coming to prominence. The old member duly announced that he would not be standing again, Unston was adopted and easily won the seat in the 1935 general election.

But while the Ludstone club was providing the path towards a political career for Unston, it was also the base for a problem he had to cope with if he was to carry out his father's plan for marrying him to Griselda Bradwell. It was the scene of yet another adventure involving the opposite sex.

Gerald and Miriam Lartin were the Conservative Club's stewards, but only stayed together because the job demanded a married couple. He was heavily involved with the part-time barmaid, leaving Miriam footloose. The opinion of many who knew them was that they thoroughly deserved each other, for Mrs Lartin, although a good-looking woman in her thirties with plenty of physical attributes, was not well-liked. The physical side was all that mattered to Jasper Unston, however, and within three years of his return to Edenhope he was in Miriam's bed on a regular basis. In fact, he developed as much affection for her as he was capable of feeling for anyone, and the affair was going strong when his father told him he would have to marry money if he wanted to keep the estate. Unston senior knew of his son's involvement with Mrs Lartin and told him in the course of his warnings: "And you'll have to give up that floosie you've got down there."

Jasper accepted the order to pursue Griselda Bradwell, ostensibly, but in fact never stopped seeing and on occasions sleeping with Miriam, although their relations were carried on more discreetly. The slowdown however made her think he was cooling towards her, and he had to tell her about Griselda. She threw a queen-sized wobbly and warned him she could ruin both his parliamentary and financial prospects if she chose. Unston managed to convince her that if he married Griselda it would be only a union of convenience and that she, Miriam would continue to be the only one he really cared for, and she accepted it. But he was left having to walk a tightrope, with forces working from both sides which could throw even a practised dissembler like him off balance. At Withymoor, he had to continue to pay court to Griselda, and eventually to marry her or face comparative penury when his father died. At the same time he must keep Miriam happy while giving the impression, to those who knew about their liaison, that it had come to an end.

§

He began to spend time at Withymoor, most of it with Griselda. With her, he could not exercise his main claim to be a conversationalist – exchanging crude bawdy jokes with like-minded males – but he did his best to cast around for subjects which might interest her. They were soon on first name terms, at his prompting – and she asked about his army and war experiences. He told her enough to let her know he had been in the thick of things, at the same time giving the impression of modesty by saying he did not really want to talk about it all. She told him about her early life, and how she had lost her mother and her dear friend the governess, and he pleased her with the way he listened and expressed sympathy. The hypocrisy was hard work, but under his father's prodding he persevered and worked steadily towards a greater intimacy.

Griselda, likewise, had not been suddenly hit by romantic passion. But she was flattered by having a man pay attention. She saw Jasper as a solitary and lonely person. He was not stupid enough to pretend that he had never had any love affairs, but managed quite successfully to give the impression that they had not been important to him, which was true in most senses of the word, and that he had not yet found anyone with whom he wanted to spend his life, which was also true. She had no entrenched philosophical or political views. She knew her father was wealthy and she simply accepted that state of affairs, of never having to worry where money was coming from although her parent's creed of waste not, want not was incorporated into her own domestic practices. But she accepted Jasper's politics, proffered with an apologetic "don't suppose you want to concern yourself with that sort of thing," and his prospects of becoming an MP. At that stage, he did not display, to her, anything of the hectoring manner, and attitude of "I am always right" which he commonly excercised on workpeople and anyone else he conceived as his inferiors, but which he had the sense to realise might have jarred on someone only two generations removed from the ranks of the working class. Nor did he attempt to exercise the talents of seduction which had figured in most of his relations with the opposite sex to date.

In fact Griselda, like his fellow officers in the early days of the war, and others who he wanted to impress that way, found him personable enough. The fact that a man, especially one younger than herself, was seeking her company was good for her ego. She had long accepted that she would eventually become an old maid and, when her father shed his mortal coil, a lonely old maid. Likewise the desire in almost every woman's breast, that she might one day be a mother, had faded almost to nothing, although Jasper's continuing attentions brought a tentative revival.

Her father, to whom, unlike her mother, she had never been close, did not like the Unstons, father or son. As a largely self-made man, he did not have much time for people who had wealth handed to them on a plate yet could not manage it properly. But the instincts that had made him join the landowning class himself had developed rather than faded. He guessed that Jasper's seeking the company of his daughter might not be altogether altruistic, in fact not altruistic at all, for he had divined the state of the Edenhope finances. Never mind, he thought, if he marries her it will establish the Bradwells as landed gentry. So Jasper was made welcome at Withymoor, and his visits increased until eventually it was a rare week which did not see him there at least once.

It could not be said that Jasper had decided he must reform, set his hand to the plough, devote himself to making a good job of running the estate and being a decent husband to his wife. The researcher would have to go back through several generations of Unstons to find people who came up to that kind of moral standard; and even then the search would probably have been in vain. But like his father, he hated the thought of losing possessions, and having to work for his living. He had accepted that marrying Griselda might be an acceptable price to pay for avoiding such a fate.

On her part, she well knew that she was not going to fall passionately in love. More, she divined that Jasper was not in love with her, which brought her to the same view as her father – tentatively, for no woman wants to think that her only attractive feature is her bank balance. But she was enjoying male company, prepared to take things as they came. A few months later, after their relationship had progressed to the extent of a theatre trip to London, including pre-show dinner and a night in an hotel afterwards, he asked her to marry him. Her heart thumping, not with love but because she had long thought that such a moment would never come for her, she said:

"I must talk to my father. I'm all he has. But if he agrees, I will marry you, Jasper." Jasper kissed her. Griselda could not help feeling something of a thrill. It was the first time in nearly forty years that any man, apart from her father, had saluted her that way.

§

Mr Bradwell was away on one of his many business trips, but when he returned two days later, she told him she wanted to talk to him about something very important.

"He's asked you to marry him, has he?"

"Yes, father."

"Well, are you going to?"

"I've told him I will, if you agree."

"It'd be you marrying him, not me. He wouldn't be my first choice of a husband for my only daughter, but he wouldn't be the last either. Are you... fond... of him?"

"I'm not in love with him, if that's what you mean. We seem to get on well... but..."

"But what, my dear?"

"I think he might want to marry me because... oh, because we... you... have money."

"Yes, I think you're probably right. But does that matter so much, if you get on well with him, like you say?"

"So you think it would be alright?"

"It's entirely up to you. I've no objection. It'd be good to see these two properties joined together."

But after she had left, Josiah Bradwell showed that care for his daughter went some way past thoughts of land and money. He said to himself: "If he plays ducks and drakes with you, my girl, I'll have his guts for garters, and I'll make sure he doesn't get a penny of my money."

Two days later, she told Jasper her father approved of her decision. There was some debate about where they would live, but it was finally agreed it should be Edenhope. Robert Unston said Griselda would be mistress of the house, and have a completely free hand in that situation. Bradwell summoned Jasper and warned him that he would take the dimmest of views if the licentious behaviour of which he had learned – "don't ask me how, just take it as fact" – was repeated. Unston kept up his facade, assuring Mr Bradwell that his past was well behind him, but went away muttering to himself: "The old bastard won't live for ever, will he."

Financial settlements, which might have been expected to be difficult, were arranged quite amicably, although they did not quite result in Griselda's bringing all her money to Edenhope with no strings attached, as Unston Senior had unrealisically hoped. Mr Bradwell volunteered a gift of £10,000 to his daughter, on her marriage, without strings. His property would go to her when he died, and his money, from which would be taken whatever proved necessary to pay death duties on both estates. If such taxes became necessary, on Edenhope, during his lifetime, he would pay them. Robert Unston and his son accepted a deal they knew they were unlikely to better.

§

Miriam, not happy when Jasper revealed that in six months time he would be marrying Griselda, nevertheless had to accept that he had no alternative if he wanted to keep the property intact. The prospect of becoming the wife of a substantial landowner had been pleasurable, but if the land would become much less substantial it threw a different light on things.

Mrs Lartin's emotions over her relations with Unston, or indeed anyone, would be difficult to pinpoint, or describe with any accuracy, apart from the hope of being one day mistress of Edenhope. She was hard as nails, not the kind of woman any person of either sex felt attracted to. Yet there was a need for some kind of personal link, or rather to always have someone in tow. Being kind, it might be described as a wish to be wanted. Yet she seemed to find it impossible to be anything but unpleasant to almost anyone. She did not pursue sex for its own sake, but at the same time enjoyed using it as a manipulative tool. Perhaps the most accurate description of her would be that she was a female equivalent of Jasper, except that she seemed to bully spitefully instead of with bluster.

To try to keep their relationship secret, he found her a cottage in the town, and under the guise of his political activities, centred on the club, was able to visit her in her off-duty periods, doing his best however to keep the visits secret. In fact she became quite pleased with the situation, still working at the club but able to spend more time away from her husband and his barmaid, in a snug little house paid for by Jasper. Their ploy was successful. No word of Unston's treachery reached Josiah, either before or after his son and Griselda were married. Then, less than a year after the wedding, came the event that eventually brought the situation reported by Marion Richards to Rachael. Robert Unston had a heart attack, and died instantly. Jasper became owner of the Edenhope estate. His father-in-law paid the taxes, and for a year and a half he and Griselda lived what appeared to those who did not know about his liaison with Miriam Lartin to be a normal married life. He did not find sex with her as objectionable as he had implied he would – Jasper did not take objection to any sex. As a result, a few months before her father-in-law died, she found she was pregnant.

She was now 41, and although she had had no-one to acquaint her with all that pregnancy and childbirth implied, she had no more than the usual fears about it. She was strong, fit and healthy, and was now looking forward to motherhood, which she had thought she would never accomplish. Jasper appeared to accept the situation quite happily, and stayed away from her bed, spending more time at Ludstone, although still exercising caution, for he knew that there were still ways for Josiah Bradwell to damage him, if he chose.

Mr Bradwell, however, having heard nothing of his son-in-law's latest moral wandering, relaxed his vigilance and, as he reached his upper seventies, thought it would be a good idea if he handed care of his own estate to his daughter and her husband. Jasper gladly accepted the associated duties, and a share of the revenues that came with them. In fact he settled down to life as a country squire, which gave him scope for his natural talent of arrogantly lording it over his underlings, including the tenants of farms and cottages. He also developed his basic tenet of ownership – that he could do exactly as he liked with what was his. The idea that ownership of land should be thought of as stewardship, caring for it for future generations and for all who lived by it, would have been an anathema. He told his gamekeeper to keep people – even cottage tenants – off all land for which they did not pay rent, even land where children had played their games for generations. He refused to acknowledge the existence of footpaths, and gave the keeper the same instructions regarding them. When he saw his Edenhope Farm workpeople's children playing in the woods and fields behind their homes he told his bailiff to remind their parents that the youngsters were there by his permission which could be withdrawn at any time. At this stage in the marriage, these attitudes and activities did not come to Griselda's notice.

His position was consolidated, as far as worries about Mr Bradwell finding out about Miriam Lartin were concerned, a few months before the election that was to take him to Parliament. Josiah died, quite suddenly, only weeks before his twin granddaughters were born. Griselda inherited the Withymoor farms and his entire monetary fortune, apart from some minor legacies to a niece and her children. There was still plenty to cover the second lot of death duties, and Griselda became a rich lady in her own right, and Unston decided he could take a step that would do away with the need for the Ludstone love-nest.

SIX

Kindergarten Stuff

There are, have been and will be many men capable of playing fast and loose with their wives or partners. But the number capable of hatching and carrying out Unston's latest variation on his lechery is surely limited in the extreme. He had spent much of his life to date pursuing activities and aims outside the pale of most moral standards, while managing to keep them hidden when it suited him. But his bullying and womanising was kindergarten stuff compared with this. He brought his "floosie," as his father called her, into the home where his wife had just given birth to his daughters.

The twins were born, as was quite usual in those days, at Edenhope. There were no complications arising from the birth, but, also as usual in the 1930s, Griselda stayed in bed for several days after the delivery.

Three days after the girls made their appearance, Jasper blandly announced, to his wife, that he had decided they should have a housekeeper, because she would be fully occupied with the babies, despite the engagement of a nursemaid. What was more, he had found one, a woman who worked at "the club" and would help in his election campaign. Griselda said she did not think such a person was needed, but he told her his opinion was different. In any case he had already told the woman in question that the housekeeping job would be hers as soon as she could get away from the club.

"Her name's Miriam Lartin, and she'll be called 'Mrs Lartin' by everyone in the house," he said.

"Do you mean you want her to live here?"

"Yes. She'll have Father's old room, as a bed sitting room." Griselda knew nothing factually about his liaison with Mrs Lartin. But she knew that he only wanted her for her money, and now the brutal announcement, her instinct, and what she had learned of his past life told her that concern for her was the last thing in his mind when he proposed to bring in a woman from outside to take over her role, in effect, as mistress of the house.

Still, she was shocked, almost bereft of words. But she asked: "When was this?"

"Yesterday."

The conversation marked the turning point in their relationship, the end of the marriage as anything more than a formality. They never again shared a bed. Or indeed a table, or a fireside.

She spent much of that night in harsh examination of herself, her husband and the situation. Next day, in a bitter exchange, and finding a resolution she never knew she possessed, she took the offensive and forced him to admit the truth about the "housekeeper."

"Who is this woman, Jasper?" she asked.

"I told you, she works at the club, and she helps me with the constituency work."

"You're carrying on with her aren't you? And now you want to carry on with her in my house. Isn't that it, Jasper?"

He wanted to bully and bluster, but remained silent. This was a Griselda he had not encountered before.

"You can't deny it, can you?" she repeated. He managed to find his bluster.

"So what if it is. You wanted me to marry you, didn't you? You'd never have found anyone else."

Griselda looked at him as though he was something she had just found under a stone.

"Just get out of my sight, you unspeakable worm," she said. "Don't ever come into this room again, while I'm here."

For the first time in his life, Jasper quailed before a female. He did not know it, but he had forced a step change in Griselda's character. From now on, the woman he had thought to use for his own ends, then brush aside, would be infinitely the stronger through every situation in which they both featured.

She warned him that divorcing him would be easy, and costly for him. He could have all the fancy women he wanted but he would never get his hands on her personal wealth. Over the next twenty-four hours she came to decisions that were to exert a huge influence on the lives of everyone at Edenhope. She resolved that, horribly unpleasant as the situation might be, she would not move out, because to do so would amount to acknowledging defeat, and now she had twin reasons for wanting to establish herself as a woman of strength. Also, Jasper was wounding her as she had never been wounded before. Not by ceasing to love her, because she knew he never had, but by demonstrating that he thought he could treat her as a non-person, who did not matter. It engendered a feeling new to her, a deep, acid bitterness, and brought a resolve that most women would have found impossible to carry out. She would live out the charade of marriage in the interests of her babies. She knew there were other ways she could deal with the situation, if she chose. Divorcing him would leave him very much worse off. But that would rob her daughters of part of their inheritance, and their welfare was now the most important feature of her existence. She had never before had a raison d'etre, a driving force in her life, but she had one now. She would become a different woman. Many in her situation would have sunk into depression. With her, it seemed to have almost the opposite effect.

As soon as she was up and about again, she gave instructions for "father's room" to be made into a bed-sitter for the new housekeeper, with a double bed. She herself moved into one at the other end of the house, big enough for herself and the infants, with a small chamber adjoining, for the nursemaid. She made no provision for Jasper. He could either stay in what had been their marital chamber or move in with his mistress.

A few days later, Miriam Lartin arrived. It was the autumn of 1934, seven months before the election. Through the next three years, Griselda manipulated the situation by gradually spending more time at Withymoor, but being careful to assert her place as the real mistress of Edenhope. Whenever she returned there, although she never stayed for more than a month at a time, she insisted on the other woman reporting to her daily on the household's running. She knew Mrs Lartin hated her, intensely. Her own feeling towards the woman was a deep disgust, a loathing, but she hid it beneath an attitude of icy cool.

And this was the situation described by Marion Richards, a few weeks after the Tophams arrived in Shropshire. No wonder Edgar thought there was something odd.

§

Jasper, flabbergasted by the change in Griselda, soon realised that he had made a terrible blunder, driven by his liaison with Miriam Lartin. The strength and resolution his wife now displayed made her the victor whenever they clashed. She came off best in every disagreement about property or finance, for she now held most of the purse strings. The clashes were not too frequent, because he was in London most of the time and she only spent enough time at Edenhope to assert her position there. Nevertheless he knew that he now had to play second fiddle to her in matters of money and the joint estates.

An example was her wish to have some Jersey cows as milk providers for the house, both because they looked good and their milk was rich and creamy. In fact she told Jasper they should have a complete herd of the breed. Which indirectly was what brought the Tophams to Shropshire.

Unston had been a hands-on farmer of Edenhope's 400 acres up to then – hands on meaning controlling the farm's activities through a bailiff, who he had inherited with the property. Now he realised that spending more than half his time in London to earn his MP's pay and perks would mean his practical involvement with the farm, and management of the other farm tenancies, would have to be cut back. At the same time, Griselda's wish – she did not put it any stronger than that, in this case – for a Jersey herd, made him think of starting a dairy side to the farm.

He investigated the economics of dairy farming, including herds of Jerseys and their low yields of rich milk. By the time he became an MP he had decided that dairying was well worthwhile, but not with

Jerseys, despite the premium their milk would bring. Exercising one of his few excursions into the acquisition of economic wisdom, he consulted advisers in the agriculture ministry and decided he would have a herd of Friesians, the black and white breed with high milk yields and excellent potential for crossing with the local Hereford beef animals. And to keep Griselda happy he would add on a few Jerseys which she could keep in a couple of small paddocks near the house but otherwise be managed with the herd.

His plan came up against problems, one of which was the need for a milk production licence, solved by using his new status to pull rank over ministry officials. Another was the situation which led to the engagement of Edgar Topham. The inherited bailiff, a dyed-in-the-wool South Salopian with a fine grasp of the practicalities of beef and sheep farming, made it clear to his master that he did not think much of the dairying plan, and knew nothing about milk production.

"It'd be a big change for us here, sir," he said.

"You mean you don't like the idea of getting up earlier in the morning," Unston said sarcastically.

"No, sir, it isn't that, there's a lot of early mornings now, and late nights. But I don't know anything about dairying, nor does Tibbott." Jack Tibbott was the current cowman looking after the beef cattle.

"In that case you can find yourself another situation,Wadham."

The bailiff looked at him unbelievingly.

"You don't mean that, do you, sir? I've been here twenty 'ear. Your father always said I was doing a good job. I just wanted to warn you, like, that it wouldna be easy, startin' something new like dairy. We'd need somebody who knew a bit about it."

"Yes, and it won't be you. I won't have somebody who argues with me."

James Wadham was devastated. He was well over fifty and the prospects of getting anything like the same kind of job were poor. By the end of the month he was gone, and never again had similar employment. But he always maintained that getting from under the dictates of the latest Unston was one of the best things that ever happened to him.

§

Rachael would have liked to ask Marion Richards what the domestic atmosphere was like at the master's end of Edenhope, with two ladies of the house apparently in situ, at least part of the time. But both she and Mrs Richards had other demands on their time, including being at home when the children arrived from school. In fact Marion's knowledge did not extend to knowing who slept with who, on a regular basis; and changes which were to help shape the future in important and eventually tragic ways were not much more than a year away.

First, down in Ludstone, was the parting of the ways of Miriam Lartin's husband and his barmaid girlfriend. She found a new lover who wanted to marry her, the girl agreed, and left her part-time job at the Conservative Club. After a few months of a lonely bed, Lartin decided he would like his wife back. She went to the club quite often, on Unston's business, and Lartin started to make advances.

As it happened, Miriam and Unston were becoming at odds with each other – it was the longest relationship he had ever sustained and he had developed a greedy eye on his bailiff's wife. Also, Miriam was becoming somewhat fed up with a situation in which the new Griselda very deliberately sought to make sure she knew her place. The upshot was that Mrs Lartin accepted her husband's suggestion that she should move into the barmaid's spot, in more than one sense of the word. There was an unpleasant scene at Edenhope when she told Jasper of her decision, but frankly,despite the void it created in his sex life, he was not so very sorry to see her go.

At the same time, the plans for dairying at the Edenhope farm hit an obstacle. Edgar had been unable to find a dairyman of the standard he thought the job demanded. The modifications to the buildings had been completed and cows from his brother-in-law delivered and he had himself been doing the milking and other work, at the same time bringing up Marion Richards' son to the job with the idea that he would soon be able to take over completely. The boy, 21 years old, was proving an apt pupil and Edgar was confident he would make a good cowman.

But on to the scene came that old imp of mischief, love. Jeremy was going out with a girl from Maestonbury and announced his intention of marrying and leaving Edenhope as soon as he could get a new job with house attached. There was no other young worker at Edenhope who Edgar thought able to take his place, he told Unston when he reported the situation and asked for permission to advertise, again. The problem was there was no cottage available for a married man, meaning the recruitment radius was small in days when almost no farm worker had a car. But the situation made Unston's eyes light up. He could see a solution that might bring Rachael Topham nearer his lascivious grasp.

"Topham," he said. "I know the answer."

§

The solution emerging from Jasper's lust-fuelled imagination was in practice quite sensible, leaving out his ideas for Rachael's part in it. He proposed to convert part of the Edenhope house into self-contained acommodation for Edgar and his family.

His father's additions to what had started out as a Welsh long house type of farmhouse had left, as already revealed, a hotchpotch of rooms, kitchens and corridors downstairs, and three separate staircases to a single storey of upstairs rooms which did not connect with each other. Altogether there were half a dozen downstairs chambers which would now be described as "reception rooms," besides the kitchens, and fifteen rooms upstairs, some moderate in size, others mere box-rooms or box-room size The kitchens were at the western end and connected with the main, or "family" part of the house via a corridor which ran from the back entrance lobby where Rachael and the children had sheltered when they arrived, along the extreme rear for the length of two rooms, turned frontwards for a one-room span, then left though the middle of what had become the squire's family residence. One staircase led from the kitchen to two bedrooms where three servants slept, and to nowhere else; one from the "family" end of the corridor to a landing and ten bedrooms where it came to a brick wall stop; and the other to four other bedrooms, and nowhere besides. All the rooms, up and down, were low-ceilinged and outside walls were damp. Altogether, there was an atmosphere of drearyness, almost miasmic, pervading the entire house apart from the most-used parts of the family end.

Unston, the ulterior motive in play, was uncharacteristically gentle in putting his "solution" to Edgar. His idea was to convert the separate part of the house next to the kitchens. He took his bailiff to inspect it.

The rooms had only been used, when they were used at all, for storage, and Edgar found them unprepossessing. But Jasper, abandoning such financial caution as he had ever exercised, almost adopted a "money's no object" attitude.

"I shall get a good architect or whatever kind of chap does this sort of thing, to look at it and see what can be done. One of these rooms could be a bathroom. But don't show it to your wife now. She'd probably turn it down, and I wouldn't blame her. Let me get some plans drawn up first. We can always offer it to young Richards if she doesn't like it then. But I think you should have it. It'll be the best house on the estate." It was probably the pleasantest he had ever spoken to Edgar.

That evening, he told Rachael of his boss's idea, warning her not to tell anyone else about it for the time being. She was not enthusiastic but agreed they should wait to see what happened to Jasper's proposals. She certainly did not want Edgar to lose Jeremy Richards. They were surprised however when only three days later a young man from a local firm of architects drove up and said he had been briefed "to start work on converting part of the 'hall' into a house for the farm manager." Violet Marchett sent the kitchen maid to find Edgar, who the man said he had been told to involve in the proposed conversion, and that Mr Unston wanted the plans to be completed as quickly as possible.

"I wasn't exactly told everything must be to your liking, Mr Topham. But I certainly got that impression. And he said that if he wasn't here when I had drawn up the plans, I was to show them to you."

In fact, the young designer turned the seven rooms into a pleasant house, with a bathroom, a luxury the Tophams had never enjoyed before, a modern kitchen fireplace to heat piped water, also new to them, and a number of built-in cupboards and other conveniences. The only element of sharing with the rest of the house was that their back door opened into the corridor connecting the kitchens with "the family." But there was a front door, with "Edenhope Cottage" on a plaque, its own letterbox, a roof over and a small entrance hall behind. All resulting from Jasper Unston's urges directed towards Rachael.

Edgar kept her informed of the progress. She was also shown the completed plan and thought it added up to a comfortable house and should be accepted, if only in the interest of the working of the farm. When Unston next returned, the proposal was top of his discussions with Edgar, in fact he almost brushed aside any other matters, on the lines of "you can deal with that, Topham, can't you." But he was most concerned that the plan for the house met with Rachael's approval, and wanted to discuss it with her. Edgar should no doubt have smelt a rat in his employer's attitude, so different from some other occasions, but he did not. The good nature that was such an essential part of his character simply accepted that Jasper was happy with the way the farm was going and was anxious to keep it that way.

The only debit point in the arrangement from Rachael's point of view was that the new house had no garden to provide her with vegetables for her kitchen and flowers and decorative plants for her rooms. But when she mentioned it to Unston, as they discussed the plans, he said: "My dear Mrs Topham, you may have all you want from the garden here. I shall tell Perkins to make sure of that." Andrew Perkins was the head gardener.

Marion Richards was of course pleased that her son was able to take over the Tophams' cottage. She knew that Jeremy liked working with Edgar, and was looking forward to taking main charge of the dairy herd. But she felt less happy for Rachael, who she felt had become a real friend, and she could not hide her worries.

"Watch yourself, love," she said. "He's a bastard."

Stephen, still only ten years old, disliked the place from the day they moved in, two years after their arrival in Shropshire. He was always reluctant to go anywhere in the house outside their own domain.

§

The outbreak of war was only days away when the Tophams moved into their new home. As with most farm people, the war made little difference to their daily life, at that stage. Milk still found its way into the workers' cans, hens still laid their eggs and produced chickens for the table, pigs occupied their cottage styes until they met their fate at the hands of the travelling butcher. Edgar found himself left even more in sole charge of the farm because Unston was detained in London for more of the time when he was given a minor job by the emergency coalition government. It boosted his ego and he always referred to himself as "a minister" although he was really two steps below that rank and had only been appointed because there was no-one else with any military experience. "Don't like the chap but I suppose he's the best we've got" was the minister's comment as he gave his approval.

The appointment also slowed down his pursuit of Rachael, although not before he had made one more move. Three weeks after she and the family moved in, he knocked on her door.

"Good morning, Mrs Topham," he said affably. "Might I have a word?"

"Of course, sir," she answered. "Will you come in?"

Inside the kitchen, usually thought of by farm folk as the main living room, he said: "Well, you're certainly making it very comfortable. Are you pleased with it?"

"Oh, yes, it's fine. Thank you very much for all you've done."

"It made sense. You've got a better house and we've got a good dairyman for the farm. Top – your husband's pleased with the way it's worked out, I think."

"Yes, he thinks a lot of young Jeremy." She thought: "How pleasant he is. Is he really so terrible? Is he mellowing?"

"Good. Now I have something I'd like to put to you." This time she wondered a little.

"You know that Mrs Lartin, the housekeeper has left us. Would you consider taking on her duties? That really means running the house. You would be properly paid, of course."

The ironical thought now was: "I hope you don't mean all her 'duties,' Mr Unston." She said however: "Well, I'd have to think about it, sir. The children take quite a lot of my time. What sort of hours would you be thinking of?"

"Oh, I think they could be flexible, to suit yourself. It's really a matter of supervising the servants and making sure I have a bed, and meals, when I'm here, which has been most weekends, although I think it might not be quite so often in future. The prime minister has asked me to do a war job in the government."

"Oh, congratulations sir." And shortly: "I'll have to talk to Edgar – my husband, of course. But I don't think I'm against the idea. I'd been thinking I ought to have some kind of job." She hesitated again, wondering whether to mention Mrs Unston, but decided against it. Jasper himself did so, however. He thought he had better bring in Griselda somewhere.

"Good. I too will have to talk about it, to my wife. She isn't here at present, in fact she's away more than she's here, which is the main reason for needing a housekeeper. I shall be here again in two or three weeks. Can we talk again then?"

"Yes, sir, certainly. Thank you."

Left to herself, Rachael pondered the wisdom of the reception she had given Unston's approach. Marion Richards' warning to "watch yourself" had been based on knowledge of what had been going on in the Edenhope household and, no doubt, on knowledge of other parts of Jasper's history. She must talk it over carefully with Edgar.

To her surprise, he already knew about it. Unston was being very careful. Edgar was wary of the idea, but had to agree with her that the job and the money it would bring would be useful. But he qualified his approval with: "You know what he's like, love, don't you. Doesn't it worry you that he might have... those kind of ideas?"

"It did at first, but now I don't think so, really. And I think I can look after myself, don't you?"

"I hope you're right. But tell me if he tries anything on, won't you?"

"Of course," she said, embarrassed that he should even ask such a question. But Edgar was serious. The thought of a man like he knew his employer to be, or at least to have been, getting his paws anywhere near the woman who had been his beloved wife for twelve years brought up instincts he never knew he had.

"I'd kill him," he thought to himself, uncharacteristically wondering where such a thought came from but meaning every word. Aloud to Rachael he said: "We couldn't stay here if there was anything like that. We'd be gone before the day was out, job or no job."

§

Unston, as he had promised, spoke to both Tophams next time he was back in Shropshire, and they readily agreed the terms he suggested. He even agreed to her request that she should speak to Griselda before she started work.

"I'd like to be sure that she approves of me, if you don't mind, sir," she said. "Even though she's not here a great deal."

"I've already spoken to her," he lied, resolving to get on the phone to Withymoor immediately. "But I will tell her you'd like to talk to her, and make arrangements."

Griselda, having learned of Miriam Lartin's departure, was wondering how to deal with the new situation. She had no intention of returning to live permanently at Edenhope, much less of getting together again with her husband, who she now despised to the same degree that she detested Mrs Lartin. But in line with her overriding desire to steer all her actions in the direction of protecting her baby daughters' interests, and making sure Jasper did nothing to queer her pitch, when he telephoned her to tell her about Rachael's wish to meet her, she told him the icy tone she now always used to him that she would be at Edenhope in two days time – when he would have left for London – and would be pleased to see Mrs Topham.

Her few encounters with Edgar had left her liking him, and intending to meet his wife, but the happenings following the birth of the twins had pushed the intention out of her mind. Now she was suspicious of her husband's motives in engaging Rachael, but her brief conversations with Edgar, and his mentions of his wife, had left her with a distinct feeling that she was anything but a Miriam Lartin. The light in his eyes, the smile round his lips, whenever he spoke of her, the odd hint of what had brought them to Edenhope, had shown plainly that she was his loving partner, above all else.

When she and her little daughters arrived at Edenhope, with their nursemaid, driven by Griselda in her Rover, she immediately followed her husband's action of weeks before, knocking on Rachael's door rather than sending for her.

Although she had never seen her before, Rachael knew immediately who this rather unprepossessing yet formidable-looking woman was, and before Griselda could speak, said: "Good morning, ma'am. Will you come in?"

To say they immediately got on like a house on fire would be an overstatement, but the empathy that was to grow into so much more was evident from the start. It made Griselda feel she had to make sure that Rachael knew the basic facts of what had happened in the past, and the situation as it now was, and after exchanges about the new house, and what a good job Edgar was making of running the farm, inquiries after the children, pleasantries exchanged genuinely rather than as mere conventions, she began the task, opting to tackle it by the forthright approach she now adopted to most problems.

"Mrs Topham," she said. "I must thank you for wanting to see me before accepting the position my husband has offered you. But I must also make sure you know the situation here, and perhaps what has led to it. Do you?"

"I know most of it, I think, ma'am."

"You know that Mr Unston and I are husband and wife only in a legal sense. No more, and never will be again?"

"Yes. At least, I had deduced it."

"Do you also know what his relationship was with Mrs Lartin?"

"Yes, ma'am, I knew that."

There was a long pause. Griselda found her resolution to be forthrightly outspoken difficult to carry out. But Rachael knew what was going through her mind, and opted to speak first.

"There is nothing like that in my case, ma'am," she said. "Nothing at all. And could not be."

"Knowing what I have learned of you, Mrs Topham, and meeting you now, I accept that most readily," Griselda answered. "But your intentions are only one side of it, aren't they?"

She was almost echoing Marion Richards' warning.

§

Rachael started the new job when Unston returned to Edenhope two weeks later. He asked her to have coffee with him so that he could explain what was needed, although she had already learned of the household's workings through Violet Marchett and Marion Richards. There were now only two full time, live-in servants, kitchen maid Betty and a middle-aged spinster house-parlourmaid, Winifred. The other maid had left for war work in a Wolverhampton factory. Clearly, with the "family" quarters almost unoccupied there was no longer the same need for a full-time cook that there had been in the past, but Unston did not suggest any reduction in Mrs Marchett's hours or pay.

Griselda's immediate liking for Rachael, and the disappearance of Mrs Lartin from the domestic scene, led to a considerable modification in her approach to living at Edenhope. Even before the so-called housekeeper's appearance she, grievously wounded by Jasper's callous announcement, had determined to make it clear to both, especially Miriam, that she was the real mistress of Edenhope. She did not admit it, even to herself, but she wanted to make the woman's life as difficult as possible, although she did not expect her approach to have any positive, practical effect. But in truth it was a factor in Miriam's decision to go back to her husband. In a battle of wills, the woman stood no chance against the new Griselda.

With her gone, Jasper, despised, almost became a cypher in her life. She could meet him, discuss financial affairs, almost impersonally. She felt superior to him, and anyone witnessing their encounters would see it. Also, having met Rachael Topham, and feeling she would like her, the idea of spending rather more time at Edenhope became attractive. Previously she had come, with her daughters and the nursemaid, for a month at a time, not only with the idea of keeping Miriam in her place but of asserting her ownership, or rather her daughters' potential ownership, of that part of the property. Now she decided she would stay most of the time at Edenhope. Almost subconsciously, she was nursing a feeling that she ought to do what she could to protect someone like Rachael from her husband's predatory intentions, the existence of which she had little doubt.

SEVEN

Young Talents

Just after the move into Edenhope Cottage, the county council's education department wrote to Edgar and Rachael to tell them that Stephen's school had put his name forward as a possible "scholarship" candidate for a place at a grammar school, and asking for their parental endorsement. Grammar schools were then, before the 1944 Education Act, fee-paying establishments but with "county special places," called scholarships by most people, awarded to bright children. They knew Stephen was bright and had wondered whether they could afford the fees for the school at Ludstone, and for appreciable associated expenses including travel. But if he could get the award there would be no question – he would go. He sat the exam and was awarded a place.

At Ludstone however, despite his innate ability, he struggled at first to keep up with his classmates and there was a question mark over whether he should stay at the school. The trouble` was that, coming from a small country school, he was behind many of the other boys, many of whom had had private education, unlike today when village schools are often seen as giving their pupils a better start. However, the extra income from Rachael's housekeeping job meant they could put matters right. They learned of a retired teacher living at Maestonbury who could give Stephen the extra tuition which enabled him to catch up in most subjects, and by the end of his second year at Ludstone he was comfortably able to hold his own with the best of his fellow pupils in most subjects, especially the sciences, and maths. Edgar and Rachael, learning the unpalatable lesson, enrolled Elspeth into the care of the same tutor.

They bought Stephen a bicycle which meant the morning journey to the train at Maestonbury took only fifteen minutes. The evening return took much longer, being nearly all uphill. With an hour for the extra tuition added on, it meant a ten hour day for him, longer if he stayed behind for extra activities like sport, on which he was keen, and good at both rugby and cricket. But once over the initial hurdles, he enjoyed school, and was popular there.

By the time Elspeth was at the age of going to secondary school, where secondary schools existed in 1941, she was also showing up as a child of academic promise, and was put in for the scholarship exam, which she passed and went to the girls' grammar, or high school as they were usually known. So that she too was bought a bicycle and joined her brother on the two-mile ride to the train. Hers was a quite different character from Stephen's, who developed a sturdy independence as he entered his teens. She was always happiest in the lee of Rachael's protection, and while her mother sometimes wished she would show more desire to stand on her own feet, and wondered what would have happened to her if she had been left as she, Rachael had been at the age of twelve, mother and daughter enjoyed a closer relationship than nine such out of ten. Elspeth's most precious hours were spent with her in readings and discussions on books and poetry, especially poetry, for the appreciation of which the girl seemed to have a precocious talent. Tennyson, especially tales of Arthur, *Idylls of the King,* was a special favourite, and kept them occupied for more hours than Rachael could spare, sometimes. There was little time for other relaxations, although Elspeth, striking up a friendship with the shepherd's daughter, occasionally wandered round the woods and fields, accompanied by the family's border collie when she was not wanted for work with the sheep. But always Rachael had one of her mind's eyes on her, sometimes worrying, especially after she went to her high school, about how she was coping in the tough outside world. Many times, she urged Stephen to try to keep an eye on her, as much as possible when he had no sight of her during most of the day. And to do him justice, Stephen talked to her as much as he could in the limited time, on bicycles and the train.

The boy himself continued his academic progress and by the time he entered the fifth form, at the end of which year would come the school certificate exams, teachers were predicting results which would take him through the sixth form and probably to university.

He was especially good at anything which required the application of his brain to problem-solving, in geometry, especially. He was still popular at the school, a member of and good-performer in under-16 or "colts" rugby and cricket teams, a good cross-country runner, and a member of the school's army cadets.

Elspeth did not show the same signs of academic brilliance in science subjects, but almost from the start of her secondary school life the love of literature, especially poetry, which had been engendered in her hours of reading with Rachael marked her out as a child likely to shine in those respects. Physics and chemistry passed her by, although she liked the logic and rhythms of mathematics; and she loved history.

In other respects, all seemed to be going as well and smoothly, for the Tophams, as wartime restrictions allowed. Edgar managed the farm to the general satisfaction of both Jasper Unston and the local war agricultural executive committee, universally known as the "war ag", the body given the task of making sure that food production demands were obeyed by farmers. It was hard work, especially when two young members of his work force elected not to exercise their right as reserved occupation workers exempt from military service, and joined up. Geoffrey Marchett, one of Violet's sons, was one, who did not return. He died in the D-Day landings on the Normandy beaches.

Griselda carried out her intention of spending more time at Edenhope, with her daughters until they had to go to school. She taught them herself for a time, well enough to ensure that they could read and write by their fifth birthday, and supervising the education for another year, when, on Rachael's recommendation, she passed them on to the same retired teacher who had helped Stephen and Elspeth.

Mrs Unston and Rachael had established a relationship that grew closer as the war dragged on. The older woman showed an interest in Stephen and Elspeth, and their education, and talked about the twins, which was how Rachael came to suggest the arrangement with the retired teacher. They rarely mentioned Jasper, unless something to do with the farm required it. Edgar developed a habit of seeing Griselda regularly, to keep her in touch with farm affairs, and sometimes to get cheques signed if there was an urgent need when Jasper was away, which was most of the time.

For the first half of the war years, he rarely appeared on more than one weekend in three, explaining his absence by pressure of "my work at the ministry." No-one at Edenhope missed him; the absence made all go smoother, was the general feeling. But Griselda could not help wondering a little. She had been sure that his lecherous eyes were on Rachael and that was the reason for spending so much money on "Edenhope Cottage." Rachael herself, despite having been presented with plenty of evidence of the man's nature and activities over the years, could not quite believe that he was as black as he was painted. Her encounters with him had pointed towards a rather different individual.

Poor Rachael. Lovingly married to a man whose character's central core was decency, and never having come across anyone whose lustful tendencies went further than a mental undressing of some girl or other; herself unable to understand any sexual creed other than that of one man and one woman, despite much worldly knowledge gained from a childhood and adolescence in which female virtue was by no means a rigid norm; and despite those slings and arrows that showed how hard the world was, and which had brought her to Edenhope; she was still ready, eager almost, to believe the best of anyone, even a man like Jasper Unston. And both she and Edgar – for he too wanted always to see good in people – were helped in an unspoken hope that Jasper might have mended his ways, by something neither they nor Griselda knew anything about.

Unston had found a new outlet for his passions, if the brute desires that drove him could be dignified by being so called.

EIGHT

Veronica

Jasper's new amour, who whatever else her function in life, served the purpose of keeping his lascivious eyes not quite so firmly fixed on Rachael Topham, for the time being, was his Westminster secretary, Veronica Bardeni. She was no Miriam Lartin, but the basis of her relationship with her boss was surely as surreally sordid as his in bringing Mrs Lartin to share a house with the wife who had just borne his daughters.

Veronica, moderately good-looking and in her late thirties, was married to a clerk in the Foreign Office, of Italian extraction. She was essentially a "good" woman. That is, she had been faithful to her husband through a dozen years of marriage, and had forgiven him for a brief and meaningless affair which had been put firmly behind them. That however was not the reason for her succumbing to the almost inevitable advances made by Unston whenever a woman he fancied came into his orbit.

She wanted a family. She and Marco put it off, by such means of contraception as were available in pre-war days, then in 1937 decided now was the time. But nothing happened. By the time she was promoted to the job as Unston's secretary she was still hoping, but in vain. She went to her doctor who carried out tests, with a result that pointed in only one direction, for she was perfectly fertile.

She did not dare tell her husband about the tests. The idea that he might be the cause of the failure would have been unbearable to his Mediterranean temperament, she believed. She loved him, sincerely, and would have done a great deal to avoid hurting him. And a great deal was what she did.

Artificial insemination was almost unknown in 1940, or she may well have gone in that direction. But when Jasper Unston started to make advances, even the crude kind he invariably employed in pursuit of fulfilling his equally crude desires, she was hit by a terrible idea.

Terrible to her, a sacrifice that could never be made by a woman with any sense of honour and decency, she thought, as she spent days and nights agonising over it. The idea of being unfaithful to her husband was anathema to her.

There was no-one with whom she could talk about it. Indeed how could there be. How could she say to anyone, however intimate a friend: "I must have a baby, and my husband mustn't know that it's his fault that I can't. So I'm thinking of having it off with my boss. He's making it clear he'd like to."

She knew that Jasper was capable of fathering a child, because he had daughters. What was more, he was not unlike her husband, physically, so there ought to be no question in Marco's mind about the identity of a baby resulting from liaison with Mr Unston. But even as these practical aspects of the affair went through her mind, she recoiled in disgust at the thought of intercourse with anyone other than Marco. And she was not in the least attracted to Jasper.

On the other side of her agony, though, was the thought of the joy she would bring to Marco if she was able to tell him: "Darling, I think we've done it." He would say: "Do you mean...?" And she would kiss him and tell him she was certain – she'd been to the doctor that afternoon.

That thought sent the blood coursing warmly through her body. It was more than enough to counter the shame of unfaithfulness and the miserable anticipation of sex with Jasper Unston. She resolved to go ahead with the ghastly plan.

In fact, she decided to expedite it, by encouraging him. She shortened her skirt, wore a blouse that exposed more cleavage, changing into such clothes at the office so as not to awaken suspicions in Marco; and flashed her legs when she sat to take dictation.

Unston took it all in his stride. After less than a week of such treatment he asked her to go out to dinner with him. She accepted after she had made sure that the venue would be one where no-one who could possibly know her would see them. She even told Marco about it, saying Unston wanted her to meet colleagues from another part of the government offices.

She did not however give in too easily to the inevitable final act. She did not want to allow him a quick roll in the hay, as it were, because that might mean it all ended before she could become pregnant. Privately despising herself as a cold-hearted schemer, she continued the programme of tittilation which invariably ended with his being brought up short and it was weeks before he succeeded in his sexual objective, during which time he had become quite infatuated. Even then, Veronica rationed their "love" sessions, trying to time them with the stage in her menstrual cycle when it was most likely she would conceive.

It all proved to be in vain, however. Two years and many sex sessions after Unston's first advances, she was still without a child in her womb. She began to be depressed, and to ask herself whether it was after all her fault, not Marco's. Then one day the balloon went up in a way she had not anticipated. Marco was present at an all-male inter-office conference when he heard Jasper boasting to someone else about his successes with his secretary, describing her as "a hot bit of alright" who"her husband obviously isn't capable of keeping satisfied." Ha,ha,ha.

Marco went home barely able to keep back angry and anguished tears. Mediterranean ancestry or not, though, he did not embark on any violence towards Veronica, physical or verbal. He sat in a chair, refused a proffered drink, and presently, as he watched the wife who he loved so deeply preparing their meal, gave vent to the restrained feelings, sobbing with his head on his knees.

"Darling, whatever's the matter?" she asked. "Whatever is it?"

After a few seconds, he looked up.

"I know about you and... that man... Unston..."

She was shattered, could not speak, went into the kitchen, collapsed on to a chair, her own head on her hands. It was quarter of an hour before he came to her.

"It's true, then, isn't it?"

Hours later, hours of distressed confession, unbelievable explanation, tearful embraces, real love worked its magic. They decided there and then that she would never go back to the Unston office, not even next day. She would plead unexpected illness. Marco wanted to seek the man out and give him "a damn good hiding," but Veronica persuaded him against it. It would almost certainly cost him his job, she said.

She stayed at home for six months, and never went to work again, for she found she was pregnant. Perhaps the magi had delivered their gift.

§

Unston's department found him a new secretary when it became clear that Veronica would not be returning, but with this one he never even thought of starting a campaign that had his usual objective. She was fifty-five, about to become a grandmother, not very good-looking, and, he could see, if he had wanted to know, that his advances would get nowhere.

The loss of Mrs Bardeni however set him off in a direction he had only abandoned because of his success with her, and because he was not at Edenhope very much. He started to again cast his eyes towards Rachael, by now, towards the end of 1943, well in command of the household and friendly with Griselda, who spent most of her time there, only departing for Withymoor when Jasper's weekend arrival was imminent. Petrol rationing restricted her travel but she would sometimes get Edgar, in his farm van, or his opposite number at Withymoor, to ferry her to and fro.

Unston began to step up the frequency of his visits to Shropshire, although his boss at the War Office made more demands on his time as preparations for the Second Front, the Normandy invasion, took centre stage in the spring of 1944. To be fair, his shortcomings did not include neglecting his work, and although plenty of others would have echoed his minister's "don't like the chap" he was doing a useful job and generally doing it well. He played a full part in the organising, kept his mouth firmly shut as part of the huge campaign of secrecy. And he did not find anything like as much scope for hectoring and bullying in wartime Whitehall as in rural Shropshire.

He managed therefore to return to Edenhope on alternate weekends, as a rule. And before Veronica's departure was three months in the past he had renewed his intentions towards Rachael, engendered years before, but which up to now had consisted only of pleasantries connected with her move, and Edgar's, into Edenhope Cottage, two years previously. He was not happy about Griselda's new routine, when he learned about it through the back door of servant references to her, but as she was never there for his weekend visits, and his only contact with her was if estate business made it necessary, he did not mean to let her presence interfere with his private life. Meaning, his determination to get to close quarters with Mrs Topham.

He was helped, fortuitously, by the farm manager himself. Edgar had been looking after the farm accounts and paperwork, prior to handing them over to the estate accountants. But as it mounted with demands from official sources, he was finding it took more of his time, which could not easily be found, and he had said as much to his employer. Now Unston saw an opportunity to set a trap.

"Could not your wife do it, Topham?" he asked. "From what I've seen of her I get the impression she is fully capable of such work."

"Yes, sir, she is, more than capable. She did all our own accounts – not that they were anything like ours here. But she's pretty fully occupied, with her work here and the children. But I'll ask her, if you wish."

"Let me talk to her, Topham. Then we can discuss pay and so on. Obviously we should have to pay her for the extra work."

Edgar thought it sounded reasonable. The fears he, Griselda and one or two more had entertained two years before had subsided when nothing untoward had happened. He said only: "Yes, sir."

That same weekend, Jasper waylaid Rachael as she went about her household duties, kept to a minimum on Saturday and Sunday.

"I'd like a word, Mrs Topham," he said. "Could you come into the office a moment?"

He was careful not to go beyond compliments on the way the house was now run, realising how busy she must be, but putting to her the proposal about the accounts. It was all done in the charming manner he could turn on and off like a tap.

"I know it would be a great help to your husband," he said. "The time he has had to spend on the paperwork has been worrying him, I know. And I know you've been helping him. I think the time has come to put it all on a proper footing."

"Well, sir, what have you in mind? I'm quite prepared to carry on as we are, only do a bit more of it. I'm sure you realise that Edgar has to be involved."

"Of course. He's doing a good job and he has to know about that side of it. But I think I should be more involved, as well. Don't you?"

"Yes, sir, of course." She would have liked to add: "And Mrs Unston," but thought it wiser not to. The thought that "you haven't bothered much about it up now" also flitted through her mind but had to be unspoken. But she was also thinking, again like Edgar, how personally reasonable he now seemed, a distance removed from the bullying despot he had been when they first came to Edenhope, six or seven years before. Perhaps he was maturing.

Jasper told her she would have a fifty per cent increase in her pay for doing the paperwork, and he would want a regular rundown before it was passed on to the accountant, through a report in his office on every Saturday he was there.

"Eleven o'clock would be a good time," said. "Yes, let us say eleven. The maid will know whether I am here or not. But I aim to get here on alternate weekends." She thought it would surely be sensible for him to see her at the same time as Edgar, whose regular appointment was at nine-thirty, but did not say so, and made arrangements for the meetings.

First time, he was no more than pleasantly polite, asking her only to point out the main points of the figures and discussing with her the general economics of the farm, which her innate business sense and knowledge of farming made easy enough. He asked after the children, and talked about "my little daughters" and "my sisters," which grated somewhat, for her growing intimacy with his wife had brought a feeling that he did not care tuppence for any of them.

Again though she had to accept that he was quite different from the individual they had seen in the past, on the surface at least.

"You know, I can hardly accept that he's the same man who put his wife through all that, and was so unpleasant to you and other people," she told Edgar that evening. He said: "Yes, love, he does seem to have changed a bit. I hope you're right."

Two weeks later, Unston asked if he could call her by her first name, which set her nerves jangling slightly, although the session, apart from that, to which she could only reply, "Yes, sir, certainly," consisted only of pleasant exchanges and questions from him, through the half hour she was there. He made no attempt to touch her, appeared to her to be careful to keep a physical distance. When she left, she asked if he would like a cup of coffee, and he replied: "Yes, please," and politely opened the door for her to go. She told Winifred to get the coffee from the kitchen and take it to him.

Britain was agog during the early months of 1944, waiting for news of the Second Front, as it was universally known at that time. Jasper Unston did not visit Edenhope at all during May, as the final preparations were made for the Normandy landings, and he was engaged in liaison between his government department and sections of the forces. As with the Tophams, he brought the pleasanter possibilities of his character to the fore as he talked with generals and air marshals and was afterwards described by a government colleague – who actually could not stand him – as "a junior minister who did an important job and did it well."

It was the weekend following the invasion on June 5 before he got to Edenhope. One would have expected that after his busy, even exhausting month, he would have been content to relax in the calm of the Shropshire countryside, his bullying and predatory instincts pushed to the back of his mind. But for Jasper, relaxation meant allowing such instincts free rein after a period of forcing himself to be pleasant to everyone in the execution of his duties – which, to again be fair to him were done well enough and even with a degree of enthusiasm.

He arrived late on Friday night, after the household had gone to bed, and immediately reverted to form by ringing for the parlourmaid and peremptorily ordering her to get his bed ready, bring his breakfast in the morning and make sure the farm manager and Mrs Topham knew he was back. He was still in bed when Edgar came at his usual time, but managed to be relatively amenable during a brief discussion of farm affairs. He was still in his dressing gown at lunch time and when Rachael appeared an hour later.

She said: "Oh, I'm sorry, sir. I'll come back later."

"No, please don't. Just get the maid to bring us some coffee, and we'll get on with the business."

They were in his office cum study, but he made no move to take his place behind his desk, instead sitting down in one of the two semi-easy chairs, and motioning to her to take the other.

"How have you been, Rachael? It seems a long time since I saw you. I've missed you."

Alarm bells started to ring. She said: "Thank you sir. I expect you've been very busy."

"Yes, my dear, I have. But that didn't stop me missing you."

Winifred the parlourmaid arrived with a tray and coffee cups.

"Put it on the desk," Unston said, and took a chair to place against his own, behind his desk.

Rachael with her usual folder containing the farm papers, rose and waited for the instruction which was obviously coming.

"Sit here, please, my dear, and we'll go through it," he said.

She moved round the desk, sat on the second chair. He had placed it quite close to his own, and she would have liked to move it further away, but could not without making it obvious she was trying to keep her distance. It was clear he was trying to imply familiarity but, up to now, nothing more, and when he spoke again it was only to say: "I'm a month out of date. Is there anything of particular importance to report?"

"I expect Edgar... my husband... told you about the sales of the early lambs. Apart from that it's been quite routine, sir. There was one bill that couldn't wait and Mrs Unston had to sign the cheque. It's all down in the accounts." She opened her accounts book at the relevant date and placed it in front of him. He ran his finger down the pages.

"It all looks satisfactory, Rachael. I'm sure I can leave it in your hands."

She took the farm cheque book from her folder. "If you could check these against the accounts, please, sir, and sign the cheques. I've made them out."

She pushed the cheque book towards him but he intercepted the movement and put his hand on hers. She tried to draw it away but he clasped her wrist.

"Don't, sir, please... please... don't..."

To her surprise, he let her go. She picked up her papers, moved round the desk and towards the door.

"Don't go, Rachael," he protested. "I'm sorry... I don't know..."

"I'm sorry, too, sir. I thought you knew... I'm not... like that..."

"You see, Rachael, I'm so lonely. And you know my wife isn't really, you know...

"Yes, sir. But Edgar is very much my husband... I wouldn't... do wrong... to him... not ever."

, "I'm sorry. It won't happen again."

Unston could not have explained what had happened to him that day. Not once before, in thirty years of one pursuit after another, had he allowed himself to be put off so easily. He had simply backed off, abandoned his attack almost before it was launched. And towards a woman he had wanted ever since he first set eyes on her nearly 10 years before. Was he now going to give up his desire because she had displayed the kind of prudery that went out with Queen Victoria, he asked himself?

Rachael did not quite know what to do. Unston had abandoned his advances when he came up against quite modest resistance from her. Was it a basic decency, a change of character coming with maturity, for which she had been prepared to give him credit in their previous dealings? Also, there was the important question of whether she should tell Edgar what had happened. But, again giving Jasper the benefit of the doubt, she was inclined not to. It would be difficult to explain her thinking, and Edgar might well react strongly. He had said, had he not, that "we'll be gone from here in no time if he tries anything like that." He would do it, and give up a job in which he was now so enjoyably immersed, and which was bringing them prosperity they had never before known. No, she would not tell him, and hope she was right in her assessment of Unston's maturing character.

She was not, of course, although she was encountering a Jasper different, on the surface, from the Unston who had spent much of his life in crude seduction and domination. Next time they met, he greeted her with a kind of embarrassed smile. He still called her by her Christian name. But although he stayed at Edenhope for most of the following week, in fact was still there when Griselda returned on the Wednesday, he very quickly reverted to his old ways on his return to London. The middle-aged secretary was temporarily drafted to another position, and he was provided with a younger woman who, although efficient enough in terms of work, was blowsily attractive, quite used to putting herself about and as fond of sex as he was. Griselda's return to Edenhope while he was still there was in fact a spur, made him think to himself what a stupid so-and-so he had been in giving up his pursuit of Rachael so easily. "Should have pressed on, shown the bitch (meaning Griselda) that she can't rule the roost with me," he said to himself. The result was firstly that he was into the new secretary's underclothes within a fortnight of returning to his office, and was still there regularly on VE day in May next year; and secondly that Rachael was pushed down the scale of his desires for the time being.

Things changed rapidly in July, two months later. The coalition which had ruled the country for ten years and through the war, under Churchill, was brought to an end by a sweeping Labour victory. Unston held on to his seat in rural South Shropshire, but lost his government job including the secretary and her obliging qualities. He reverted to regular weekend visits to Edenhope, and renewed pursuit of Rachael, the flickerings of decency she had brought out of him extinguished like a candle in a gale of wind.

NINE

Timetable to Tragedy

One of Unston's first moves on beginning the new routine was to tell Edgar and Rachael that the regular Saturday morning briefings – the term he used – would resume. At first, he was quite peremptory with the bailiff, almost giving the impression of "now I'm back, Topham, and I'm in command" but the attitude softened as he realised, as he of course knew very well, that the farm was being well run, and he kept his bullying to occasional choleric outbursts on minor matters, which Edgar mentally shrugged off.

He was however well and truly back on the trail of pursuit of Rachael. The sight of her set his pulse racing in a way no woman had done before. Not yet 40, she was as physically attractive as she had ever been, not that her kind of good looks had usually been the sort that turned him on. But now he seemed to thirst for her. Again he wondered, coming as near as he ever could to that kind of introspection, what had made him hold back more than a year before.

He again began to speak to her in intimate tone, calling her "my dear" and even "sweetheart," indulging in risque double entendres as though sharing a joke with her. It was however weeks before he made a physical pass at her, and at first it was no more than a pat on the bottom as she leaned over a table. It was quite different from the kind of tactic he had employed through most of his life, no doubt because she was a very different woman from most of the types who had satisfied his lusts previously. And was in fact so gradual that she allowed herself to accept it as nothing more than a type of hearty comradeship, common to men like him. Subconsciously there was also a wish for nothing drastic to happen that would mean the end of their comfortable life at Edenhope, and especially the kind of fulfillment Edgar now enjoyed. Her husband asked her occasionally "how he was behaving" but she would always say something like: "Oh, just like him, you know how he is, but nothing to worry about."

She still had little chats to Griselda, of whom she had become increasingly fond, but who she still addressed with the occasional "ma'am." They talked about the children, their individualities, education, illnesses. Mrs Unston, although she never said so to Rachael, was pleased that there seemed no signs of the Unston character coming out in her daughters. And she always made quite a fuss of Elspeth, now entering her teens, on the few occasions they came into contact.

She too, although more circumspectly than Edgar, inquired how her husband was behaving in the office, although only by asking how Rachael was getting on with him, and receiving a parallel answer to the one given to Edgar. But more pungent comments came from Marion Richards, who still worked in the house, doing the laundry, although she now had an electric iron with the advent at last of the new power. She told Rachael: "You still need to watch 'im. I wouldna trust 'im as far as I could throw 'im."

§

It was a Saturday in March. Rachael attended Unston in his study at the established time, eleven o'clock, but was told he had other things he must see to. She would have to come back at three. Not terribly happily, for she had other plans for the afternoon, she went away, mentally rejigging her timetable, not easy for she had arranged to spend the afternoon going through some work with Elspeth, who had gone out with Marion Richards' daughter and could not be contacted to be told of the new schedule. But after lunch with Stephen and Edgar, who was relief milking on cowman Jeremy's weekend off, she knocked on the study door.

Jasper was sitting in one of the two semi-easy chairs in the corner of the room, and when she went in, signalled her to the other. Before she sat down, she opened the little attache case in which she kept her farm documents, and took out the accounts folder.

He said: "Never mind that now, Rachael. Just talk to me. I've had a hard day. I need some pleasant company."

"I'm sorry to hear that, sir – I mean about the hard day. I'll try to be pleasant company, but we have to get on with the work, if you don't mind. I've got things to do at home."

He got up as though to move to the back of his desk, and she did the same. But instead of sitting down, he put his arm round her shoulders. She tried to wriggle away, but he clasped her tighter, in both arms.

"Rachael, don't. I want you. I've wanted you for ten years. You must know. You're meant for me..."

She could smell whisky on his breath, something she had never noticed before. She thought quickly. A plan formed.

"Let me go, please – Jasper," she said. "Then we can talk, about anything you like. Let us sit down." He released her, and she sat, on the nearer of the two armchairs. "Come, sit here," she said, indicating the other chair. He dropped himself into it. "Come here. Sit on my knee," he said.

She started to rise, but instead of turning towards him, moved the other way, grabbed the attaché case from the desk, and tried to open the door.

It was locked. He had meant to be sure she could not get away and had quickly turned the key as he first clasped her. Now he was up again and had his arms round her.

"You're not going... not this time..." He pushed her towards the wall, thrusting his hand up her skirt. With a mighty effort, and helped by the skirt being up round her hips she brought her knee up into his genitals, with all the force she could muster. He dropped away, clutching himself. "You bitch," he mouthed. She grabbed a big glass paperweight from the desk and swung it, again with all her strength, against the side of his head. He dropped back, and she again made for the door, turned the key and ran out, along the passages and into her own kitchen.

There was no-one there. Stephen was upstairs, doing schoolwork; Edgar had gone to start his milking chore; Elspeth had not returned from her walk. She dragged herself up in the stairs, flung herself on the bed in her – their – room. Not crying, her eyes rarely shed tears, but racked by silent sobs.

"Oh God, I should have let him," she mourned. Then: "No, no, no. But I should have listened to them. Edgar, Edgar, my love, I've ruined your life. I've let you down. Why couldn't I manage it better?"

§

Elspeth returned moments later, never thought to look in her parents' room but went into Stephen's.

"Yes, Tadpole, what do you want?" It was his pet name for her as she grew towards an attractive but somewhat gangly fourteenth birthday.

"Where's Mum?"

"She'd got to go and see his lordship because he wasn't there this morning, I think. Expect that's where she is. Don't think she'll be long, though. She said she'd be back about half-past."

"I've got to see her pretty urgently."

"What about?"

"Oh, it doesn't matter."

"Can't be so awful urgent, then, can it? But if it's so important, why don't you go and look. Nobody'll eat you."

Elspeth's "pretty urgent" need was the one which comes on young girls about that age, and which her mother had warned her would be with her "one of these days." She had a tummy ache and, she thought, the first signs of the rest of the trouble that would be with her for the next thirty or forty years. She and Stephen got on well together although he tended to make it clear she was "only" his kid sister, but she could not possibly tell him about this.

Now she went first to the kitchen but only Violet Marchett was there, and she knew nothing of her mother's whereabouts. She went off down the rambling corridor and came on Winifred the parlourmaid who told her she thought her mother was with Mr Unston in the study. She went to listen at the door, but could hear nothing, and knocked. His voice said – muttered, really, she could only hear it faintly: "Well?" She went in.

Unston was slumped in his chair behind the desk, staring straight in front. But he said: "Hello, my dear, come in. My, you're a pretty girl. What can I do for you?"

"I'm looking for my mother, please, sir. They told me she might be here."

"Oh, yes, she's gone. Left me all alone. You wouldn't do that to me, would you, sweetheart? You wouldn't go away and leave me all alone? Come and sit here with me." He got up, stumbled round the desk, caught hold of her.

She was afraid. She said: "I'd better go and find Mum, sir. I need her urgently."

"No, stay with me. I'll look after you." He put his arm tighter round her. She struggled but could not get away. In another few minutes, despite her struggles and screams, she was half naked across the desk and he was on top of her.

§

Rachael heard Elspeth in Stephen's room, and managed to raise herself out of her near stupor to get off the bed and move next door to ask him where the girl was.

"She's gone to find you," he said. "She said she needed you urgently."

"Do you know where?"

"I thought you were with Mr Unston, and I expect that's where she's gone to look."

"Oh, my god, my god..."

She ran down the stairs, out into the corridor and along towards "the house." She met Winifred, asked her if she had seen Elspeth, and was told. Her heart in her mouth, for she feared the state Unston might now be in, she almost ran the remaining yards to the study and heard her daughter's screams before she opened the door.

Summoning strength she never knew she had, she pulled him away, grabbed the crying Elspeth and half dragged, half carried her back to her own house. She told her, in a voice amazingly firm and even: "Go upstairs and get in the bath." She herself went downstairs, opened a kitchen drawer and took out two 12-bore cartridges, lifted down Edgar's gun and loaded it, as she half ran along the corridor. At the study, she went straight in. Unston was slumped in a chair. She put the gun to his head and pulled the triggers, one after the other. His blood and brains spattered the room.

Winifred heard the shots, met Rachael coming from the study, still carrying the gun.

"I've killed him," she said, her voice still calm and steady. "Send for the police."

The maid, opened-mouthed, looked in the study, screamed when she saw. Rachael carried on to her own kitchen, hung the gun back on its pegs, for all the world as though she had just come in from shooting rabbits. She moved towards the stairs, but never reached them as she fell in a heap on the floor, where Stephen, alarmed first by Elspeth's violent sobs, in the bathroom, found her minutes later.

§

Telephone calls brought a car load of police, quickly followed by an ambulance, and the questions began. Rachael, now conscious but hardly able to speak, answered some of them in a barely audible voice. Edgar, called from his milking by Winifred who fetched one of the men to take over, did likewise. A woman officer, summoned from a distant office, took Elspeth away, trying to calm the child through her tears and protests.

Rachael, as soon as she was able to answer coherently, told the senior police officer exactly what had happened, starting with Unston's own attack on her, and making no attempt to hide the fact that she had deliberately shot him.

"He was... doing that... to my little girl... and he had tried to do it to me," she said. "He was an evil man, and I killed him."

She was told she would be charged with murder, to which she responded with a quiet: "Yes. Of course."

Everyone concerned, policemen, Violet Marchett, Winifred, Edgar and Stephen wondered at her apparent state of quiet calm.

Edgar was in a much more openly emotional state. Stephen tried to comfort him. Edgar asked, when they took her away, if he could go with her, but was told he could not. He could perhaps see her later, at the Shrewsbury police station where she was being taken.

Violet and Marion Richards prepared some food, which Stephen ate but Edgar refused. He tried to call the number the police had left him but was told it was too soon for him to be given any information, about either his wife or Elspeth. But later he was told he could see Rachael for a few minutes.

Griselda, as Jasper Unston's wife, had been told of her husband's death, including that it appeared he had been shot by Mrs Topham. The inspector who delivered the information could not understand why the dead man's wife seemed to be more worried about the killer than the killed, her own husband.

"Oh, Rachael, Rachael, I tried to warn you," she burst out in an unusual display of emotion. Leaving the twins in the care of their nurse, she got straight into her car and drove to Edenhope, still swarming with police examining the fatal study, taking samples, fingerprints and statements. Near to tears herself, she told Edgar: "Oh, Mr Topham – Edgar – why did you come here? Why ever did I marry him? He was a bad, bad man. None of us should have allowed ourselves to get anywhere near him."

Later, when Edgar was told he would be allowed to see Rachael, briefly, she offered to drive him to the county town. Stephen could not see her, for the time being, they said.

It was a sombre journey, in which, through the beautiful hills and valleys, she would otherwise have taken much pleasure, after a period when car journeys had been severely restricted. She was already thinking about the future, what was to happen to the Tophams, to Edenhope, its other people, now her sole responsibility, and those things would have to be talked about. But not now. One thing however she wanted to say, and did.

"Edgar, I want you to know one thing," she said. "Whatever happens, you and your family will always have my friendship, and support when it's needed. I have grown very fond of Rachael, and I have a great respect for you and the work you have done here. Please remember that, and count on it. Whatever happens."

"Thank you, ma'am. You're very kind."

§

Rachael's apparent calm had disappeared by the time Edgar was allowed to see her, for about quarter of an hour with two police officers present. He wanted to hold her, comfort her, but he was told he must not touch her. Through nearly twenty years of sharing happiness, financial ups and downs, bouts of misery, he had never known her shed a tear. Now, although she looked into his eyes for all the few minutes they were allowed together, with a burly police sergeant keeping watch, she never stopped crying. All he could do was return her gaze and tell her, softly: "I love you, I love you, I'll always love you." She spoke hardly a word, only, as he was told he must go: "Look after the children, look after the children."

Afterwards, the detective chief inspector who seemed to be in charge of the case told him he wanted to ask him some questions. Edgar thought he did not seem an understanding or sympathetic individual.

"Did you know your wife was having an affair with Mr Unston?" was almost his first question.

Edgar was taken aback. The very idea was monstrous. He could hardly reply in any way that made sense. The policeman seemed to take his confusion for embarrassment at a liaison being discovered.

"How long had it been going on, Mr Topham?" he asked.

Edgar managed a few coherent words of protest.

"She wasn't having an... affair... with him. She isn't like that... she couldn't be less... like that..."

The chief inspector looked hard at him. To be fair, he did not think that Rachael and Unston had been having an affair. He was probing, trying to make some sense out of a situation he found difficult to comprehend. He was not used to dealing with killings – they happened rarely in Shropshire, especially killings of MPs and former government ministers. There seemed to be an implication that the dead man had been shot while he was assaulting a young girl. Chief Inspector Rawlings found it hard to believe that such a person, in such a position and from such an old-established county family, could do such a thing.

He asked more questions, but they related to the actual incident, and Edgar had not been in the house when any of it happened. He asked the chief inspector for news of Elspeth, but was told he knew nothing at that stage. She was being cared for at "a children's facility" elsewhere in the town, there would be a medical examination, and he would be informed of its outcome "in due course."

Edgar of course also asked what would happen to Rachael, was told she would be taken before a magistrate next day who would no doubt agree that she should be "remanded in custody" pending further inquiries and an eventual appearance at an Assize court.

"Will she be kept here?" he asked.

"Oh, no, it will be a prison somewhere. Probably Strangeways – they have women there." Edgar's heart sank even further. Manchester was nearly a hundred miles away.

As he joined Griselda in her car, she asked: "How was she?"

"Terrible, ma'am," was all he could say.

As they drove, she told him: "Edgar, you can't stay there" – she meant Edenhope. "I think you and Stephen should come to Withymoor, for the time being. And Elspeth, as soon as you get her back. There's plenty of room."

§

Next day, Griselda insisted on taking Edgar to the magistrates' court hearing where Rachael was remanded "to the custody of His Majesty's Prison Service" and he learned she was indeed going to Strangeways Gaol. He was able to see her only for a few minutes. He was also told that unless he could bring her some clothes, she would have to wear prison dress, whereupon Griselda insisted on going out to buy new garments for there would not have been time to fetch her own from Edenhope.

"Oh, no, ma'am, you can't do that. It's not your fault..." Edgar protested, but she said it did not matter whose fault it was, she could not abandon Rachael for the sake of a few pounds worth of clothes.

He also inquired again about Elspeth, was told where she was, and he could see her briefly, but she would have to stay there for another day or two until police officers had interviewed her. They made the short detour necessary, both went in to see her and found her in a desperately low state. She cried in Edgar's arms, begged for news of her mother and became almost hysterical when she was told what was happening.

"Will they... will they... *hang* her?" she almost screamed. Edgar could not speak, but Griselda caught her hand and said: "No, my dear, I'm sure they won't. Not when everyone knows what happened." And she told the girl that her father and Stephen were staying at Withymoor and she hoped she would do the same as soon as she was allowed home.

Stephen seemed to have gone into a state of almost morbid introspection. He was polite to Griselda or her household staff, but he never spoke, even to her or his father, unless he was spoken to, and he would disappear into his room, or the farm buildings, for an hour at a time. On Monday morning Griselda said to him: "We'd better tell your school what's happening, Stephen, hadn't we?" He replied only: "Yes, Mrs Unston, suppose so. Don't want to go back though." But he did, the following week, after the headmaster assured Edgar he would keep a very careful eye on how he fared. In fact, he coped well, even when he overheard comments about what had happened from his fellows. But to be fair to them, no such insensitivies came from any of his fellow fifth formers. The head boy, three years older, made a point of chatting to him.

As soon as she was allowed by the police, Griselda, with Violet Marchett and Marion Richards, set about cleaning up Jasper's study. She also got them to sort out the Tophams' house, involving Edgar on the basis that he must not be allowed to sink into a morbid refusal to go there. She asked him what he wanted to do about the farm, and he told her he would of course do whatever she wanted.

"I think we should carry on as we have been, if you're prepared to do it," she said. "I don't want to lose you, Edgar. In fact..."

But she did not say what she had in mind. It was much too soon.

TEN

Fight for Life

It was Griselda who took the lead in getting what she had no doubt would be justice for Rachael. Of course she had done wrong in shooting Jasper – taking life, even the life of such a man as she now knew him to have been, was always wrong. She knew the letter of the law would demand that Rachael forfeit her life, in retribution. An eye for an eye. But oh my god, what a ghastly, one-sided bargain. To take away the life of a good, hard-working, loving wife and mother in recompense for the life of a man like Jasper Unston, even allowing for the work he had done in the war, as a government official. The fact that he was her husband, the father of her children, was irrelevant, set against the way he had treated her and behaved to so many other women throughout his life, and had finally sated his lust on a thirteen-year-old child.

She told Edgar what she thought they should do. Through her own solicitor, Edward Boulton, who she knew would think along the same lines, they should first of all make sure the facts of what had happened on that Saturday were known and corroborated. That was not easy as far as the events in the study was concerned, for only Rachael and Elspeth knew the facts, and they were both severely affected, emotionally. But the medical evidence would surely help, and Rachael must be brought to a state where she could state the facts plainly before a court, jury or whoever. And she, Griselda, would foot all the bills, she said.

"I can't think of any more important use for my money than to make sure that justice is done for your wife," she told Edgar. "And I mean real justice. Not the 'eye for an eye' kind."

Griselda also determined that her husband's real character, as far as his dealings with women were concerned, must be brought out, openly. It would be an important factor in the judicial system's decisions on Rachael's fate, she reasoned. But bringing it into the open would be hugely difficult. After all, she herself knew little as fact apart from his affair with Miriam Lartin. And she guessed, accurately enough, that family and political allies would close ranks if there was any attempt to dig dirt which might rub off on them.

Edgar had not known Griselda before that brief encounter in her husband's study, so was not aware of how her character had changed. The rather dull, uninspired and uninspiring woman of her father's mill-owning days had given way to one of purpose and determination. More than one event had brought it about. The birth of her twin daughters, Jasper's inhuman treatment of her, even her growing regard for Rachael, Edgar and others at Edenhope had been and still were factors.

Before the week following the tragedy was out, she had set her efforts in motion, first of all by consulting Marion Richards and Violet Marchett. Both had heard of the event that had brought Unston back to Edenhope in disgrace from his job on a family connection's estate – the attempt to seduce a sixteen year old girl. Edward Boulton set in train efforts to find out the truth, but the enquiry agent he employed came back quickly to say that he had been "warned off – in no uncertain manner." Enquries in London did not run into the buffers quite so quickly. There had been rumours about Jasper's in-office affairs. But no-one knew enough to enable the enquirer to run to ground anyone willing or indeed able to testify in court. Veronica Bardeni heard of the enquiries through her husband and contacted Mr Boulton. Griselda went to see her, and was told, in a long, tearful session, of *that* sordid if in the end happy story, but Veronica said, quite understandably Mrs Unston felt, that she could not give evidence in public. Boulton said that of course Griselda could not relay the story in court, for it would be hearsay evidence and not allowed.

Boulton made efforts to get Mrs Lartin to give evidence on the same theme, but completely without success. She wanted to know how much she would be paid.

In the end the lawyers – a top barrister had been employed – came to the conclusion that the only evidence pointing to Jasper Unston's depraved character would have to come from Griselda herself. Bringing Miriam Lartin into the house, in the way he did, was a telling point enough, anyway.

§

Rachael's trial was fixed for the end of May, only seven weeks from the day of the terrible event. Edgar was allowed to see her weekly, and saw a steady improvement in her condition. She greeted him more cheerfully each time, discussed her situation and his quite normally, expressed her enormous gratitude to Griselda, and spent most of the time they had together talking about the children. She did not want to talk much about the coming trial, she said – she had enough of that with the lawyers.

"I can only tell the truth, can't I, love," she said. "I know I shouldn't have done it, but I did, and I'm not sorry, as far as he was concerned. The awful thing is that I've got to leave you, and the children."

On another occasion: "I'm not afraid of... what might happen. You've only got to die once, haven't you?"

And on his last visit before the trial: "You will make sure the children have good lives, won't you, Edgar, my darling. Try not to let them think badly... of me."

But she never shed a tear. That was for him, every time he had to leave her.

He fetched Elspeth from the children's home midway through the first week. She was in a very low state, said she could not go back to school. Griselda worked a minor miracle with her, Edgar thought, went with him to the school, explained the situation, and brought back all her books and a schedule of work with which she promised to help the girl until she was fit to return.

A lady who has been missing from these pages for a long time also came along to play a part in helping Stephen and Elspeth through the most traumatic period of their lives. It was Griselda again who told Edgar's sister Ida of the awful happenings and asked her to stay a few days at Withymoor. She had been a regular if not very frequent visitor at Edenhope, usually with her husband Arthur who was always pleased to see how "his" cows were doing, and Mrs Unston had met her there. Edgar, in his distress, never thought of contacting his sister but Griselda, fearing that she might learn of the tragedy through the newpapers, took it on herself. Stephen had always been a favourite with Aunt Ida, who had no son, only two daughters, and she took both him and Elspeth under her wing, driving them to school while she was there, returning to watch a rugby match in which he was taking part, and helping in supervision of their work.

"It won't help your mum if you neglect your school work," she told them. "It would drag her down."

Edgar continued to supervise the Edenhope farm, although for one reason or another he was often unable to spend all his time there. Griselda had a foreman, George Davies, inherited from her father, to look after Withymoor Home Farm's two hundred and fifty acres. He and Edgar got on well and Davies could be relied on to keep an eye on Edenhope if necessary. Mrs Unston had a part-time secretary to help keep track of affairs on the estates – seven farms and a dozen other houses – and the farm accounts were handed over to her.

Griselda knew that Edgar would sooner or later wonder what was going to happen regarding Edenhope. Frankly, she had to admit, she did not know herself, although one or two possibilities wandered through her mind. She could not see herself or the Tophams going to live there. But she wanted to assure Edgar, and through him the children, of the continuing validity of what she had said to him as they travelled to the county town that day: that they would always have her friendship, and support if it was needed. The opportunity arose when one day, on receiving his pay, through the secretary, he sought her out to tell her: "I don't want to seem presumptuous, ma'am. But I think we need to make some, er, adjustment in our financial arrangements."

"What do you mean, Edgar?"

"Well, you've just paid me my normal wage, but I'm living on you, and the children. I don't suppose you'd like me to give you money, like a lodger, but I think my pay ought to be adjusted."

"Don't talk rubbish, Topham." But she smiled. Edgar thought she could look quite attractive when she smiled, nowadays. "Didn't I tell you, the other week, that you could always rely on my friendship? Friends don't ask their guests to pay for their keep, do they, Edgar? We'll talk about such matters when the time is right."

§

Although Rachael seemed to become more composed, even cheerful, as the Monday set for the trial approached, Edgar and the children, Griselda, Ida and the Edenhope women became increasingly downcast. Griselda's daughters, now away at school, had been somewhat insulated from the events. Edgar drove Griselda's car, with her and the two children, to the assizes at Stafford.

Elspeth, as a possible witness, had to surrender to officials before the proceedings began.

Edgar had been told by the lawyers of the form the trial would take, and that the prosecution was intending to keep its case strictly factual, but he was still surprised at the brevity of their presentation. He was also surprised when, after Rachael was asked how she would plead, and she said, firmly, "guilty" that the judge directed that a not guilty plea be recorded, as was common in murder cases where the life of the accused was at stake.

Prosecuting counsel said the basic facts were clear, and indisputable. Mr Unston, the deceased, was a respected member of parliament, a junior minister in the wartime government, and a landowning member of a long-established Shropshire family. The defendant Topham was his housekeeper and farm secretary and lived with her son, daughter and husband, who was the farm manager, in part of Edenhope House. She had discovered the deceased in the act of sexually assaulting her thirteen year old daughter, who the prosecution did not propose to call because of her age. Medical evidence from an examination immediately after the incident confirmed that she had been sexually violated. Mrs Topham, after coming on the assault, in the deceased's study had traversed twenty yards of corridor, from the study to her own family quarters, deliberately loaded her husband's 12-bore shotgun, traversed the same distance to return to the study, and killed Jasper Unston by firing both barrels at his head, at close range. She had then returned to her own kitchen, telling a servant maid on the way "I have killed him, call the police," and replaced the gun in its usual place. The prosecution accepted the sexual assault as a fact.

"The provocation the assault invoked cannot be and is not disputed," counsel added. "But the deliberate, apparently calm way she went about acquiring and loading the weapon, then deliberately shooting Mr Unston in the head, twice, can leave no doubt that this was a premeditated act of murder which calls for punishment by the extreme measure demanded by the law for this crime."

He was asking for the death penalty but doing it in a manner that clearly left the way open for Rachael's defence to bring in all the factors they had been assembling in the last seven weeks.

Edward Boulton had engaged a young London barrister, Rupert Maconachie, who had been recommended by a friend of his, Charles Jameson. Maconachie had done a sterling job in pleading the case when Jameson's son became foolishly involved with a gang of arms and drugs smugglers. The barrister made full use of the opportunities left open by the prosecution to first of all allow Edgar, Violet Marchett and Marion Richards to tell the jury as much as the judge would allow of Rachael's character, about which there was no problem, and the situation at Edenhope vis-a-vis Unston and Miriam Larkin, not much of which could be stated openly, by them.

Griselda was the prime witness. The jury's eyes nearly popped out of their heads when she told the court, in answer to Maconachie's questions, that she was Jasper Unston's wife and thought Rachael Topham was a wonderful wife, mother and worker. Bringing out what had happened when he had brought Mrs Larkin into the house was a much trickier business, but he managed it, although the judge brought him up short once or twice.

Griselda herself was however determined that her husband's character should be exposed as far as was possible. When Maconachie's questions at one stage were clamped down upon by the judge, who questioned their relevance, she said, loudly: "I think all that is very relevant, your honour. May I say something about it?"

The judge, taken aback like the jury, said he would allow it but warned that it must be relevant to the case before the court and he would stop her immediately if it was not.

She said: "I think it is very important, your honour, that the jury, and yourself, should know what kind of a man my husband was. The kind of man who would bring his mistress to live in the house with his wife who had just borne his daughters, as he did. And who through all his life had been a womaniser and seducer, who..."

She was sharply interrupted by the judge, who also told the clerk that those words must be struck out of the record. But she had made her point. The jury had heard. Maconachie asked more questions which enabled her fears about Jasper's designs on Rachael to be brought out, although he was warned by the judge that "Mr Unston is not on trial here, Mr Maconachie."

A murmur went round the court when Maconachie called Rachael herself. After the preliminaries of establishing her position at Edenhope, he asked her to tell the court exactly what happened on that Saturday afternoon.

"Mr Unston asked me to go there at three o'clock to go through the farm accounts with him."

"And did you?"

"I took all the papers with me but he said he did not think we should be bothered with them.I thought he had been drinking."

"And then what happened?"

"He caught hold of me, and pulled up my frock... and... tore my underclothes..."

"And?

"I hit him with a paperweight, and kicked him, and managed to get away, to my own house. I ran up the stairs and lay down on the bed. I was very upset."

"Please go on, Mrs Topham."

"I heard Elspeth come upstairs, and go into Stephen's room, so I got up and asked him what she wanted. He was doing his homework. He said she wanted me, and it was urgent. He told her I was probably in Mr Unston's study."

"Would you like to tell the court why she wanted you, Mrs Topham?" Maconachie asked.

"She had just found that she was starting her periods, and was very upset." There was an almost audible gasp from all round the court.

"So she went to Mr Unston's study because she thought you were there?"

"Yes."

"Where you had just managed to ward off a similar attack?"

"Yes."

"You went to the study because you thought she had gone there?"

"Yes, I was afraid of what might be happening to her."

"Will you tell the court what happened when you got there?"

"I pulled him... away from her... and carried her to our own house, and told her to go upstairs and get in the bath."

"And then?"

"I loaded my husband's gun and went back to the study, and shot him."

"Did you not think that was a wrong thing to do, Mrs Topham?"

"No, not at that moment. I thought he was an evil man."

"But if you thought that, why did you work for him, in as close quarters as you obviously did?"

"He had been quite... nice... to me, and to my husband, recently. I had been warned about him, but I thought perhaps he had changed."

"Had you encouraged him at all?"

"How do you mean?"

"When he attempted to make love to you on previous occasions."

"He didn't... at least... he only asked if he could call me by my Christian name."

"You told him he could. Was not that an encouragement?"

"No. I would have preferred him not to, but I thought it was normal."

"Is that all – calling you by your Christian name?"

"He became – a bit familiar sometimes. And then..."

"And then?"

"He caught hold of my hand one day, and asked me to sit by him, and talk to him."

"And did you?"

"No. I just left. He apologised for it next time I saw him."

"You accepted the apology?"

"Perhaps I shouldn't have. I had been warned, I suppose, by Mrs Unston and... others. But you see, there was my husband's job to consider... we'd had a hard time before we came to Edenhope... and he'd been quite good to us, lately."

"Apart from what the law says about it, do you think it is right to take someone's life, Mrs Topham?"

"No, sir. It is very wrong."

"So why did you take Jasper Unston's?"

For the first time her voice dropped, almost to a whisper. "Because of what he was doing to my little girl. I know it was wrong, but not as wrong as what he was doing. It was evil."

"Thank you, Mrs Topham."

Prosecuting counsel said: "I have no questions, m'lud." All he would have asked had been put by Mr Maconachie. And in his closing address he did little more than repeat what he had said in his opening. The prosecution had clearly decided in advance, from all they had learned through police investigations, which in fact had revealed a great deal about Jasper Unston's character, and Rachael's, to leave a clear field for Maconachie, who before he made his own plea, asked the judge to allow him to re-call the pathologist who had reported on the deceased's health and injuries. He asked if the level of alcohol shown by tests on Mr Unston's blood was enough to seriously affect his behaviour and was told that it might be. The question had been prompted by Griselda, who suspected, although nobody, then or ever, could know the truth, that her husband, determined that afternoon to finally achieve his conquest of Rachael, had deliberately drunk more than his usual amount at lunchtime, to make sure she could not dissuade him as she had previously.

The barrister in his own statement simply asked the jury, and the judge, to bear in mind all that had been said about the defendant, who admitted her wrong but was clearly under the most severe provocation.

He concluded: "I ask you, members of the jury, and you, m'lud, to try to put yourselves in the place of a woman, who you have heard described as a loving mother and all round good person, who has come on her daughter, just entering adolescence, being sexually assaulted – raped – by a man who has minutes before attempted to assault her in the same way."

After the judge's summary, which was brief, not amounting to much more than "You have heard the evidence," but with references to what had been said about Rachael, the jury retired and was back inside an hour.

"Have you reached your verdict?" the judge asked.

The foreman said: "Yes, your honour."

"Do you find the defendant, Rachael Topham guilty or not guilty of the murder of Jasper Unston?"

"Guilty, your honour, as you directed. But we would have wished to return a different verdict. And we would add the strongest possible recommendation for mercy to be shown."

The judge said he would pass on the recommendation to the appropriate quarter, and took a few minutes before he spoke again.

"Rachael Topham, you have been found guilty of the gravest crime this country knows, the crime of deliberate murder. The law says there can be only one punishment. Before I pass sentence, have you anything to say to me in mitigation of this crime?"

Standing up straight, she looked directly at him and said, quietly but firmly: "No, your honour. I know it was terribly wrong, but I am sure I would do the same thing again, in those same circumstances. If that means I have to die, so be it."

Her voice faltered for the first time as she then looked across at a silently weeping Edgar and said: "Please, my love, take good care of them."

But as the square of black was placed atop the judge's wig, and he pronounced the sentence, and hoped God would have mercy on her soul, she again looked him in the eye, and at the end said: "Thank you, sir." As she was led away.

ELEVEN

Agony

The weeks after the verdict were as agonising for Edgar and the children as any part of the ordeal, although throughout the lawyers were optimistic of the eventual outcome. No woman who had killed under the level of provocation to which she had been subjected had been executed, for many years.

Griselda did not attempt to discuss the future during those weeks of agony. She left any talking to him, and it was always on practical matters, the children, the farm. She could see, in his silences, his reluctance to even mention Rachael, how he was being torn to pieces. Oh my god, she thought, what it must be like to love and be loved like that. Yet, it seemed to her, he had found some kind of new strength. Rachael had been the stronger partner in their life before Edenhope, it had become clear to Mrs Unston from their conversations in the months leading to the tragedy. Now she was sure Edgar was determined to find resources within himself to cope with misfortune far greater than the loss of his farms and his independence.

The execution date had been fixed for five weeks after the verdict, and there were only two weeks to go when the reprieve was granted by the Home Secretary, and communicated to Edgar via telephone and Mrs Unston. Griselda could hardly contain her joy. Edgar was supervising haymaking; they knew the news, good or bad, was imminent, but he had told her: "It's no use hanging about when there's work to be done." When Edward Boulton called, he told her: "I should speak directly to Mr Topham, but I know how important it is to you, Mrs Unston. Will you tell him?"

She was in her car and driving to Edenhope and the hayfield in minutes. The harvesters could hardly believe their eyes when they saw their normally staid and reserved employer run across the field and throw her arms round Edgar, pitchfork and all.

"It's alright, it's alright, she's reprieved," she half laughed, half cried.

"Oh, Edgar, isn't it wonderful? She'll come back to you, someday! And the children!"

It was an indication of Edgar's new ability to compose himself and deal with practical matters that he said, after a few moments which saw him back to his tears: "I think we'd better tell them" - meaning the men – "what this is all about, ma'am. They're always ready to get wrong ideas."

But the harvesters were almost as pleased with the news as Edgar. All shook him by the hand. Ted Marchett said: "You get off, gaffer. We'll make sure it's all done, no fear. Go an' tell 'em up at the house. An' get my missis to open that bottle o' bubbly 'er won at the fete."

§

When Edgar asked if the reprieve meant Rachael would one day be released, he was told there could be no certainty about it. It would depend on "His Majesty's pleasure," to use the official jargon. Imprisonment for life was most unlikely, the lawyers said, but she could not expect to be freed for at least ten years, and even then it would be on licence, subject to supervision and liable to recall if she committed any further misdemeanour.

She was told she would stay at Strangeways Prison, for the time being. It was as near as any gaol housing women, at that date, but still meant a round trip of nearly two hundred miles for Edgar and, eventually, the children. He was allowed a special concessionary visit almost immediately, and it was as joyful an occasion as any could be in such surroundings. She was much more concerned about his and the children's well-being than her own, wanted to know what he thought would happen at Edenhope, and to him and the farm. He was able to tell her that Mrs Unston had already made it clear that she wanted the farm to carry on with him running it, but no details such as where they would live had so far been discussed.

"I couldn't live in that house, love. And I'm sure the children would hate it. Come to that, I don't think she'll ever live there again. I've got to talk to her about it tomorrow, after I've seen you, she says. She's a good 'un, love, isn't she? You know what she told me – we'd never be without a friend as long as she was around. And I believe her. She seemed as pleased with...the news about you...as I was." And he told her how she had brought it to the hayfield, and the men's reaction.

Next day Griselda told him her plans, and how they affected him, if he agreed. First of all, she proposed having Edenhope House modernised, internally, after which it would be put on the rental market. The farm she proposed to keep on, as it was, with him to manage it, but with one variation from the present set up. He would have a twenty per cent share in its net profit. And, shutting him up before he could say anything, he and the children should continue to live in part of the Withymoor farm house, as at present but with a rather greater degree of separation from her own part of the house. Until, she said, George Davies retired in two years time.

"Then I intend to offer you his house, Edgar, and ask you to run this farm as well as Edenhope. I'd like to do that now, but George is a good man and I wouldn't do anything like that until he reaches retirement. I wouldn't even make him leave the house then only I know his daughter wants him to go to her. She and her husband have their own farm but he's had an accident and he's more or less disabled. Her father would be a big help to them."

Edgar was almost overwhelmed. He told her: "Oh, ma'am, I hardly know what to say. I think you're offering far too much. We've brought all this trouble on you and now you want to reward us."

"Edgar, I think I'm making proposals that add up to a good bargain for me and the girls. I don't know what financial state the farm was in before you came, but I know it's in a very good one now and I suspect it's down to your running of it. I think I'm on to a good thing. And just remember, although I don't suppose you want to be reminded, this trouble as you call it was brought on us all by my husband."

"That wasn't your fault, ma'am."

"No, and it wasn't yours, but you're having to pick up the pieces. But there you are. Those are my proposals. What do you think? Do you want time to think about them?"

He did not, of course. Stephen and Elspeth were delighted, although the poor girl was still in a state of mental collapse, of which more later. And so was Rachael when she received his letter, telling her all about it.

§

Inevitably, many people – even her friends, to some extent – wondered about Rachael's state of mind. The provocation of seeing her thirteen year old daughter raped by a man who only minutes before had attempted to do the same to her, was in itself enough to send any mother beyond the edge of reason or sanity. But even under such extreme provocation, could a woman who had, apparently calmly, certainly deliberately, killed her employer, be completely normal, they could not help wondering.

She herself had wondered, in the long days leading up to the trial, and since, whether she had been driven temporarily insane, especially as she could not now, even with the threat of the gallows looming, find within herself any shard of regret for what she had done. She knew that she must have "flipped" when she opened the study door to witness perhaps the most awful scene that a mother could. Perhaps that was temporary insanity, she told Edgar, and, later on, Griselda. Mrs Unston's response was: "Rachael, we all know, don't we that the most potent instinct in a mother, human or animal, is to protect her young. I don't know whether that could be called temporary insanity and I don't think it matters very much. Anyone who didn't go mad, to an extent, in circumstances like that must have been a strange kind of mother."

But neither Edgar nor Mrs Unston had the slightest doubt about her mental state now. Before the reprieve, he wanted only to comfort her, to emphasise his love for her, as always. To himself, and partly to Rachael, he echoed Griselda's words, adding to himself: "I only wish Elspeth had never got to him. I'd have beaten the living daylights out of him for what he did to you."

He never found any reason to doubt her sanity now. And despite her searching examination of herself, neither could she. The same essentials that had occupied her life at Edenhope – care for her children and her husband – filled her mind even when she was waiting to know her fate. Afterwards, she knew she was going to be in prison for a long time, and her preoccupation in those early days was in trying to work out how she could achieve what must be her objective: to still fulfill the essentials of being a mother to her children, and a wife to Edgar.

Prison life in 1946 was still harsh, for women every bit as much as for men. The principle prevailing among many, in society at large and in and out of the judicial system, was that they were there to be punished. Besides which, official resources – money available for spending on anything which would make the convicted criminal's life easier, including food – were in short supply, just after the war. Rachael's daily breakfast, at 6.30am, during her first months at Strangeways was a dish of barely palatable porridge and a thick slice of bread with a scraping of margarine. Midday dinner was better but its meat content if any was minimal. Last meal of the day, at six o'clock, was more bread and margarine with, some days, a tiny teaspoonful of jam. While anything but a glutton, she liked good food and through the war years had made a priority of providing it for Edgar and the children. Improvements soon began to be made in the standard of food, but she had been there for five years before it reached a level she would previously have thought passable. Visitors were not allowed to take in extras, for years after she started her sentence.

She was allowed no visitors at all for two months, apart from that one concession for Edgar at the time of the repeal. And the number of letters was limited. But in her very first, she set the pattern for all her years in confinement by spelling out, to Edgar, what he must please do to keep himself and the children on an even keel, and try to make sure they made good progress in all aspects of their lives. "Please try to make sure they know I am alright," she wrote. "I am not sitting miserably in my cell. I am thinking about them, and you, my dear love, and working out how I can still be a mother to them. Try to talk about their schoolwork with them, and if you can, discuss the books she is reading with Elspeth." Not a word was said about the miseries of her routine, the inadequate food, the strip searches, the cell and its toilet bucket, stinking after more than twelve overnight hours when with the best will in the world, she could not avoid using it.

Happily, the governor of the women's section of the prison was possessed of a larger slice of humanity than many in the service, and was already trying to make the lot of his unhappy charges at least a little easier. One result was that more letters were allowed. He and his deputy were the censors, and the content of Rachael's correspondence as the love poured out of it soon showed him that this woman was a million miles removed from most of the inadequate creatures filling many of the cells. Not sentimental, pity-seeking love, but down-to-earth exchanges about their schoolwork, their sport, their daily lives, books they were reading. She and Elspeth again discussed, at long range and after a period when the poor girl was almost unapproachable, the *Idylls of the King,* and soon *Jane Eyre,* and Mary Webb's quintet of Shropshire novels, as well as some of her poetry; and much more. As soon as she was able, she used some of the greater allowance of letters to write to Griselda, Ida and Marion Richards.

She wrote fewer to Edgar than to the children, because he was her most frequent visitor. But her letters to them were full of admonitions to them to "take care of Dad," and theirs to her of references to how Dad had helped them do this, or they had gone with Dad to do that. And when he visited, even from opposite sides of the dividing screen the love that would flow between them as long as they lived was as tangible as when they had sat on opposite sides of a fireplace.

Then, as she had promised, Griselda Unston offered the Tophams, Edgar, Stephen and Elspeth the substantial cottage where George Davies had lived, when he retired and went to live with his daughter, two years after the terrible events at Edenhope. She would take no rent from him but deputed one her two domestics at Whittymoor House to spend a few hours each day cleaning and cooking at the cottage, and asked Edgar to pay her; which greatly pleased the lady in question for Griselda did not reduce her own pay to her. "She needs a little extra now her husband can't work," she told Edgar.

She also provided her manager with a new vehicle which she insisted was for his personal as well as farm use, brushing aside his protest. "The farm pays for all my needs, and the girls' education, and a bit over," she said. "And I'm quite sure it would not do all that if it was not for your running of it." Edgar was left with a warm glow, only damped by the thought of Rachael in her prison, when she should have been sharing the new prosperity with him and their children.

And as they moved into their new home, Whittymoor Cottage, the first tenants, a wealthy financier and his wife, entered Edenhope House. They did not stay long – none ever did.

PART TWO

PART TWO

ONE

"Don't let them Touch Me!"

B y the time they moved into Withymoor Cottage Stephen was
back on something of an even keel, after a period of terrible
emotional turmoil, the inevitable result of the traumatic events of
that Saturday afternoon two years before. Not so Elspeth.

Griselda marvelled that she was not permanently affected, as
she told her new friend and confidant, Aunt Ida Maginness, who
spent weeks at Withymoor and became another tower of strength
supporting her brother. Ida was not completely surprised that
Rachael bore it all the way she did, almost seemed to grow stronger,
for she had felt her young sister-in-law, who had herself been
orphaned at the age of twelve, to be a person of great character,
from the day they met. But the child – savagely raped at the age of
13 by a man she had never liked but was told she must respect; put
through the ordeal of a medical examination; and seen her mother
sent to prison under sentence of death – how could she possibly not
be seriously affected, her psychological core twisted and weakened,
perhaps beyond recovery, the two ladies asked each other, in various
word formats as they got to know each other.

There was physical evidence of the poor girl's terrible state
of mind. Through the weeks before the trial, and then up to the
reprieve, she would not work, read little, hardly even listened to
the radio which Griselda had installed in her room. Her beautiful
auburn hair, which Rachael had allowed her to grow long, became
dry and lifeless. Only under pressure would she eat. She had been
growing apace, but growth seemed to have come to a stop, almost
to have gone into reverse. Mrs Unston, consulting Edgar, brought
in her own doctor, and a specialist. They were going to do nothing
but talk to her, but as soon as she knew they were doctors, Elspeth
cried, almost screamed: "Don't let them touch me, don't let them
touch me." The education authority, through her school and the

attendance officer, as he was then called, expressed much, and justified, concern, and Edgar, Griselda and the doctor had to work hard at assuring them that forcing her to go to school, or removing her from her father and all around her who cared for her must be counter-productive. And once again the aid was sought of the retired teacher who had helped her, Stephen and Mrs Unston's own daughters. The concerned officials were placated, although Miss Johnstone, now in her seventies, was as much of what we now call a counsellor as a tutor. She would spend hours reading from poetry that Edgar told her was loved by his wife and daughter. For many days, there was little active response from Elspeth, although sometimes the teacher would note that she had gone to sleep, which she and Griselda both thought was a positive result.

Signs of improvement came with the first letter from Rachael. Edgar had tried to avoid letting his wife know of his worst concerns about Elspeth. "She's low," he said. "She couldn't be anything else, could she? But we've got Miss Johnstone coming most days, Mrs Unston's fetching her, and she'll stop her getting too far behind. It would be good if you could write to her, though." And it was good. The letter was the nearest possible substitute for physical contact with her mother. She read it over and over, pressed the miserable prison paper, with its censor's stamp, to her lips, came alive when she told Griselda, Miss Johnstone and, at lunchtime, her father about it.

"Listen," she said. "She says she's alright. She's getting books, and I must tell her about what I'm doing, and please will I go back to school as soon as I can, and I must kiss you all for her..."

And indeed, not many days later, as the summer holidays approached, she asked her tutor if she and her father could talk to the school about going back for the new term. She was sent books and some written work to do. It was extremely hard going at first. An hour a day was all she could manage before collapsing in tears. "I can't, I can't," she said. And Miss Johnstone would try to soothe her and read, in a voice that seemed to be made for poetry, from verses of Keats and Tennyson, or Mary Webb, that had held the child spellbound when she and her mother had read them together.

So back to school she went. It was before "special needs" became an officially recognised part of educational responsibilities, but Elspeth's needs and problems were recognised by at least some of her teachers, who knew of the background to them and that she was essentially a bright, intelligent and sensitive child. More than once Edgar or Griselda – his phone was an extension of hers – were telephoned with the message :"We think it would be better if you fetched Elspeth home at lunchtime today, Mr Topham. She's alright, but I think she's finding the going a little too hard, today." And he would go for her and, depending on the needs of the farm, would either spend the rest of day with her, talking about Rachael, or reading, or leave her with Griselda or Barbara Johnstone who would apply similar soothing medicine.

Through the Christmas holidays, she got to know the Unston twins, Deborah and Ursula, almost her own age. Griselda was pleased that her daughters seemed not to have inherited the worst aspects of their father's character. The nearest to it was the "jolly hockey sticks" manner engenderd by their girls boarding school. But they were not bullies, and their mother was firm in clamping down on any tendency towards snobbery or their father's creed of "I can do what I like with anything that's mine." A few years later, when they became mildly involved in discussions about what should be done with a certain piece of land, and Ursula suggested that "surely, Mum, you can do what you like with it" Griselda told her: "Yes, but that doesn't mean I can ride roughshod over everyone concerned with it. Being owners of land means you're its guardians, not just its possessors, and I hope you'll always remember that." So they spent time with her farm bailiff"'s daughter and they as well as she gained from it. Their relationship with Elspeth was friendly rather than affectionate, but Edgar was pleased to see it; and he and his three female collaborators in the girl's rehabilitation, Ida, Griselda and Miss Johnstone all thought it could do nothing but good.

But hard as they all worked on restoring her to normality, it was the letters from her mother that had the most marked effect. "You can see her perk up and stay perked up every time one comes," Griselda told Miss Johnstone. And gradually she perked up to an extent where all but those closest to her thought of her as a normal girl and eventually, a normal and charming young woman.

But never, in her secret life, could she escape recurring visits to the black abyss of despair into which she had been plunged by the awful happenings of that Saturday afternoon. And never, never, could she have been persuaded to return to their scene. For very many years.

§

It may be remembered that a second-hand Meccano set, bought by Rachael from a market stall at Ludstone, delighted Stephen, then aged nine, as no other toy ever could. And almost from the day it appeared, it fed a love of things mechanical and fostered an inventiveness and a need to know why and how; which as he grew towards adulthood became a driving quest. Not for long was he content merely to build models from the set's manual. Within a year he was making devices of his own design, devising gearing systems, automatic brakes, lifting operations. "Look, Dad," he would say to a delighted Edgar, who was himself not devoid of practical creativity: "See how this balances out that weight and I can make it lift that..." And so on.

At his grammar school, he automatically gravitated towards the sciences, physics in particular. He had just taken his school certificate exams, and was waiting for results, when the horrors of that Saturday afternoon, in which he played an unwitting but disastrous part, blasted the family's life.

He was not psychologically affected as badly as Elspeth. In later years, he sometimes wondered whether there was something lacking in his make-up that caused him to ride out the emotional storm which damaged his sister so severely. He need not have. He was only on the periphery of the tempest. He could not have known to what awful experience he was sending her when he suggested she go search for their mother. And in fact he suffered a great deal in the next weeks, unable to shrug off guilt and remorse. It was no use Edgar and Aunt Ida telling him that he could not have known that any harm would result. He *had* sent her, hadn't he?

He did not and was not expected to go to school that next week, and no concern would have been expressed if he had not gone for the rest of the term, when attendance, after the conclusion of a fortnight of exams, was not much more than going through the motions. But at the end of the week Stephen himself asked Edgar: "Dad, do you think I should go to school?"

"What do you think, son? Do you want to go?

"No, but I think I'll be letting Mum down if I just moon about doing nothing. I don't think it'd be what she wants."

"I think you're right, lad. I'm sure you're right."

So he went back. It was not easy. Nobody, among boys or teachers, was unpleasant to his face, in fact the reverse. The headmaster sent for him when his form teacher reported Stephen's return, spoke kindly and urged him to seek his or other staff's help and advice and help if either was needed. He was also told he must go home at lunchtime if he wished. Although he never did, partly because there was no train at a convenient time. The head boy made a point of seeking him out, not an everyday occurrence between senior prefects and boys not yet promoted to the sixth form, to tell him: "I say, Topham, everyone thinks it's terrific that you've come back, you know. It must have been damned hard." There were a few unpleasant moments, for example when he heard a boy saying to another: "That's the kid whose mother shot the bloke she caught shagging his sister." He asked not to be chosen for the under-16, or Colts, cricket team, and his wish was honoured.

Before the end of the holidays, his mother's fate was decided, after an awful three week period before the reprieve. He spent most of the holiday working on the farm, his father and Mrs Unston agreeing that getting physically tired was just about the best antidote to mental and psychological torment. He also had the satisfaction of learning his School Certificate results, and being able to write about them to Rachael. They were the best in the school – four distinctions and four credits, the distinctions in the subjects he cared most about: physics, maths, English and chemistry. He went into the sixth form to tackle those four for Higher School Certificate and, by now spurred on through regular letters from his mother, came out with more top grades. By then, he had already decided where he wanted his path through life to take him: into engineering research and development. It led to some debate in his mind, and with Edgar and his teachers, about the best way to pursue that aim.

"What have you in mind to do now, Topham?" his headmaster asked before the presentations on speech day, a tradition still honoured by many grammar schools in 1948. "You ought to go to university, you know."

"Wouldn't an engineering apprenticeship be better, sir?" Stephen asked. But the head thought not, in his case. And Rachael, from her prison, thought the teacher was right.

Edgar thought the expense would be far too great, even in the light of his new circumstances. However, the county education authority was by then funding outstanding students, they were told. That is, it would pay the fees and give a grant which would go some way towards living expenses. Stephen sat the Cambridge entrance exam, came through with more high grades and survived the interviews, a tougher test in days when the elite universities seemed only to want pupils from elite schools. Although sometimes, when we hear of the proportions going to Oxford and Cambridge from the public schools, one has to wonder whether it is so very different today.

He enjoyed Cambridge, made some good if not terribly long-lasting friendships, played rugby and cricket for his college, came out of his three years with a top-class engineering degree and confirmation of the urge that had been building within him ever since that year of the Meccano.

Surprisingly, perhaps, in view of all that happened, the trials and tribulations of adolescence had almost passed him by. Or perhaps not so surprising. He never had any doubts about his sexuality, always thought that his life would include marriage and fatherhood, indeed positively wanted it to. But when his fellow sixth formers boasted about their exploits with the opposite sex – making it up, more often than not – he did not join in. His need was as strong as theirs, but at that stage he wanted to keep it to himself. When he dreamed of the future, it was to see himself with a wife and children, in a comfortable home, as unlike Edenhope as could be, with ponies in the paddocks, a "posh" car in the garage. Occasionally, a girl on the train journey to school, or in some other sphere, like the daughter of the bakery shop owner where he bought his lunch when there had not been time to prepare his sandwiches, would arouse his interest, and she would be the wife in his vision of the future. But none of them featured in sexual fantasies.

Like his father, Aunt Ida, Griselda Unston and Miss Johnstone, he worried about Elspeth. He occasionally came across her in one of her periods of depression, and would try to persuade her to go for a walk with him, in the woods and fields. He even tried to share in her love of poetry, but although he was an avid reader, hardly ever could he find himself stirred by the verses that seemed to penetrate her soul. He appreciated the words, the characters and the stories in the works of most of the great writers, but poetry seemed to pass him by.

TWO

Susan

By the time Stephen finished his Cambridge studies, and completed the national service which at that date was obligatory for most young men, Rachael had been in prison for six years and Edward Boulton the solicitor was beginning to talk of the possibility of release. She had been a model prisoner throughout, becoming respected by officers and inmates, and doing well all work to which she was allocated. But it would be years before she saw the outside world again. Public opinion in those days did not allow politicians to go soft on murderers.

She could therefore only witness his graduation at second hand, through the glowing descriptions of Aunt Ida, who went with his father to the ceremony and by now was able to visit, and photographs taken by Edgar, who would have liked to play down what he might have called "all the fuss" were it not for the delight he knew it brought to his wife. But they discussed future possibilities by letter and at his visits. And when, through the university's careers advice system, he was offered a place with a firm in the van of advanced engineering technology, she, his father and everyone else urged him to go for it. The offer was made before his national service, which he served with the RAF, but was there to take up when he came out. The firm was based near Manchester, which although a long way from home at Withymoor, meant he could more easily take advantage of opportunities to visit his mother.

He came as near as possible to enjoying his time in the air force, bearing in mind that he was itching to get on with his real career. And towards the end it was made quite different by an event that was to exert an influence on his life greater than any he had encountered so far, even the Meccano set and the horrors of his sister's and his mother's ordeal.

The event's name was Susan Baines, a part-time waitress in a cafe attached to the RAF base at Cranford, to which Stephen and friends among his fellow "erks" would sometimes resort in evenings when their meagre resources did not allow of anything more exciting. The manageress was her aunt, and Susan was recruited to fill gaps in the staffing, and provide herself with pocket money. Two years after leaving school at 15, she was a student at a local technical college, working towards diplomas in shorthand and typing, and basic accountancy. Her father was a small tenant farmer who struggled to make his holding provide for his family of wife and two daughters, of whom Susan was the elder. Her parents knew she was a bright girl, but a job in an office was the height of their ambition for her, as for so many parents of girls in 1951.

Susan herself, at barely 18, had no particular ambition, except perhaps to one day marry a young man with a good job who she would love and be loved by and who would provide them and their two children with a comfortable home. Her mother warned her, when Aunt Kathleen offered her the few hours work at the cafe, to "just watch your step with those young airmen." And she did, was always cheerful and polite but never responded any further to the cheeky invitations, advances and witticisms that inevitably came from young men far from home and, they hoped, on the verge of a range of romantic adventures.

There was one group of three however, rather older than most, who did not ask her what she did with her spare time or variations on the same theme. They seemed to want to talk between themselves on, from fragments of conversation she heard, topics featuring words like "energy absorption coefficient," "mach unity" and "ailerons." But she thought they were three very nice young men. Then one afternoon she heard one say: "Christ, it must be awful to be in gaol and not know when you're going to get out. How's she stand it, Steve?" And Steve's quiet answer: "My mum's a remarkable woman." After which they were all silent for a few minutes.

She could not get the scrap of what was obviously a deeply personal and perhaps tragically-inspired conversation out of her mind. The young man Steve looked anything but a type to have come from a criminal family. Yet his mother was in prison. For life? Susan could not help looking at him and wondering, every time he came in, often with the same two friends. He looked such a nice boy, she thought. Blue-grey eyes seemed to smile ahead of a mouth itself a fine shape. Medium brown hair and eyebrows the same colour, high cheekbones tapering to a firm chin. A slightly snub nose bearing on its bridge marks made by glasses worn for reading. She noted none of these features for themselves. You don't when you're sixteen. They simply added up to "such a nice boy."

She did not know that Stephen had noted her in the same way. Such a nice girl, reminding him of the baker's daughter. Grey-green eyes, nearly black hair, full eyebrows that almost met above a straight, slightly snub nose, a mouth that seemed to smile warmly but with nothing of the coquette about it. Not a beauty in the conventional sense, but she attracted him, made him want to talk.

A week after the intriguing conversation, he came in on his own, sat down and when she approached the table said: "Do you mind if I don't order for a few minutes? I'm waiting for someone else." Quarter of an hour later he was still alone, and was the only one in the cafe. She could not have said, then, what made her do it, but she asked him: "Would you like a drink while you're waiting? We're just going to have one before people start to come in, We won't charge you."

He replied: "Oh, I couldn't dream of not paying." Then adding, out of as sudden an urge as her own: "Why don't you bring a pot of tea for two, and have a cup with me?"

"Someone might come in, and I'd have to serve them," she said.

"I wouldn't mind."

With the teapot, milk and sugar between them, cups filled, she asked: "Do you think your friend isn't coming?"

"I don't know. But p'raps he's forgotten. He's a bit like that."

They were quiet for a few moments, then both started to speak at once. "Sorry," he smiled. "I was just going to ask your name. Mine's Stephen."

"Yes, I know. I heard your friends call you Steve the other afternoon. My name's Susan."

Another slight pause, and: "You're doing national service, I suppose."

"Yes, another six months to go."

"Then what? Have you got a job to go to?"

"Yes, I'm looking forward to it. It's with a technology firm at Sale, near Manchester. What about you? This is only part time, I guess."

She explained. "Is your home near Manchester," she asked.

"No, it's in Shropshire, near Ludstone, on a farm."

"Oh, my dad's a farmer, at Beriden." Beriden was a village very near the RAF station.

"Mine's the manager of the home farm on an estate."

"Have you got any brothers or sisters?"

"One sister. She's two and half years younger than me. In her first job, in a library."

She would have gone on to ask about his mother, but the memory of that conversation a week ago stopped her. Instead she said: "I've got a young sister, as well. She's still at school."

The little cafe was still empty, and they continued to talk, searching for items of mutual interest in the way of young people with little in common, as far as they know, except the feeling that they want to pursue the attraction that has brought them together. They were both too intelligent to fall back on the often near-inanities of adolescence, indeed Stephen was well beyond that stage, in years anyway. Younger though she was, however, it was Susan who sensed there was a path he would like to go down, and she started along it.

"What are you going to do in your job?" she asked.

"Well, I won't know the detail until I get there. They're well up in R and D, though, and it'll be something on those lines."

"R and D?"

"Research and development, in engineering. It's what I've always wanted to do."

"Not farming?"

"No, although I think that would have been my second choice, believe it or not." He was on the verge of telling her that his mother came from parents both involved in things mechanical, but that would have led to places he did not want to go. As it happened, two customers came in and Susan said: "Sorry, I'll have to go," and got up, gathering the tea things. He tried to help, and managed to say: "I was enjoying that. Can we talk again sometime?"

It was a little time before they could. On two of the next three occasions he went to the cafe, she was not there. The second time he asked "Aunt Kathleen": "Is your niece, Susan, not working here any more?"

She answered: "Are you Stephen?"

"Yes."

"Oh, she's mentioned you," she said, her eyes twinkling. "She said she'd had a nice talk with you, the other day. Yes, she's still here, but she's had exams lately so we changed her shifts. She'll be here tomorrow afternoon."

Tomorrow afternoon brought another problem, however. Stephen's two particular friends insisted on going with him to "the caff." But when she brought their tea and buns, he asked her: "How did the exams go?" And when she hesitated, added: "Tell me later."

His friend Geoff said: "Been getting off with her, eh, Steve? You're a bit of a dark horse, I can see, boy." And his suppositions were confirmed when Stephen insisted on paying for the refreshments, giving him the opportunity of talking briefly to Susan.

Both knew they wanted the acquaintance to continue. After another couple of chats in the cafe, he asked her what time she finished and could he walk home with her – the farm was little more than a mile away and her two feet were her usual mode of transport. Yes, she said, but not all the way, her mum would not like it. The walks home continued, on each of the three days in the week that she worked, and their intimacy grew. They talked about books they'd both read, his sister's obsession with poetry, his work on the base, he said he'd never gone out with a girl before; she said it was almost the same with her, and they discussed films, and music.

One day, three weeks after their first meeting, Stephen drew her into a gateway where they often stopped briefly, and asked: "Do you want us to go on seeing each other?"

"I'd have thought that was obvious, or I wouldn't be here now, would I? Why, don't you want to, Stephen?" And he did not know how the question was accompanied by a little sinking feeling in her stomach.

"Of course I do. But there's something I've got to tell you. P'raps you won't want to know me then."

She knew at least some of what he was going to tell her. But she tried to make it easy for him.

"Is it – something about you? Have you done something bad, or something?"

"It's not me, it's my mother." He hesitated, turned away.

Susan said, very softly: "It's alright. I think I know. She's in prison, isn't she?"

Stephen looked back at her. "How did you know?"

"I heard you and one of your friends talk about it. It makes no difference, Stephen. No difference at all, to me."

But of course, more than sixty years ago, such things could make a considerable difference to many people, especially parents of a girl who wanted to marry the son of a murderess, for that was soon how it was between Stephen and Susan. He told her everything about it. She gasped in horror when she heard how Rachael had caught Jasper Unston in the act of raping his young sister, after attempting a similar assault on her mother. Like his father and his Aunt Ida, she told him, lovingly by this time, that he must not blame himself for unwittingly sending Elspeth to the fateful study.

By the time he had told her everything there had been several more walks home. And inevitably, they were seen by her mother, one evening when Mrs Baines was picking blackberries and had gone along the road to beyond the point where they usually parted.

"Golly, it's mother," Susan said as they rounded a bend and came in sight of her, less than a hundred yards ahead.

"It's no good – I didn't want it to be like this, but she must meet you. Come on."

Olive Baines stopped her blackberry gathering and waited for them to come up to her, saying nothing.

"Mum, this is Stephen," Susan said. "He's been walking home with me."

"Hello, Stephen," Olive said. "Have you far to walk back?"

"Just to the camp," Stephen said.

"Well, thank you for seeing my girl home. Good night."

Susan said: "Good night, Stephen. See you next week."

Stephen said: "Good night. Good night, Mrs Baines," and turned round to start his walk back. God, what an awful start.

Susan and her mother walked towards the farm. "I hope he hasn't got ideas," Mrs Baines said. "I told you to watch those airmen."

"He has got ideas, Mum, and so have I. When can I bring him to meet you and Dad, properly?"

§

It took a little time, but it worked out after, two months later, Susan took him home in good old-fasioned manner, to meet her father, mother and sister. She had not, by then, told them about his mother. They both wanted Stephen to do it himself. Which he did, on that first occasion. He did not want them to get the idea that he was holding anything back about himself.

"Now, lad, Susan's told us it's serious between you and her. Is that right?" Ben Baines asked, filling his pipe with Old Stoker as they were left alone in the front parlour while the womenfolk washed up after Sunday dinner.

"I want us to be married, some day, Mr Baines."

"Ay, it seems that's what she wants as well. Ye'd better tell us a bit about yourself, then, hadn't ye?"

"Well, I'm 22. I got a good degree at Cambridge and I've got a good job waiting when I've finished my national service. I think it offers reasonable prospects. I like playing rugby and cricket. My father's manager of a farm in Shropshire."

"Susan tells us the job's in engineerin' – research and development, I think she said."

"Yes, that's right. It's what I've always wanted to do."

"Ye didn' want to go farmin', then?"

"It would have been my second choice. I'd have gone to Harper Adams or somewhere."

Further questions, about plans for the more immediate future, some regret that going to Manchester would take Susan a long way from her home, and a warning that she could not expect much in the way of financial support from her parents.

"We've talked about it quite a lot, Mr Baines," Stephen said. "We don't think we'll be in a position to get married for at least two years. Probably three or four."

"It looks as though you're being pretty sensible about it," the older man said, as his wife came into the room.

"We've had a bit of a chat, Mother," Mr Baines said. "I don't think we need to show Stephen the door."

"No," Olive said. "I have to admit, Stephen, that when I saw you first time in that air force uniform I was worried. But Susan's told me a lot about you an' its a bit different, now."

There was a little silence as Susan came in with cups of tea, and Stephen gathered his courage for the big disclosure.

"Mrs Baines, Mr Baines, that's very nice of you. But there is something very important I've got to tell you."

They looked at him wonderingly. Susan moved to his side and caught his hand, but he took it away, gently.

"I've told you I've not done anything wrong, I mean seriously wrong, in my life. But there is something I've got to tell you now. Susan knows about it, but I asked her not to tell you because it wouldn't be fair. It's got to come from me." He stopped, looking down at his feet, between his knees. Susan again caught his hand, but again he would not have it.

"It's about my mother," he managed to get out. "She's in prison. Perhaps for life. She killed someone." His head went down between his hands. Mrs Baines gasped. But nobody spoke for seconds until Susan said, almost in tears: "Mum, Dad, don't think bad of her. Until you know everything about it. You won't then, I promise you." She knelt down by the arm of Stephen's chair, put her arm round him.

This time he did not break away. Mr Baines got up, left the room, and came back with a small glass of whisky.

"Drink this, lad, it'll do ye good," he said.

"No, it's alright, Mr Baines. I'll be alright."

"Drink it, then ye can tell us."

Stephen obeyed, drank half the whisky, felt his courage return as the liquid burned its way to his stomach.

"What happened, Stephen?" Olive asked.

"He was an awful man," Stephen said. "My dad's boss, and my mum's. He tried to... you know... force himself on her... my mum. She got away but then he got my sister in his study and he was doing the same to her, only this time he... was doing it, and my mother saw. She got Elspeth away and fetched my dad's gun and..."

He stopped, but Susan said: "She was only thirteen, Mum." Olive gasped again.

"He was a really bad man. He'd brought another woman into the house just after his wife had twins, and kept her there, as his mistress," Susan added. "And he'd had... women... all over the place before that. And he was a Member of Parliament, and he'd been some kind of government official in the war."

"If he was like that, how come he'd been an MP, and a government minister or something?" Olive asked.

"Oh, he was so clever, and he could be nice to people when he wanted to," Stephen said. And from that point, prompted by many questions from Susan's parents and a few from Susan herself, as much of the story as he knew or could remember came out; including the terrible effects of her ordeal on Elspeth, the kind friendship and support of Griselda Unston and, most importantly, how Rachael was continuing her role as wife and mother from her prison captivity. It was teatime before the questions ceased, and when Stephen left, well into the evening, Mr Baines shook his hand warmly and Olive put her arms round him and kissed him on the cheek.

They were married rather less than three years later at Cranford Parish Church, Leicestershire, in a quietly formal ceremony with Susan's young sister Marie, and Elspeth, as bridesmaids. Most of the guests were Susan's friends and relations. Edgar and Edward Boulton had attempted to get permission for Rachael to attend, but failed. Griselda and Aunt Ida agreed privately that the refusal was probably a good thing. Her attendance might have cast a shadow over the ceremony. She would no doubt have had to be accompanied by a prison officer to whom she might, horror of horrors, have been handcuffed. But the Topham family was as fully represented as its limited numbers allowed, with one of Ida's sons-in-law best man.

Stephen had taken up his job with Techmaster on leaving the RAF, found himself a modest lodging in a village on the Cheshire side of Manchester, lived equally modestly out of an excellent salary for so young a man, and salted away most of the remainder with one object in view – to marry Susan as soon as possible. She had finished her courses and found herself a useful post with the local council before he left the area. The result was that they not only had enough to set up home by the date of their marriage but had actually bought a house, an unusual achievement for a young couple in the 1950s. It was a former farmworker's cottage in the village of Bollingbury, where he had his lodging, and came to them for the sum of £700. They did not even need a mortgage. It had no amenities apart from a water supply but the price meant they had cash left over to instal a bathroom and hot water system.

THREE

A Peccadillo and its Results

Their first years at Bollingbury were quietly happy. Although neither was highly sexually charged, they had tasted the pleasures of the flesh more than once before they were joined together in the parish church of her Leicestershire village, taking precautions which they carried on afterwards for they did not want to start a family just yet. Susan found herself a part-time job as secretary to an author who lived in the village. They played tennis at the village club, and were among its best players, went to cinemas and the local theatre, walked in the easily-accessible Pennine foothills, exploring Macclesfield Forest, Wildboarclough and the Goyt Valley.

Stephen was well thought of at Techmaster, and applied an agile engineering brain to good effect. One of his innovative ideas was adopted by a big aircraft engine concern in America, bringing more kudos to the firm, and himself, and before he and Susan had been married for three years, he was twice promoted. But the second promotion brought with it a development that came near to ruining his marriage. He was installed in an office next door to his immediate superior's secretary.

Caroline Jenkins was a brassily attractive, basically intelligent, highly sexed but emotionally unbalanced young woman, a year younger than Stephen. Most of her life to date, outside work, had consisted of a series of romantic entanglements into which her male counterparts entered with enthusiasm but soon found they could not take the pressure of her uncertain response to one situation or another. She was married, officially, to a young architect, but after she had thrown a wobbly every time he did not get home for his tea at the proper hour, accusing him of staying behind at his office in an affair with a female colleague, the young man decided he had had enough and left for greener pastures. Since then, two years before, she had had a series of liaisons as she searched, like the Belle of Barking

Creek, for her great romance. When Stephen arrived in the office next door, it did not take her long to decide he might be the man to fill the bill, married or not.

She took him morning coffee and afternoon tea and soon began to use the opportunities to engage him in conversations about films, books and pop music, which she turned into ogling encounters designed to show him she was ready, willing and available. Flattered, he responded as most other young men would have, with a routine of cheeky ripostes extending into double-entendres, not intended to have any greater meaning than to show he was as with it as she was. He joked about her to Susan, called her a saucy little hussy but a good secretary, for she was allowed to do small jobs for him, like typing memos to his younger colleagues. But when these were long enough to involve dictation, she would take the opportunity of flashing her legs as she sat down opposite his desk, and making sure her considerable expanse of bosom was well displayed. To remain totally immune to such treatment would have been more than young male flesh and blood, even Stephen's, could stand indefinitely, when Susan was called away to care for her sick mother. She was gone for three weeks and towards the end of that time his defences, growing weaker all the time, were eventually breached when Caroline found herself stranded at the office one night, by a bus strike.

When she took in his tea, she said: "Don't you feel sorry for me? It's pouring outside and I've got to walk home, three miles. I've tried to get a taxi but there are none free until nearly seven o'clock." Actually, she had been told a taxi would be available at six-fifteen, but Caroline was making hay while it rained. "Mr Tomlinson said he'd take me but he's going early and his wife needs his car as soon as he gets home." Which in this case was true. He had been apologetic about not being able to offer to drive her home but said: "Go and cry on Mr Topham's shoulder, Caroline."

Stephen said: "I'll take you, Caroline. Can't have you getting pneumonia, can we?" But the onslaught was launched almost as soon as she got into the car. Before they reached her flat she was telling him how marvellous it was to have someone going home with her.

"You'll stay and have tea with me, won't you?" She knew Susan, who she had met briefly and thought of as dull and plain, was away.

"Yes please. But call me Stephen."

The rest was easy. Her well-practised arts of seduction were hardly needed. The meal for which she had asked him to stay was never eaten, not even prepared. Abstinence of nearly a month had left Stephen with a different appetite. They spent the whole night in a sexual romp with only a brief interlude to eat, drink and sleep.

"Do we have to go to work, Stevie darling?" she asked, as he disengaged himself for the second time in less than twelve hours. "Couldn't we just stay here?"

"No, I can't," said Stephen. "I've important things to do."

"More important than me?" Her petulance was already showing.

"Come on, sweetheart, you know we have to go. I'll come back tonight."

At tea-time that afternoon, as she put the cup and saucer on his desk, she caught his hand and put it on her breast.

"You're coming, darling, aren't you?"

"What do you think?"

It became another evening and night like the one before, although this time the meal was prepared and eaten. But at breakfast Stephen said: "I'll have to go – home – and get some clean clothes, and check the post."

"You'll come here tonight though, won't you?" She pleaded in the tone that had superseded the office banter. "Let this be your home, Stephen, darling. I want you – always."

To be honest, he was in a turmoil. He was already feeling ashamed of himself. Caroline, while being a good secretary, was little more than a sex-kitten in personal character, he knew. The idea of deserting Susan for her was not on his agenda. Yet, the thought of telling her, lightweight character though she was: "Bye-bye, it was great fun but I'll have to get back to my wife now" made him writhe with embarrassment. Quite apart from the scene that would obviously result, perhaps with others involved, it would create a situation at Techmaster that would at least complicate his working life.

"Damn, damn, damn," he said to himself as he drove home at lunch-time. "Why ever, why ever... I'm not even in love with her... I'm just being an animal..." He resolved however that he must take the bull by the horns and tell her, that evening and before he could be drawn into any further physical encounters, that the liaison could not go on. But his resolution was never carried out.

When he returned to the office, he found a memo on his desk from his boss, via Caroline. "Please see Mr Tomlinson, soonest." And underneath the typing, handwritten: "He wants you to go to Sweden, today. Don't go, please, darling. Stay with me."

He went immediately to his boss's office, saying only as he passed her desk: "I'll have to go," and barely hearing the sobbed "No" as he went through the door.

Tomlinson told him what it was all about and said he had asked Caroline to make travel and accommodation arrangements. He went back and asked her if she had done so.

"No," she said. "You're not going, are you? You can't."

"Caroline, please. I've got to go. It's my job."

"I don't care. You can't go."

"Caroline, it could cost me my job."

"Do you care for your job more than me?"

He looked at her. For goodness sake, how stupid he had been. He had never thought that there was any real depth to her, but to take this attitude...

"I'm sorry," he said. "I'll have to go."

She started to cry.

"I'll make the arrangements myself," he said, and left. It took him an hour to do so. It meant he was unable to contact Susan to tell her what was happening. He had meant to go home that evening, call her and, even if it had to be done on the phone, make a clean breast of it all. He spent two difficult, hard-working days in Gothenburg, hardly able to force his mind to concentrate on the problem he was there to solve, and leaving his Swedish colleagues wondering what was the matter with him. At night, despite a luxurious bed in an equally luxurious hotel, he could not sleep, and spent hours wandering round the harbour and parks.

§

Susan arrived home two days after he left, only hours before Stephen was due back from his Swedish trip. Putting her own clothes away, she noticed that some of his were missing, guessed he had been called away, and phoned Techmaster to find out whether she was right. She was put through to Caroline – Stephen's calls were diverted to her in his absence.

"Hello – is that Miss Jenkins? It's Susan Topham here. Can you put me through to my husband, please?"

There was a pause. Then: "He's not here."

Susan was surprised at the girl's hesitant yet offhand tone, with no explanation for Stephen's absence. "Will you ask him to ring me, please," she asked.

"I can't. He's in Sweden." And after another pause. "He won't want to speak to you."

"I beg your pardon?"

"He's staying with me."

"What do you mean?"

"He loves me. He's been staying with me for a long time, ever since you left him." Which of course was not remotely near the truth.

Susan could not believe what she was hearing. She hung up, and half collapsed, in tears. A few moments later there was a knock on the door and Stephen's Aunt Ida walked in.

"Susan, love, whatever's the matter?"

Susan tried to dissemble, but Mrs Maginness could not be fooled, and eventually got to the truth as far as Susan knew it.

"It sounds to me as though this woman's trying it on, or got a screw loose," she said. "Is there any way you could find out a bit more?"

Susan wondered about speaking to Mr Tomlinson, but apart from any other considerations, that would have meant going through Caroline. Eventually she said: "I could speak to Brian, p'raps." Brian Forster was a colleague and friend of Stephen: they had joined Techmaster at the same time and were pursuing broadly parallel routes within the firm. Susan liked him. She phoned him.

"Oh, Susan, I'm terribly sorry," he said. "I think there might be something going on. But it'll be her doing, if there is. She's no good. No good to anyone."

"Has he... has he been... staying with her, as she said?"

"I know he took her home that night when there was a bus strike. That was two days ago. I think that was the first time, but I can't be sure.

"Look, it's a bit awkward, but would you like me to have a word with him? I hate the thought of... that stupid little huzzy..."

"Oh, no, Brian, don't you get involved. It'll either come right or it won't."

She told Aunt Ida what he had said, and started to weep again.

Ida comforted her, made tea and made her drink it, and when Susan had recovered to some extent, said: "Look, love, I think I know what you should do. Believe it or not, but I was where you are, once."

§

Mrs Maginness drove her to Sale and the Techmaster offices, in time to see Caroline leave the building and go straight to Stephen's car, and wait beside it. There was no sign of him. It looked as though the other girl was expecting him. Aunt Ida said: "Have you got a key to the car, Susan?"

Susan rummaged in her handbag. "Yes," she said.

"Go and get in and wait. You know how to handle her if she speaks to you. I'll see if I can find your husband. I won't say anything to him about it, but I'll tell him you're waiting for him."

Susan approached the car. Caroline walked away when she saw her coming. Susan got into the passenger seat. Caroline moved fifty yards further away, stood near the office entrance. Ten minutes later Stephen and his aunt emerged. Caroline threw herself at him. Two typists who had followed them out stared. Stephen pushed her away, gently but quite firmly. "No, Caroline, no. I'm going home," got into his car, beside his wife, and drove away.

Aunt Ida spoke to Caroline. "Come with me, my dear. I'll take you home."

§

As they drove home, the resolve, inspired by Aunt Ida and apparently so cool and collected, that had enabled her to deal with the situation at Techmaster could not be maintained any longer, in its entirety. She knew she could not and did not want to keep up an icy front towards her husband. Yet neither must she behave as though it was just one of those things that would be forgotten with a little time.

Neither spoke during the fifteen-minute journey. When they arrived at their cottage, he went into the little room he used as an office, still without saying anything, and sat down, not at his desk, but in a chair in a corner, staring gloomily into nothingness. But five minutes later she came in with a cup of tea.

"Drink this, Stephen," she said, and held out the cup and saucer. He took it, without looking at her, and put it on a nearby shelf.

"Don't. Don't be nice," he said.

"Drink your tea," Susan said quietly.

She went back to the kitchen. She cried again, even more bitterly than when she had first learned of the catastrophe that was going to wreck her life. She was still weeping when Stephen brought his cup and saucer. His mind was back in turmoil. He had thought he could put things to rights, or at least start to, with a confession, of shame; and a new avowal of the love he knew was the most important thing in his life. But he knew now that however genuine it was on his part, such a confession, such an avowal must seem to Susan to be a mere excuse, an attempt to creep back into her favour. Nevertheless, he must try, to get over to her the shame with which he had been wracked for the last three days.

He wanted to put his arms round her, but such a gesture must have been the last thing to do, he realised. He waited until she stopped crying, and said the only thing he could: "Susan... I'm sorry, I'm sorry... Susan... I'm sorry..."

She lifted her head and looked at him: "I'm sure you are, love. Of course you are. But how long will you be sorry for? 'Till next time?" He said nothing.

"Do you want something to eat?"

"No, thanks."

Both again sat in silence. After a while, he said: "I'm going for a walk."

He was gone half an hour, walking down the road and along a circular path past the recreation ground. He met two people, both men, hardly spoke to them, although he knew them well enough. Near home he leaned on a gate and this time it was he who cried, although tearlessly. Then he turned round to see Susan standing at their front gate, looking towards him. He went to her and they went indoors, without speaking.

She asked again: "Won't you have something to eat? There's some stew ready."

"No, I don't want anything. I'd better go to bed. I'll have a bath first."

She said: "I've made your bed in the back room."

"Yes."

"That's where you sleep. Until we've got things straightened out."

Shamefacedly, he picked up the holdall containing the clothes he had taken to Sweden, went upstairs and straight into the bathroom. But he did not bathe, sat down on the toilet and sobbed. He heard Susan moving about next door, then go down the stairs. He went into the back bedroom and saw the bed, beautifully prepared with a clean pair of pyjamas on top. He picked them up, and saw the wet marks on the pillow. He knew what they were. He went downstairs and found her at the bottom of the garden, leaning on the fence, adding more tears to the stream that gurgled just beyond it.

"Susan, can we talk, please? I'd like to talk."

She turned to him, her face streaked by the tears.

"Not tonight. I can't. Tomorrow. We'll talk tomorrow." With another sob, she walked past him, through the flower beds and into the house.

He stayed where he was, for half an hour. His mind, his whole body felt horribly vacant. But he could not just do nothing. He trudged to the house, found her in the kitchen.

"I'm sorry, Susan, I'm sorry. Please let me talk..."

"Tomorrow, Stephen. Try to sleep well."

§

Emotionally drained, he slept better than he expected, waking with the first inkling of dawn. He lay for an hour longer, an hour of mental scourging. Now, back at home, the warmth of Susan's gentle affection seemed to penetrate the doors and walls between them. Why, why had he ever allowed himself to be lured as he had, he asked himself for the umpteenth time. It had been nothing but animal lust, and it must never happen again, however strong the temptation of a pretty face, or body. The thought of it set his brain burning, almost physically. She was his wife, his partner in life, as no other could be. He went out to the landing, listening for signs of Susan in bathroom or kitchen, but making no attempt to enter her – their – room. Neither did he go downstairs, instead went into the bathroom, quickly washed and shaved before dressing in cotton trousers and polo shirt and going downstairs, debating with himself whether to take her a cup of tea, but deciding against it, if it meant waking her. Instead, he prepared the breakfast table, strangely embarrassed by a routine that he had regularly carried out at weekends before... But he made a cup of tea for himself and took it to the end of the garden, watching the burbling stream beyond the fence, and a vole diving in and out of the water.

The little animal's activities in the end diverted him from the introspective anguish, and he became so engrossed that Susan was almost on him before he realised her presence. She had gone into his room, seen him through the window. Neither knew what to say, but after a few moments she asked: "Did you sleep?"

"Pretty well. Better than I deserved. Did you?" She did not answer, instead, after another pause, said: "Would you like some breakfast?"

"Just some toast. But I can get it."

"No, I'll get it."

They ate their toast and drank coffee in silence, sitting on adjacent sides of the little kitchen table. But finally she asked: "Do you want us to stay together, Stephen?"

"Yes. Yes. Yes."

"It's easy to say that now. How do I know this won't happen again? How do I know there won't be... another?"

He looked directly at her for the first time in twenty-four hours.

"I don't think I can say anything to convince you. I can only say that right now I've never felt so ashamed of anything in my life. And I want you, Susan. Not just... like that. I want you with me, always. Always."

She looked back at him, directly.

"I want you with me, always. I want you to stay. But I'm going to say something, and I mean it." He looked at her again, and she at him.

"If anything like this happens again, ever, it will be the end. I love you, but I couldn't take another... like this. I couldn't take it, Stephen. I couldn't take it."

There was no wonderful, instant, reunion. The atmosphere was pervaded by too much angst. Time was needed. He spent that morning– it was Saturday – again in the office, Susan doing chores around the house. After a lunchtime still heavy with constraint, he asked, searching for some way back but anxious not to let her think he was assuming that he could simply slip back into his place as the man of the house: "Would you like me to cut the lawns, and tidy the beds up a bit?"

"That'd be good, if you can spare the time." And the afternoon was spent working in the garden, mowing the grass and moving, trimming and digging up plants under her direction. It was the best possible treatment for the aching anxiety. No therapist could have prescribed better. There was no deliberate physical contact, but when she struggled to uproot a shrub she had long wanted to transplant he caught hold of it with her in a successful joint effort. He saw her trying to lift a planted, heavy wooden tub and again hastened to help. After tea of ham, eggs and chips that had often been their Saturday evening meal unless they were eating elsewhere, he again went back to his desk. At ten o'clock he came out and said: "I'm going to bed.

Goodnight, love," brushed her hair with his lips as he went towards the stairs, up to the bathroom, and into the back bedroom. The bed was made up again, but his pyjamas were not there. He went down again, said: "I can't see my pyjamas."

She said: "They're on the bed. In the other room." And they were, with her nightdress.

He went upstairs again, got into the night attire, and the bed. A few minutes later she came up and did the same. He lay still as she climbed in beside him and put out the light. Although he was aching for her, in a way he had not ached for months, he must not touch her, must not make it look as though *that* was all he wanted her for. It was not, anyway. Not now. But after a few minutes Susan capped the situation she had engineered.

She asked, very softly: "Are you asleep?"

"No."

"Come here, my darling. Love me."

FOUR

Elspeth

She still gave her father, Aunt Ida and Griselda Unston cause for anxiety, even after she went back to school and appeared to be doing well academically. They – Griselda especially, when she was in the big house library, of which she had always been urged to make use – would sometimes catch her in a spell of introspection difficult to penetrate. Mrs Unston, consulting Barbara Johnstone, hit on a ploy that often worked. She would take out a book of the child's favourite poetry and read from it, aloud but without doing anything else to "wake" her. And Elspeth would usually, almost invariably, "come round" and start to talk.

But of course Edgar, although there were good books including poetry at Withymoor Cottage, was not usually in a situation where he could take such a step, and would not in any case have known which verses to read. He had always been reluctant to worry Rachael about their daughter, but he knew that her mother's letters were the most important thing in her life and he had to walk a tightrope between causing anxiety for Rachael and getting her to help lift Elspeth out of her personal slough of despond.

He wrote, about the time Stephen was finishing his first year as a Cambridge undergraduate: "We are all fine here. Ida has just been for a week. She came on the train but Arthur drove down to fetch her back. They're both very well and send their love to you. Mrs Unston and Miss Johnstone also. Both those ladies are a big help to me and Elspeth.

"My darling, I hate to worry you about anything. But it would not be right if I did not tell you that I am a bit concerned about Elspeth. I think that what happened is still affecting her. Her school work is good and as you know she did well in her exams. But she has little turns when she seems to shut herself off from everything, and I can't get through to her. Mrs Unston seems to have hit on a way of doing it, which is to read poetry to her without "waking" her, and it usually works. I wonder, love whether you could write to her, through me, with some verses that you know she likes especially. Then I could keep your letter by me and if I find her in one of these moods I would read it to her, and tell her it is a letter that has just come from you. I know it would be a little lie but would that matter?"

Rachael, in the next letter she was allowed, told him not to be too worried. She thought it would have been remarkable if Elspeth had not suffered some psychological effect from her experience, and that the love she was getting from him and everyone round her would eventually be more powerful than the trauma. But she would of course do as he suggested, and enclosed a letter for Elspeth including some lines from "Morte d'Arthur" which were among her favourites.

Rachael was right. Elspeth gradually emerged from most of the nightmarish consequences of that Saturday afternoon and its associations. She was able to work hard during her last two years at school and came out with good Higher School Certificate results – not as good as Stephen's but good enough to make Edgar and Rachael think she ought to go to university, which in 1951 was unusual for girls in the Tophams' level of society.

Before that however came an encounter that, like her brother's in the air force, was to be as significant in her life as, even, the terrors of Edenhope. At that time, the first steps towards integrating boys' and girls' education post-16 meant that a number of girls were transferred from their own schools to the boys' equivalent, where the range of subjects was somewhat wider, although usually on the science side. Elspeth was thoroughly immersed in literature, poetry especially, but she also liked biology, particularly as it related to plants and animals. Stephen's old school was strong on the sciences, and indeed in literature, and Elspeth's transfer there, after her school certificate successes, was almost automatic. She did not relish the idea of being lost in a school of 600 boys, and being one of only a dozen girls in a lower sixth form of thirty, but her mother told her it would be a case of the boys being in awe of the newcomers, rather than the other way about.

Among the boys in her English group was a shy, somewhat effeminate-appearing lad by the name of Lancelot Percival, honoured, completely inappropriately, with the nickname of "Pimply Percy." He had no more facial eruptions than many of his classmates. With the advent of girls, the school decided that Christian names should be used all round, and when Lancelot's was revealed, it brought some ridicule from the Johns, Richards, Roberts and Michaels, most of whom had little knowledge of and less sympathy with Arthur's knights and the poetry they inspired. "I reckon he's a poofter," one could have been heard to say to another. But the name and its connotations had quite a different effect on Elspeth. He was the only one in the group, girl or boy, who not only had a name that struck an immediate chord but turned out to be interested in poetry.

Lance was not homosexual. At that stage in his life, when his school compatriots spent much of their time in wishful thinking, and talking, about girls, he was just not interested. He had more worthwhile fish to fry, he might have said if he had used that kind of language. Although apart from the mild ragging about his name, he was not bullied, certainly not disliked, and from time to time objects of his interest would strike a chord with one or another of his classmates. But when they started relating their (alleged) exploits with the opposite sex, he would quietly retire to his desk and get out a volume of Browning, Wilfred Owen, Edward Thomas or others of the war poets, sometimes John Betjeman, then becoming quite widely known and whose humorous, rather bumbling style had much appeal for him. He liked narrative verse, however, including much of Tennyson, although *Idylls of the King,* which set Elspeth's nerves tingling however many times she read them, had nothing like the same effect on him.

Just as Lance veered away from the other boys' bawdy talk and tales of conquest, Elspeth did not involve herself in the girls' parallel chit-chat, and would often take herself apart with her book of the moment, as often as not a volume of verse. And it was on one of these occasions, halfway through her first term at the school, that Lance happened to see what she was reading. It was the *Rime of the*

Ancient Mariner, which he had read and re-read until he knew many sections of its 600 lines by heart.

"Oh, I say, do you like that?" he asked.

"It's the first time I've read it. Mr Bradbury (an English teacher) lent it me. He said he thought I'd like it."

"I think it's terrific. I must have read it a dozen times. Bradbury read it with us last year. What do you think?"

"It takes a bit of following, but I think I shall like it when I get to know it. Do you think it's *real* poetry, though? Isn't it just a story in verse?" A somewhat surprising comment from one who thought *Idylls of the King* was the epitome of poetic creation.

"Oh, it's that alright, but Coleridge meant a lot more. He was..." Lance stopped, but resumed in a few moments, as she looked at him wondering what he was trying to say. "I think you should read it all first. Then let's have a talk about it. With Bradbury if you like. It would please him."

It was the start of a literary companionship that lasted through their school life, and far beyond. Elspeth had developed into a pretty girl, with a willowy but shapely form, auburn hair like her mother's, and plenty of boys eyed her appreciatively. But there was an aura about her that somehow inhibited the kind of approach sometimes suffered by other girls, and welcomed by some.

At that stage in his life however, Lance hardly saw her as a girl, pretty or otherwise. As they sat together, quoting lines of verse to each other, discussing them and their authors, no thought of her attractiveness entered his head. One or two boys remarked that "Percy seems to be getting off with that Topham girl," but if they had said it openly he would have wondered what they were talking about. As we have already said, he was not homosexual – "gay", at that time, still meant merry and bright – and had not developed affection for anyone of his own sex, except his father, a village parson on the Herefordshire border with his own idiosyncracies which did not extend to Lance's passion for poetry. Neither did that passion stem from his mother, whose life revolved happily round village affairs, the Mothers' Union, the W.I., the annual fete, and care for her much loved if not fully understood husband and son. But neither parent found anything strange in Lance's literary tastes.

He also found pleasure in the novels and verses of Mary Webb, and when he saw Elspeth with a copy of *Precious Bane,* a few days after their *Ancient Mariner* encounter, it brought another little sensation of pleasure as he recognised a literary fellow.

"Hello," he said. "You like Mary Webb, then."

"Yes, I love her."

"Have you read her other novels?"

"I haven't read the one they're making the film about, but I have all the others."

"*Gone to Earth.* It's quite different, I think. Have you got one you like best, out of the others?"

"I read *The Golden Arrow* with my mother, when I was only ten or eleven, and I keep going back to it. But they're all good. And the poems. I really do like this one, though."

It was a conversation like many over the two years leading up to their Higher School Certficate exams, and which grew more sophisticated with their developing knowledge and tastes. Each found the other a natural target when they wanted someone with whom to discuss the books, authors, plays and poetry which formed a large part of their curriculum. The English teacher, Keith Bradbury, was delighted to find pupils so eagerly engrossed in his subject, and ready and able to discuss it, often to his own level. More than one lunchtime was spent in three-cornered debates.

Apart from their literary interests, the two liked each other from the start, found near-unanimity in such extra-curricular likes and dislikes as came into their discussions. But it was the kind of friendship that could be found among many boys. If Lance had been told it was obvious he "fancied" her, he would have said something like: "What do you mean, 'fancy' her? She's a good kid and likes the same kind of things I do, that's all." Which indeed it was, and the same with Elspeth, who only came to realise a great deal later how important a part Lance had played, through those two years of school, in helping rid her of the worst effects of her ghastly experience. No "romance" could have done so much, in fact if Lance had shown a tendency to move in such a direction she would have recoiled, much as she liked him.

§

Near the end of her two years at Ludstone, Elspeth, her father and mother and Mrs Unston puzzled over the next steps in her life. The prospect of a university scholarship such as Stephen had obtained seemed practically nil. Her results were good, but not that good, and women's places were still comparatively few and far between. She could go for training as a teacher, she was told by the Ludstone head, but the prospect of trying to control bunches of unruly youngsters of either sex, most of whom would have little or no interest in the literature that fuelled her life, made that idea an immediate non-starter.

"Oh, Dad, I don't think I could do it," she told him. And Griselda, when Elspeth discussed the idea with her, as she discussed most things of importance, had to agree that it was not for her.

It was Barbara Johnstone who came up with the suggestion that she accepted more readily than any coming from the others, even her mother, racking her brains, in her prison cell, for ideas that would start her daughter on a road that might lead to fulfillment.

"I think you should think about becoming a librarian," her former tutor said. "I'm sure a lot of the work would be pretty humdrum, but I'm sure as well that there'd be a great deal to interest a girl like you. You'd meet some interesting people, too. I'd bet there wouldn't be many days when you didn't have someone looking for a book that led along channels that interested you. I know when I was a girl, in my first teaching job, one of the people in the local library at Stafford was wonderfully helpful, and we spent hours – well it must have added up to hours – talking about books and poetry we both liked."

"But wouldn't it mean I'd have to go away?" Elspeth asked. "I don't want to. I don't want to leave Dad, and you, and Mrs Unston... and not be here when... when... Mum comes home."

"My dear, your mum would hate the thought that you might spoil your life, because that's how she'd see it, I'm certain, by staying at home and doing some boring job and ending up as a boring old maid like me -" Miss Johnstone started before she was interrupted by Elspeth as sharply as she could ever interrupt anyone.

"Oh, how could you say such a thing! You're the least boring person in the world, except my mum. And Mrs Unston."

"Well, it's nice of you to say so, but that's not the point. What I mean is you must do something that will broaden your horizons, if you don't mind another cliché. Teaching does that for some people, it did for me, but to do it well and be happy in it, it must be a vocation, and I honestly think it wouldn't be the thing for you. Your vocation is in literature, Elspeth. Perhaps you'll be a writer, a poet perhaps. It would be lovely if you were. But you've got to have something to make a living. Poetry can hardly ever do that, for anyone. Librarians are not terribly well paid, like teachers, but they get enough to keep a roof over your head, and provide food and clothes and... like I said, it would not be a life of boredom."

Miss Johnstone talked to Griselda, who did not know too much about libraries or indeed teaching, but caught on readily to the idea as a possibility for Elspeth. She agreed with her friend's view that teaching, in a normal school at least, would not be right for the girl she thought of almost as a god-daughter; and other possibilities, like working in an office as a shorthand typist or secretary, were such a no-no, for Elspeth, as to make her almost throw up her hands in horror. The two ladies summoned Edgar to a conference, as his daughter's last term at school drew to an end.

"Edgar," Mrs Unston said. "Miss Johnstone and I have been talking to Elspeth about what she should do now. Would you like us to tell you what we think?"

"Oh, yes, please, ma'am. Her mother and I have been worrying about it. I don't think there's much chance of her getting to university. And in any case she doesn't want to go away from home."

"Well, I'm afraid what we're suggesting might mean she'd have to. Barbara thinks she would enjoy work as a librarian. It would keep her in touch with literature, and poetry, which is what turns her on, isn't it? And I agree with her."

Edgar looked at them. It was not a possibility that had occurred to him, or even to Rachael. But after a few moments he said: "Yes, I see what you mean. I think you might be right. It's certainly worth thinking about. I'm going to see her mother next week. I'll see what she thinks."

In the meantime, Miss Johnstone suggested, he and Elspeth should speak to the school. Careers advice was quite skeletal, at that stage, but teachers who knew their sixth form pupils were often able to help, and in Elspeth's case the English teacher, Mr Bradbury, with whom she had a warm understanding, would be keen to further any plan that would keep one of his star students in touch with the things that, in Griselda's words, "turned her on."

Keith Bradbury had had similar thoughts himself, he told Edgar, Miss Johnstone and Elspeth, who by then had become attached to the idea, although the idea of going from home for more than a day at a time was still not on her agenda. And Mr Bradbury said he would make inquiries, with the object of finding a trainee librarian spot more or less locally, if possible.

And Rachael told her husband to "go for it." "Of course," she said. "It's the obvious thing. I don't know why I didn't think of it."

FIVE

At Lufton Eye

The children of clergymen had many disadvantages, sixty-odd years ago. They often lived in too-large, cold, expensive-to-run vicarages with their fathers – Anglican priests were all men, at that date – struggling to bring up their offspring on inadequate incomes, although there were not many in straits as dire as Trollope's Mr Quiverful with his tally of 14. Nowadays, many parsons' wives have incomes of their own, from a profession or job, like teaching, and no-one among their parishioners thinks any less of them for it, but in 1950 such a sideline would have had eyebrows shooting off into the ether.

The Rev Arthur Percival, Lance's father, was vicar of Lufton Eye, a North Herefordshire village about as far south of Ludstone as Withymoor, Edenhope and their parish of Maestonbury were to the north. His was a modest living, and the vicarage as inconvenient as the next, but he and his wife Elizabeth, who had married him when he was a city curate, before the war, had one huge advantage over the Quiverfuls of a hundred years before. Their blessings were just one-fourteenth as great; Lance was their only child.

Helping also to balance the disadvantages of ecclesiastical fatherhood was another plus. Some Oxford colleges gave scholarships to the sons of clergy, of enhanced value if the parent had himself graduated from the college. It meant Lance was eligible for a hefty contribution towards his fees and costs, to a level which would have today's students gasping in disbelief. He sat the exam, passed with a high mark and impressed the interviewing fellows. He opted to read English and theology, although with no intention of entering the church. The news of his achievement came through before the end of the school year, and he of course told Elspeth about it.

The two were still in a relationship based on their literary loves and tastes. It was the words, they *way* they told of Lancelot, Guinevere,

Elaine, Gawain and all the others at Arthur's court, rather than the stories themselves that excited them. The outside observer might have said it was obvious the two were made for each other, but Lance and Elspeth did not see it in those terms. She did not look forward to any physical contact with him, because there was none, beyond accidental touches as books changed hands; or eye contact, sometimes intense, as one tried to convince the other of the merits of this book or that, one poem or another.

But Lance at least was beginning to feel the glimmerings of something else. Not love, in the way most eighteen-year-olds think of it. It was just that apart from his father and mother, Elspeth was the person he most enjoyed being with. The thought had hit him that when he went away to Oxford they would no longer have their almost daily discussions and debates on all the things that he cared about most. It led to conversations that brought in more personal matters.

Like most in the upper echelons at Ludstone School, he knew broadly what had happened at Edenhope four years before, although it had never been spoken of between them. Elspeth still shied away from any mention of it, outside her immediate family, and even there, when it had to intrude into their practical lives, as occasionally it must, she would withdraw into the shell that had worried them all for some time. Only once in her life, far in the future, did she initiate the subject herself. At this time Lance instinctively knew that he must not mention it. But as their school days neared their end, and they were waiting for the results of their Higher School Certificate exams, and there was even more opportunity to talk together, he began to ask her about Withymoor, and it led to hearing about her father and his work with the farm, and Stephen, Aunt Ida, Mrs Unston and Miss Johnstone. In turn, she asked about his own home life, and what he was going to do in the holiday that would shortly be on them.

"I expect I'll spend a lot it helping my father in the garden," he said. "It's huge, and the only help he's got is one chap who comes for a few hours once a week. When we came here, in the war, when I was little, he ran it as a kind of market garden, and supplied people in the village who couldn't grow things themselves. It's not like that now, but he still cultivates most of it. Mother thinks it's good for him, and for me – stops me spending too much time with books, she says. She helps as well, but she doesn't have much time, with all her committees and things. I think she spends as much time on parish affairs as my father, almost, and then she has housework. It's a big house, and she only has a lady come in to clean one day a week."

As the idea of becoming a librarian developed, Elspeth told him about it, and he thought it sounded a good suggestion, for her, if she could not go to university. He asked his father what he thought. He had spoken of her to his parents more than once, and how she was passionately interested in literature, especially poetry. His mother detected the start of a romance, and was delighted, for she had been worried that her son might not be quite normal in that respect, as she would have put it. Not that she had anything against homosexuals, "they can't help it," but she did not want her son to be one of them. She wanted him to have a wife, who would bring grandchildren to her and Arthur.

"Oh, sounds about as interesting a job as she could do, given the interests she obviously has," Rev Arthur said in answer to his son's question. "She won't make much money at it – might as well be a parson. But I don't suppose that matters."

Mr Percival obviously thought a little more about the matter, however, for a day or two later he said to Lance: "You know, you should keep your eyes open for anything in the libraries at the colleges that might suit your young lady friend. It might be just the thing for her."

"She's not my lady friend, father. She's just a friend. But I will. I hope she'll have found something by then, though."

Another day or two later Lance's mother made a suggestion of her own, the product of a maternal mind questing for romance and grandchildren.

She said: "Arthur, you know you've been wishing you could sort out your books, or get someone to do it. Well, I've an idea. Why don't we ask this friend of Lance's to come and stay for a day or two, and tackle them. If she's thinking of becoming a librarian, it would be just the thing for her. We've plenty of room, and we could pay her something, I'm sure."

Her mind was also running along the lines of "and then I could see what she's like," but she kept that one to herself.

Mr Percival had a library of more than 2,500 volumes, ranging from books of sermons to detective fiction, hardbacked and paper, acquired, many of them second hand, over twenty-five years of church and married life. They were in no order whatever, scattered round shelves, glass-fronted cabinets and boxes. He asked Lance what he thought of his mother's idea.

"I could get George (the garden assistant) to help me put up a few shelves in the study, there's plenty of room, and make it into a proper library. D'you think she'd come?"

"I don't know, father. She doesn't like the idea of going away from home to work, I know, but I'll ask her."

His mother had another idea however. "Get her parents to bring her down one day, then she could see what's involved."

Elspeth took a little persuading. Meeting strangers, even the parents of someone she would have described as her best friend, if she had been asked to classify him, did not come easily to her. But she agreed, and Edgar drove her down one Sunday afternoon when Arthur Percival had no evening service. She and Lance's mother liked each other at once, and Arthur told his wife later that it was a good job he was married to her or he might have been tempted, holy orders or not; and Elspeth, shown the books and asked whether she thought she could put them in order, catalogue them and put those that needed it out for repair, said she didn't know but would love to try.

She spent ten days at Lufton Eye shortly after the end of term, the first time in her life, apart from those awful few days after her ordeal, that she had ever been away from home. She slept in one of the vicarage's five cold, lofty bedrooms, washing and bathing in the house's equally lofty and unheated single bathroom. There was a fireplace in her room but Mrs Percival, apologetically, told her the last time they had attempted to use it and some of its fellows in other rooms the whole house had been invaded with smoke that ruined curtains and bedclothes. She thought the chimney was probably blocked by nesting jackdaws, who swarmed in the trees between the house and the church. Elspeth spent much time, some of it with Lance, watching the hooded mischief-makers from the room's high, stone-framed window, fostering a latent interest in feathered and other wild life that would grow with her years. Once, just as dusk was playing tricks with the light and her eyesight, she was startled by a movement in the little spinney, then amazed when the motion resolved itself into a fox, obviously a vixen, and three cubs, skirting the lawn. When she told Mr Percival, with delight, what she had seen, he said: "Oh, yes, we call her Lady Martha. She's got an earth out of the old well at the top of the garden. Been there three years now. We don't mind her at all. We've got no poultry and she keeps the rabbits down."

Jackdaws and foxes apart, she liked her bedroom. Perhaps the little bookrack by her bed, with seven or eight volumes new to her but which Lance had told his mother he was sure she would like, had something to do with it. Indeed she liked the whole house, despite its lack of many of the modern amenities with which Withymoor Cottage was now endowed. And she could not help feeling a warm appreciation of its senior residents. Mrs Percival was not unlike her mother, she thought, except that she did not appear to care much for poetry, and she candidly admitted that her taste in reading was lowbrow. "I just like a good story, especially a good love story," she said. If she had added that she liked a good romance in real life it would have been just as true. As soon as she had got to know Elspeth she was sure she wanted her to become the daughter she had never had, by marrying Lance. Although with the accompanying question mark: "Will she ever be able to have babies, or even look after a house? There's nothing of her. She's like a willow wand. But she's so good for Lance. And she's so nice. Perhaps she'll develop. Then there's... but that doesn't matter... oh, I do hope..."

What "did not matter" had come to light after the Sunday visit when Edgar talked about his son, Mrs Unston and Miss Johnstone but never mentioned his wife. After they had gone, she wondered why, to her husband.

"Don't you remember, four or five years ago? She caught her employer assaulting... raping... her daughter... and she shot him. She's in prison."

Elizabeth's eyes widened as the horrible meaning of her husband's quietly delivered revelation sank in. "Her daughter – you mean..."

"Yes, I'm afraid so, my love."

"Oh, my God... the poor child... the poor child..." And after a moment: "Does Lance know ?"

"He's never mentioned it to me, but I'd be very surprised if he doesn't know something. But please don't say anything to her. Andrew Joslyn at Maestonbury told me it affected her very badly. They were afraid at one time she might never be normal again. And I believe they have a hard time even now getting her to meet new people."

"But she came here today."

"Yes, and I think she'll come to stay, and do that job with the books. I know what your idea was in suggesting it, you naughty little schemer, but I think it'll mean we can play a part in helping her get back to normal, whatever happens between her and Lance."

"Oh, Arthur, I do hope so... oh, how awful... she must only have been thirteen or fourteen..."

"Thirteen, I believe."

"Arthur, I know the commandment says 'thou shall not kill' but I can't help thinking he deserved shooting. Was he as bad a man as that makes him look?"

He told her as much as he knew of Jasper Unston, as an MP and junior government minister, a little of the sordid side of his life, and how his wife was the Topham family's great friend and patron.

"Oh, Arthur, how wonderful. Do you know her? Have you met her?"

"No, all I know is what Andrew's told me. But he says she's a really good sort. She organised and paid for Mrs Topham's defence at the trial, and goes to see her in prison."

"Did they sentence her to prison for life?"

"No, she was sentenced to death." Elizabeth gasped. "But she was reprieved. I understand she can apply for release after so long. I'm afraid it will be a few years, yet, though."

The revelations inevitably had an effect on Mrs Percival's feelings about Elspeth. She was no longer simply a girl who might make a fitting wife for her son, she was a creature who had been battered by evil and must be helped and nurtured in every way she could. Yet it must be without any reference to what she had learned from Arthur. Elizabeth's intellectual powers may not have matched those of her husband and son, but she had something far more important – a fund of common sense, and a great capacity for liking and loving, which she employed when Elspeth came to stay.

§

Elspeth and Mr Percival, with some input from Lance, decided the two and a half thousand books which were the ostensible reason for her presence should first be sorted into half a dozen categories and within those put into alphabetical order, by author, where possible, and catalogued, in a ledger complete with pounds, shillings and pence columns, dug out of the vicar's desk.

"Bought it when we were selling the garden stuff about ten years ago but never used it. We seemed to give most of it away," Rev Arthur explained. "The book'll do for this, though, won't it?"

She spent four or five hours a day at her task, some of the time while Lance and his father were working in the garden. Several times, when Mr Percival had sermons to write or parishioners to visit, Lance joined her, but it was doubtful whether the result was faster progress, for they would then spend as much time as his help saved in investigating the content of a book they had arrived at, and discussing its merits.

Once, Elizabeth, bringing coffee, opened the door to a scene that might have got her excited, had she not already learned that the relationship of the two did not, yet anyway, add up to daughter-in-law and grandchildren. Two heads, Lance's with its crown of long, fair locks – much too-long,she thought – Elspeth's and its auburn waves, bent over the table, almost as close as they could get, then touching as their eyes wandered up and down the poem they had found. The proximity was due to nothing more than an eager delight in the new words they had discovered, and Mrs Percival, after an emotional second or two, knew it.

But she did not lose hope. They were indeed made for each other, she was utterly convinced. And in the meantime, she, her husband and Lance would all play their part in helping Elspeth put the horror of Edenhope where it belonged.

That their efforts were rewarded with some success was shown when Elspeth's ten-day stay came to an end with the book-sorting project not quite completed. She had indeed got them all into their categories, apart from a hundred or so still in the loft which Mr Percival said he was not allowing her near until he had at least cleaned the mould off them. But he had not yet got George the garden assistant to put up the shelves, which was what Rev Arthur's promise to do the job really meant. And the volumes needing repair should be dealt with before the final triumph of Elspeth's work could be realised, he ruled. It all brought a suggestion from the girl that she should return in another few weeks to complete the operation. Elizabeth did not quite know the strength of Elspeth's reluctance to be away from home for more than the length of the school day, but she knew enough to realise that this was a breakthrough, real progress.

She had been in touch with Edgar by phone, who was anxious to know how his daughter was doing, and was delighted when Elspeth sounded quite bubbly, clearly enjoying her stay. Mrs Percival was also surprised, and pleased, when Mrs Unston called to ask after the child, and Elspeth, handed the phone, spoke as intimately to her as to her father. She decided she wanted to meet them both, and called Edgar, the day before Elspeth was due to return, to tell him she would be bringing her, with Lance, and Mr Percival if he could be free. He was, they did, and all at Withymoor were delighted with Elspeth's new friends and the progress they had made in helping her out of her personal black hole.

Lance went away to Oriel College at Oxford soon after the vicarage library reorganisation was completed. Elspeth, now at ease with the prospect of becoming a librarian, although anxious that it should not take her too far from home, started to search for possible situations, but found nothing. Local authorities, the main employers in the field, were often encouraging when she told them of her literary interests and achievements, but regretted they had nothing to offer at present.

Her father and the female cohorts who had done so much towards restoring her psychological equilibrium, and who now included Elizabeth Percival, at a longer range, thought she had become a quite different person, after her stays at Lufton Eye. They all, even Edgar, looked on Lance as her boy-friend. Fortunately, none of them put the thoughts into words. Elspeth was still not far enough removed from the state when she had screamed that the doctor was not to touch her. Mention of anything that implied carnality could have crippled her recovery. Poor child; and poor Elizabeth.

§

Lance quickly became absorbed in his university, once over the initial freshers' period of socialising which did not hold much attraction for him. Studying for a double-headed degree meant attending more lectures than most other undergraduates, and more tutorials, but by the end of his first term he had learned to sort the wheat from the chaff, helped by a natural aversion to most of the diversions seen by some of his fellows as the main reason for being at university at all, even at such an august and allegedly sober college as Oriel. And he was helped in having a tutor, James Torreson, who was as enthusiastic as he was about English language literature, from Chaucer and Shakespeare to contemporary poets and novelists. It led to allowing his natural curiosity into the background of his student's literary passions, bringing to light his frienship with Elspeth and her role in reorganising his father's library. But the tutor scented a romantic attachment.

"She's your girl friend, is she, this young lady with an obvious talent for organising books?"

"Oh, no, sir. There's nothing like that. She's just a good friend. We spent a lot of time talking about this kind of thing at school, with Mr Bradbury, often, our English teacher. She's very keen on poetry, Tennyson especially. Morte d'Arthur and all that seems to set her on fire. My father thinks she'll be a poet herself, one day." And he went on to tell of some of the ways their thoughts had gelled through the school years, and how Elspeth's appreciation of more kinds of literature had developed, along with his own.

"What's she doing now, then? Is she here, or at some other university?"

"No, she didn't think she'd get in. And her father couldn't have afforded it, although there's a rich lady, her godmother I think, who would have helped. But she didn't want to leave home. It was hard work getting her to come to us to do the books. There'd been an awful tragedy..." He broke off, but continued: "She's trying to get a job in a library, but she hasn't found one yet."

Torreson thought Lance's denial of any attachment to the girl would not bear too much examination. He seemed quite animated when he talked of her. But the tutor said only: "If she doesn't want to leave home, she's going to find it hard to get a job in a library, isn't she?"

"I think she's realising that now. I had a letter from her yesterday. She said she thinks she might have to try further afield."

Torreson looked thoughtful. Then he said: "Lance, I think I might just be able to help. I think I know of a position, here, that might suit her. But it would involve a personal recommendation from me. I can't do that without knowing your friend. Do you think she'd come up so I could meet her and talk to her?"

Lance thought, briefly. "Yes, I think she might. Either her father or Mrs Unston – that's the lady I mentioned – would bring her, I think. Shall I write to her?"

"Yes, and don't waste any time about it. This situation won't be there for ever."

Lance wrote immediately, keeping the letter short so it would catch the college post, but telling her it might lead to a position for her. Two days later he had a reply, from Griselda, asking him to telephone her, reversing the charges. By the end of the week she and Elspeth were with Mr Torreson, and on their way to a quickly-arranged interview with one of the Bodleian's senior librarians.

He almost got off on the wrong foot by assuming Mrs Unston was her mother, but was told by Griselda: "No, I'm Elspeth's godmother (as near the truth as made no matter). Her mother is a dear friend of mine but she's away at the moment."

Elspeth's own diffidently-delivered but coherent and intelligent answers to his questions, including about how she had tackled the Percival book collection, along with her obvious knowledge of and love for literature of every kind, impressed him. A week later she had a letter offering her a position, and within a month had become a trainee in the world's premier university library.

§

Lance came out of his three undergraduate years with a top-class degree but decided he would like to pursue academic life further, possibly to the extent of becoming a lecturer. His scholarship did not run to funding an MA course but his father said he could manage that for one year or even two. Beyond that they would "have to see what happens."

What had already happened was that the young man had realised that Elspeth was much more to him than a literary friend. He would have hesitated to say that he was in love with her. Theirs was still not that kind of relationship, and that was not the kind of language he would have used in reference to himself. In their academic discussions, they of course came across many instances of people in love or who loved. They had for example quite animated debates about whether Harry Esmond was in love with Beatrix, or whether his passion was all along for her mother. Did Stephen Southernwood really love Deborah Arden or did he only want to get one over the rural society of the day by getting her to live with him without their being married? But they discussed these and many other enigmas with intensity but, apparently, quite dispassionate detachment.

Apparently, because the appearance of disinterest became one-sided as time went on. Lance came to know that, call it what you like, he had a special feeling for Elspeth; she was the one he wanted to be with for as many hours of the day, and days of the week, month and year, as was possible. For her, it was not like that. She liked Lance, liked him enormously, and the liking was augmented by the pleasure she found in their joint excursions into literature. If he had said he was going to the other side the world she would have been deeply sorry, would have missed his company for itself as well as for their intellectual companionship. But, at that stage, she would not have been heartbroken. If anyone had been able to analyse her emotions, they might have said her heart had been broken, or rather its growth stunted, years before. She truly loved her mother and father, came near to the same feeling for Griselda Unston. But that other kind of love, the kind that made Edgar and Rachael ache for each other after twenty years of marriage, was not in her psyche, then. The nearest she came to it was in her passion for poetry.

She enjoyed her new surroundings in the libraries, though, and the work involved in her training. She met students and staff and often had interesting conversations with them, in spite of her lowly status. With the help of James Thoresen, she found a bedsit lodging with the wife of a college porter, and was comfortable there. At first, she found being away from the folk at home a heavy burden, even with the solace of Lance's company. She usually saw him two or three times a week – most of her spare time was taken up with writing to her mother, her father, Mrs Unston, Miss Johnstone and Aunt Ida. He would meet her at her library at the end of her working day, and usually they would go to a cafe she liked for an hour or so before it was time for her evening meal. It could not be said that she rejected his advances, because he never made any. Somehow Lance divined that there was a psychological barrier between Elspeth and the male sex that prevented anything further than the kind of relationship he had maintained with her for years. The idea of "trying it on" with her would have been anathema to him. His own nature saw that kind of thing coming only as the climax to gentler feelings that grew, mutually, with time. Some who knew him thought he should have been a girl, but that was nonsense. He was just a very gentle boy. Nevertheless, the intensity grew. He could only hope that one day the barrier would come down.

As the term neared its end, and the Christmas holidays neared, he asked whether she would like to spend a few days at Lufton Eye, and she said she would, if it was alright with her father. She did not know how it made his pulse race.

SIX

Freedom

By 1955, when Stephen and Susan were married, and Elspeth was three years into her library traineeship, Rachael had been in prison for eight years and hopes that she might soon be released were rising. Edward Boulton the solicitor, prodded by Griselda Unston, although he did not need much prodding, kept up the pressure on the Home Office and thought her chances of parole before too long were good. But the wheels of justice, as usual, became regularly bogged down in bureaucratic mud and it was to be another two years before she again saw the skies over Shropshire.

Perhaps, though, the delay might have been to her benefit, in the end. In the spring of 1957, while she and the family, including Elspeth, by now a full-blown librarian at Oxford, and beginning tentatively to write poetry of her own, were daily hoping that the phone would ring with the news they had been awaiting.

It did, but not to tell them that she had been paroled. It was something far more. There would be no supervision, regular reports to police. She had been granted a full royal pardon. She would be as free as the day she married Edgar.

It came about through a fire. She worked in the kitchen of the women's block, and while designated with the lowly title of prisoner assistant, was in effect one of the cooks, regarded with respect, after an initial period while the officer in charge made sure she knew her place. The food was still dreary, by her country housewife standards, partly because the ingredients they had to work with were often second rate. The suppliers of meat – the little there was – and vegetables thought they could get away with sending produce from the lowest end of their stock to the prisons; and they were right, because the officials on the receiving end were happy to accept it, as being good enough for the scum it was to feed. Which although generally true was unfair on some like the women's governor at Strangeways, who battled for years to get better food and conditions for his inmates. Rachael however, when her abilities and personal qualities became recognised, managed to get one or two minor improvements made which brought the resulting fare to something slightly more acceptable.

The fire resulted from an accident of a type duplicated in many kitchens. A huge chip pan full of boiling fat was accidentally upset on top of a lighted gas cooker and almost before anyone realised what had happened flames erupted, setting alight anything combustible anywhere near including the clothing of the prisoner who had upset the pan. While everyone screamed, Rachael ran into the burning mass, grabbed the girl, pulled her clear and, using a sharp knife to help, ripped off most of the clothes, at the cost of burns to her own hands and arms and the risk of worse. She helped officers take the young prisoner to the sick bay, and stayed while both their burns were treated.

The governor, investigating the incident, knowing that Rachael's parole was imminent, having learned much about her during the ten years she had been in his charge, and after talking to her for half an hour about her family, made a decision. After contacting Edward Boulton, he wrote to the Home Secretary.

His action in fact had the effect of delaying her release as the wheels again churned slowly. But a month later she was told that "in recognition of your courageous acts during the fire in the kitchen of H.M.Prison, Manchester, Her Majesty has granted a free pardon etc etc." In fact, although no-one only the Home Secretary and one or two senior officials knew it, the Queen herself, learning Rachael's story, had almost insisted on the pardon.

It was ten years almost to the day since he had last touched her that Edgar wrapped her in his arms as she emerged from the prison gates, made a detour on their journey to have lunch at the little hotel that had hosted Stephen's christening party more than 25 years before, and arrived at the home of which she had only seen a photograph. No-one else was there. Griselda, Ida and the children had all agreed that they should "just let her and Dad be alone," and they would have a welcome celebration next day.

"It was just like a wedding night," she thought afterwards. He showed her the house, and as much of the farm as could be seen from the front window, ate the beautifully prepared sandwiches and cake that had been left on the kitchen worktop, under a glass cover but mysteriously fresh.

Upstairs, in the bedroom where he had spent those thousands of solitary nights, now hastily but delightfully redecorated, by the side of a cologne-scented bed, they undressed each other, like the teenage lovers they had never been, he taking great care not to hurt the hands and arms still tender from the scorching flames, but marvelling how beautiful she still was.

"Edgar, my love, my love," she moaned softly, afterwards. "I'm sorry... I shouldn't have done it... I shouldn't have put you through all that..."

"Don't, love, please, don't. You're here now..."

§

Elspeth and Griselda were the first to appear, followed by Stephen, Susan and Aunt Ida for a welcome home celebration that went on for days as Barbara Johnstone, the farm men and their wives, Marion Richards and Violet Marchett and the others, more neighbours, Lance and his parents and even the Maestonbury vicar came to add their congratulations. Rev Joslyn, who hardly knew the Tophams, for they had been only occasional churchgoers, but who had had several conversations with Arthur Percival about the Edenhope tragedy, kept religious elements out of anything he had to say to Rachael, until her question to him: "Do you think God will forgive me, Mr Joslyn?"

Edgar could have sworn there were tears in the parson's eyes as he answered: "Mrs Topham, God has already forgiven you, I'm certain. Can you doubt it when you see how everyone around you, all these good people, are so happy for you?" Rachael was not at all sure that she believed there was a God, but the words brought comfort to a soul now entering territory it had never yet trod. Before the tragic events ten years before, she had been a capable young woman struggling, at first up steep hills of adversity, later along a pathway more even but still with its darker stretches and pitfalls, to support and keep happy a husband she loved dearly; and to bring up their children. She had been sustained through the years in prison by the same need, so desperately felt that the privations went, not unnoticed, but shrugged off as unimportant compared with what she must continue to do for them. Now she returned to a life of prosperity, a husband highly respected for his farming abilities, a fond patroness in the wife of the man she had killed but who regarded her, not the wretch she shot, as the victim of the tragedy. To children doing well, Stephen making rapid and valued progress in his profession and married to a girl she liked enormously; Elspeth apparently happy in her work and her efforts to write her own poetry, and with a young man in tow who Rachael also liked immediately and who, she was as sure as everyone, the girl would one day marry. It was all too good to be true. There did not seem to be anything to struggle for any more. She was looking for the next thing to go wrong, almost from the time of her return. Happiness like this was impossible, wasn't it? Some may have said she was asking for trouble, wishing it on herself.

Her sister-in-law Ida was the harbinger, three months after the release. Living not far from Stephen and Susan, she could not help learning, at close quarters, of their estrangement. She had found Susan weeping, and her down-to-earth advice helped the girl deal with the situation in the way she did.

Ida did not mean to tell Rachael and Edgar about the affair, but somehow, when Rachael asked her about them on one of Ida's many visits, she divined there was something being kept back, and it had to come out. She did not telephone, or ask Edgar to take her to Cheshire – Rachael had not at that stage learned to drive – but she wrote, to both of them, the shortest of notes.

"Dear Stephen and Susan," she wrote. "Aunt Ida has told me you have had some troubles. Please come and see me. Please."

The anguish showing plain in the brief little appeal brought them to Withymoor, almost next day. They were able not only to reassure her but to tell her that they thought, only thought, but hoped, that she was going to be a grandmother.

§

It was a different story with Elspeth. At first, Rachael thought the same as everyone else who knew her and Lance: that they were a natural pair and would sooner or later be married. But as the years went on and it did not happen she began to worry. Elspeth was beginning to be recognised as a poet and Rachael was always the first to see her verses, often lyrically romantic and not indicating any form of personal stress in that direction. She came to Withymoor every three or four weeks and Lance often came with her. But still no hint of engagement or anything like it. But one day when they were talking about books and poetry, as they had done so often when Elspeth was a child, and what Lance thought about it came into the conversation, Rachael asked her: "Have you never thought about getting married, you two?"

"Oh, Mum, it's not like that. We – we're not – we're just friends."

"I don't think Lance thinks about it like that, darling. I'm sure he'd like you to be more than just a friend."

Elspeth did not answer, looked away. Rachael thought she was near to tears. But she said no more, then.

A few months later, Lance came with his father. He had been spending a few days at home and Rev Arthur wanted to visit Withymoor. Rachael found herself alone with him while Mr Percival went to call on his fellow cleric at Maestonbury. They talked about his work at Oxford and, inevitably, about Elspeth's poetry.

"You're very fond of her, aren't you, Lance?" Rachael said – it was more a statement than a question.

He looked at her, embarrassed, but still pleased to talk about her to her mother.

"Yes, Mrs Topham, I am."

"In love with her?" He did not answer.

"Fond of her, anyway," she substituted.

"I don't know what you'd call it, Mrs Topham. I'm more than just fond but – oh... yes, I love her."

"She says you're just friends."

He sat quiet, looking the other way. When he turned to her again, she could see the anguish. Tears were not far away. She reached out and put her hand on his arm.

He said: "We *are* friends. I know she enjoys all the things we do, and talk about. Books, poetry, music. We like nearly all the same things. The same things seem to catch our eyes. I don't think I've ever asked her to go somewhere with me that she wouldn't, unless there was some reason like work or something. But..." He paused again.

Rachael asked, quietly, still with her hand on his arm: "Have you ever said... have you ever told her how you feel?"

"I daren't, somehow. I'm afraid of what would happen. I might lose her. You see, I think..." He stopped again. And now Rachael was afraid. Did he think the unthinkable?

"Tell me, Lance. She's my child, isn't she?"

"I think she'd like to love me. But something's stopping her. I think she's... afraid, perhaps."

"You mean, afraid of committing herself?"

"Perhaps that, but I don't really think so."

Rachael was worried. The boy hadn't tried it on with her, had he? That didn't fit. Not this boy.

"What then, Lance?" Her voice betrayed her own fear.

He hesitated, as though summoning courage to take a fearful plunge: "Do you think perhaps it's what happened... I mean... that man..."

"Oh, God, Lance, I hope not. Her father and Mrs Unston have told me how she was. I think it was worse, pr'aps than they ever let me know. And I was worried that there might be some permanent effect. But then there was you, and going away to the library, and staying with your parents. I thought she was well on the way to putting it all behind her. And lately – the poetry she's writing. It's full of love, isn't it? I mean love between men and women, boys and girls..."

"Yes, I know. How could anyone who's afraid of... those kind of relations... write like that. But there's a little bit more. I've never... tried to kiss her, or anything like that. But once or twice, when we've been walking or something, I've touched her hand or... and she's... almost jumped away... as though touching me was something she couldn't stand."

She looked at him again. Surely no-one could possibly find him repulsive.

"Perhaps it's just shyness," she said, but without any degree of conviction in herself. "Give her more time, Lance. But don't give up. You shouldn't give up." She stood up, leaned over and kissed his forehead.

She pondered, over the next week, before Elspeth came again, how or if she should pursue it with her. Edgar did not dismiss her fears, by any means but thought more time was probably needed. His daughter had certainly been seriously affected by what had happened, and there was the instance when she had protested with screams: "Don't let them touch me." But that was only a few weeks after the awful event, when she was encountering all kinds of horrors, especially her mother's arrest and trial, besides the assault. Since then, he argued, she had made huge strides towards a return to normality, from returning to school to going to live on her own, seventy miles away. Surely this remaining illusion would eventually disappear. Rachael hoped he was right.

SEVEN

A Row of Lettuce

Susan's hopes that Edgar and Rachael, Olive and Ben would soon become grandparents were fulfilled when Benjamin Edgar appeared, a healthy infant brought into the world with no complications. He was born at their cottage home at Bollingbury, Stephen anxiously waiting downstairs – this was long before it became the norm for fathers to participate in their offsprings' births – until he was summoned by his mother-in-law to go see his son. And there was a repeat performance two years and two months later when Oliver Ian – the nearest they could get to Ida – made an equally undramatic entrance. As did Edward to make it three within six years.

By now, at 32, Stephen had put his misadventure well behind him. His pulses and his loins were still capable of being stirred by one female or another, as are most men's, but he never allowed temptation to take hold. He was so proud of his wife, the way she coped with three small boys, still had excellent meals on the table at the proper times, kept the house in apple pie order – although accepting the few hours of paid help on which he insisted – and even finding time to do a share of the gardening.

He never forgot the time he came home midway through the afternoon to find Susan planting a row of lettuces, Ben passing the plants to her, Ollie under a cherry tree, asleep on a blanket, and baby Edward gurgling in his pram, under the same tree. He came round the corner of the house before she saw him, giving him a few seconds to drink in the scene. Ben saw him first, and shouted: "Daddy!" Susan took the remaining plants from him, laid them on the ground, with her dibber, came to him. "You're early, darling. Are you alright?"

He kissed her, picked up Ben, said: "Yes, I'm fine. I had to go to Birmingham and I thought I'd come straight home. I've got a bit of work to do but I can do it here. Look, Ben and I will finish planting those. You put the kettle on."

Later, in his little office, he found it difficult to get down to the work. He could not get away from the feelings engendered by the garden tableau and how, five years before, he had nearly ruined the canvas before the brush could create the picture that truly reflected his life.

§

Stephen was highly regarded at Techmaster. He had already led development projects which had brought the company important orders and recognition, in Britain and overseas, including the USA. The latest inspired a headhunting approach from an American concern. A UK representative came to see him at home, to make him an offer, a few weeks after the incident in the garden. It was for an initial three-year contract on the west coast, at nearly double his current salary, and included many extras including a subsidised house and holiday travel to and from Europe for himself and family. He talked it through with Susan.

"Would you like to go?"

"I wouldn't mind," she said. "I'd like to see America. But what would happen if we didn't like it? If you didn't like the job and neither of us liked living there? And there's your mum. She was without you for all those years... and my mum and dad... and the children. Ben'll be going to school in September. If he went to school in America he'd... oh, I don't know."

"I've thought all those things, darling, and one or two more, and I'm like you. I don't know."

In the end, they decided to consult both sets of parents, arranged to go that weekend, to Withymoor on Saturday and Leicestershire next day. Not entirely to Stephen's surprise, all were adamant that they should not turn down such an offer.

"What if we don't like it and we have to come back with no job to go to?" he asked his father.

Edgar was inclined to scoff. "I don't believe you wouldn't find a job, and a good one. And if you didn't, you could come and work here. Don't suppose you'd be much good, but we could take you on at half pay," he laughed.

That part of the dilemma was solved however when Stephen revealed the American approach to the big boss at Techmaster, managing director Tom Manningham.

"Look, sir, I'm not asking for a pay rise or anything. But I wonder if I went and we didn't like it, would you consider taking me back?"

"Steve, I don't want to lose you. And you're in line for a rise, anyway. But I think you should take the job. It's too good an offer to refuse, and it will broaden your horizons. And I hope that answers your question. Of course we'd want you back."

After that, they quickly made the decision, and by the end of September, 1962, were in a pleasant house in a pleasant suburb of Portland, Oregon. Stephen liked the job, did it well with at least one notable success, Susan got on well with her neighbours, Ben liked his school and made good progress – except that he learned "that awful American spelling," according to his father – and Oliver was found a good nursery school. They took trips into the Rockies and to the coast, and once north to British Columbia, and returned to England for the firm's two-week holiday. Which was when they decided that the USA was not for them.

They were teetering on the edge of a decision to stay. Stephen had been assured of a substantial promotion, both had come to like north-western America and (most of) the people. They wanted Edgar and Rachael to visit, started to make enquiries about the procedure, to find that Rachael might not be allowed in the USA.

"They can stick their visa," Stephen almost ranted. "We're coming home next year. If I can't have my mother to visit, they can't have me." And Susan agreed.

He had an interesting conversation with Mr Manningham when he went, by invitation, to ask if he could have his old job back.

"Afraid not," Manningham said. "You'll have to make do with another. I want you to be development manager."

They had rented out their house at Bollingbury. Now they put it on the market because they wanted a bigger one, to give a bedroom each for their three boys. They found one in the Cheshire village of Alderley Edge, the hill which gave the place its name just behind their back garden.

EIGHT

The Poet

Dreaming spires, quadrangles
Wind-flown gowns and Sunday teas
Students, eager, knowledge-thirsty
Others, only seeking for they must
Isis, blade-tipped oars in harmony
Rippling muscles, sweating brows
Punts and god-like forms a-poling
Willows, weeping tears for lovers
Fabled seat, O can there be
A place on earth to match with thee

Woods and fields, ponds, whinb'ried hills
Circling farmhouse, barns and byres
Big red tractor, three-share plough
Dog jumps down, and Jack climbs after
Overalled, and features weathered
Muddy, oily, cap askew
God-like? Ask the lass there, calling,
'Dinner's ready, don't let spoil'
Thinks naught of Isis, spires or fable
Has gods, high-chaired, and John, at table.

Elspeth had climbed to a senior position in her library at Oxford by the time her first poems were published, in the literary magazine, *Verse*. She had been writing poetry almost since her schooldays, but had never thought any of it warranted submission to publishers or editors. Lance, to whom she showed almost everything she wrote, disagreed, and urged her to try. There was one in particular that he thought especially good, a long, lyrical ballad to which he gave the title *Beauty* – she never gave a heading to any of her work. It ranged over almost everything she found beautiful, from her mother's hair to "Lady Martha," the vixen and her cubs seen from her window at the Lufton Eye vicarage. It was not the subjects, but the juxtaposition of perfectly chosen words, the lilt and feeling of the lines, that thrilled Lance.

Beauty was not the first of her poems to catch the critics' eyes, however. That was a simple two-stanza, twenty-line composition, posing the beauty she had found in her university city against rural love in a modern setting. It did not scan too well and the last two lines in each verse rhymed, not a format likely to set the typewriters clicking madly among 1960s critics. But it immediately caught the eye of Verse's editor, as he showed in his intoduction.

"It is pleasing to say we think we have uncovered a new talent, although we cannot make the claim with honesty, for the talent has uncovered itself, by passing through Verse's letter box. The lady who has sent us the lines below included another three of her compositions. Time and space prevented us from including them all, but we look forward to doing so in our next issue."

§

The literary intimacy with Lance had never waned through nearly twenty years, since it began at school. And it had become more. Gradually, they came to share almost all their thoughts, philosophies, ideologies. Lance, like his father, was a natural conservative with a very small "c," so small in fact that it could almost have stood for what most people thought the exact opposite, except that father and son were equally disgusted by the excesses perpetrated in the name of that creed, in Soviet Russia. A few years later Lance became almost as appalled by what he saw as the every-man-for-himself approach, and the jingoistic attitude, of Mrs Thatcher and her cohorts. Elspeth would not have put her beliefs in quite the same words, but in essence they ran parallel.

He spent many hours agonising over the other aspects of their relationship, however. Their abstract thoughts seemed so close, almost as though they were twins, nurtured in the womb together.

But Lance, gentle as his feelings were, wanted something more like the bond between Edgar and Rachael, or his own mother and father. In other words, he had come to love her in the way of man for woman. It was not that he dreamed of going to bed with her, achieving orgastic heights, although occasionally the thought of children, his and hers, would send shivers down his spine. Sexual fantasising did not come into thoughts of her, but the idea of Elspeth nursing a baby, their baby, was almost more delightful than he could bear.

He believed that Elspeth did indeed have some kind of feeling for him apart from one of intense mutual interest in books and poetry; even though, as he had once told her mother, she seemed to shrink from physical contact, however slight or accidental. More than once, he thought he would ask her to marry him, even just live with him. The rest would surely develop, he thought. It was not that she knew nothing of love. Her poetry was full of it, between boys and girls, girls and other girls, even boys and boys, as well as between mothers and children, husbands and wives, grandfathers and grandmothers. Anyone reading it would say she obviously believed that love made the world go round.

Lance was right. Elspeth had come to love him. It was perhaps a more passionate love, even, than his for her. It fed many of her poems – witness her first published. But facing it was a black fog of denial she could neither dispel herself nor allow any male, even Lance – especially Lance, indeed – to penetrate or disperse. She knew the source of the miasma. Logical consideration would have scattered it to the four winds. Perhaps an hour of weeping on her mother's bosom would have brought a cure. Perhaps if Jasper Unston, caught in the act of raping a 13-year-old girl, had been punished by society rather than suffered his fate at the hands of her mother.

Nobody knew about the black wall, apart from her mother and, eventually, Lance. The years when she worried everyone, when they wondered whether she would ever return to normality, were long past. Starting with her visits to the Lufton Eye vicarage, she had increasingly adapted to a place in the wider world, especially the Bodleian Library. Almost everyone liked her, as they had at school despite the perceived idiosyncrasies which made her more interested in literature than girly gossip. As she progressed up the library scale she found herself increasingly sought, as a point of contact, by students, lecturers, tutors and even professors. "Try Miss Topham in the library – she'll point you in the right direction," students might be told when uncertain exactly what book or books they needed. She was always ready to talk to any of them, within the constraints of time and the working day, especially if they wanted to discuss books or poetry. More than one "fancied" her and made it clear. But she never had any difficulty in brushing them off, in the nicest possible way. And often they would get to know about Lance, and come to the conclusion that they were wasting their time – to the accompaniment of some distress, in one or two cases.

Outside the library, she and Lance continued to spend a great deal of time together. For the first two years of her life at Oxford, she stayed in the original bedsit. Then, as she began to accumulate more personal belongings, books, clothes, she found a flat she could afford. Eventually, as her financial situation became quite comfortable, she moved into a small terraced house, not far from the college lodgings occupied by Lance, by then a well-thought-of lecturer and member of the literary societies. They would meet three or four times a week, at first in a quiet cafe – neither cared for pubs or the fare they offered – later in her house. Everyone who knew them thought she was his girl-friend. She was often his guest at society evenings, where he tried in vain to get her to read, or allow him to read, some of her verses. She always gave an impression of shyness, and strangers would think her dull, until a mention of something in which she was interested, a book, a poem, an author, brought sparkle to her eyes and intelligent vivacity and sophistication to her conversation. And sometimes it could be other topics, wild creatures in particular, that had a similar effect.

It was however Lance who finally persuaded her to send some of her work to Verse, and who showed her the first they published.

"I've brought something to show you," he said as he knocked on her door and walked in. From his pocket he produced the magazine, opened it at a carefully marked page, and displayed the twenty lines and the editor's appreciative comments, laid out in a panel.

Her face glowed. "Oh, Lance," she said, and he thought she was going to put her arms round him, perhaps kiss him. But as always, the inhibition stepped in. He wanted to embrace her, and thought that if ever there was a time to take the plunge, this was it. But he was terrified that he might ruin it all, even though she had by then stopped shrinking away at the accidental touch, and they stood shoulder to shoulder as they read the verses.

"I'll get tea," she said, assuming that he would be sharing the meal with her, as he usually did. How two people, in their mid-thirties and loving each other sincerely, could maintain such an artificial situation, would have been difficult for even the most perceptive of psychologists to understand, if they did not know of what happened twenty years before. And even then, for many women who had been savagely raped had put it behind them. But spurred by the way she had greeted him as he showed her the poem in the magazine, he decided to risk all.

"Can I talk seriously to you?" he asked.

She trembled. She feared she knew what was coming.

"What about?" she asked, in a voice she tried to make as normal as possible.

"You, and me. We've been... friends... for a long time..."

She looked directly at him, their eyes met and stayed together. His hopes rose.

"You're a lot more than a friend, to me, you know..."

Now she looked away, but did not move. She was standing no more than four feet from him, as he folded the copy of Verse, trying to hide his tremors.

"I love you. I've loved you for a long time," he managed to say, quietly.

Her eyes came back to meet his. She was shaking like a leaf. But she said, barely audibly: "I know."

"So will you marry me? Please, my dearest."

He made no move to embrace her. But she collapsed on to a sofa, her face in her hands, sobbing violently. He still did not touch her. It was perhaps five minutes before she sat up straight, and looked at him again. When she spoke, it was in a whisper, but clearly and steadily.

"I can't. I can't. Oh, Lance, I'm sorry. I can't."

He took her hands – the first time ever, and amazingly she did not snatch them away.

"Will you tell me why?"

She did not answer.

"Is it because... of what happened... at Edenhope?"

Again she said nothing.

"I'd accept that... there couldn't be anything like that... between us. If I could just be near you, night and day, and look after you... and..."

"Oh, no. It wouldn't be fair... on you... it wouldn't be fair..."

Neither said anything for minutes, but he still kept hold of her hands, and she made no attempt to disengage herself. Finally he took his hands away, and sat down beside her.

"Can I just ask you something else?"

"What?"

"Do you perhaps love me... a little?"

"Oh, Lance," she whispered. "More than a little. I'm sorry, I'm terribly sorry..."

§

Elspeth had been reading Penelope Mortimer's recently-published novel, *The Pumpkin Eater*, and after the desperate revelation, she wondered whether she and the tormented Mrs Armitage had something in common, some strange female abberation. But she quickly dismissed the thought, as ridiculous. Mrs Armitage had an urge – a destructive urge, someone in the book called it – to have more and more children, and was obviously, therefore, happy to indulge in the activity essential to produce them. It was strange, Elspeth also said to herself with what she categorised momentarily as sudden clarity, that she could think of the sex act in this detached way yet shrink with indescribable horror at the idea of herself taking part in it. Then in the same breath of thought came the vague but even more horrific memory of that Saturday afternoon twenty years before. She did not want to deny that she loved him, as a person, not just as an intellectual friend and companion. She could happily have lived alongside him, cooked his meals, washed and ironed his clothes. Even the thought of his arms about her, through the night, was pleasing. As long as... and here she hit the black wall, shrunk into sickened revulsion at the very idea. The impenetrable fog shut her off from accepting what she knew, in another burst of clarity, ought to be one of the finest things in her life. She spent most of that night trying, and failing utterly, to tell herself that her fears were baseless, to find a way through the blackness.

She saw her mother regularly, especially after she learned to drive and bought a car of her own, and sometimes Lance went with her, or took her, and they would see both sets of parents. On one occasion when she went alone, Rachael probed a little about Lance, and Elspeth could not avoid telling her about his asking her to marry him. But the way she did it told Rachael what the outcome had been without it being spelt out. And instinct told her why.

"Are you sure?" she asked. "You care for him, don't you?"

"Oh, Mum, of course I do. But I won't ever be married, to anyone. Even him."

They were in Elspeth's old bedroom at Withymoor Cottage, looking out over the fields towards Edenhope. Rachael caught her hand, drew her closer.

"There's nothing to be afraid of, love. Not if it's someone you feel like that about. It's part of... loving."

Elspeth threw her arms about her mother. "Oh, Mum, I know. But I can't help it. The thought makes me... oh, I don't know what... I like being close to him... but I couldn't... I'd die, Mum."

Rachael stroked her hair, just as she had, nearly every night twenty years before. She did not feel there was anything she could say. She would have liked to tell Lance what she thought he should do: to urge him, as she had a long time before, not to give up, to keep as close to Elspeth as he could, in every way, to continue to make his feelings for her clear, in the gentle way that was the essence of his nature. Sooner or later that approach would work, she was sure. But the opportunity did not arise. She suffered for her daughter, mentally, almost as much as Elspeth herself. Rachael had never been sexually hyperactive, but sex had been a glorious, soul-lifting part of her love for Edgar, and of their relationship. Still was, half way through her sixties and Edgar eight years older. She talked with him about it. He appreciated her worry, and joined in it, but was more ready to accept that it was a long-lasting result of that ghastly event, and that there was nothing they could do about it, only hope.

NINE
New Rule

If anyone had asked him, as he neared his seventieth birthday, to name the best decade of his life, Edgar would have said, without hesitation, "this one;" or any parcel of years since Rachael returned to him. He thoroughly enjoyed running the Edenhope/Withymoor farm, knew he was doing it well, with his wife's help and support; and alongside his work, gloried in the success of their two children; and in the approbation and affection that came his way from Griselda Unston and many others. But the onset of three score years and ten brought the knowledge that his supply of good things, like all such, may be finite. He developed a heart condition and was told that he must get rid of the burden of management; at the same time an arthritic hip began to hamper mobility.

He, Rachael and Griselda knew they had to face up to the fact that he must soon retire. The problem was, how was he to be replaced. Mrs Unston was even older, by two years, and she was beginning to dislike the idea of upheaval, even such upheaval as would be involved in finding and then getting to know a strange new manager. Edgar, and Rachael, had become such an intimate part of her life, the closest friends she had had since those halcyon days of her mother and her governess.

Mainly for this reason, she and indeed the Tophams, especially Rachael, knew that replacing Edgar would be extremely difficult. Not from the point of view of the practical elements of managing the farm, for there were plenty of eager young agriculturists who would make a good job of it, and between them he, Griselda and Rachael would have sorted the wheat from the chaff. But it had to be someone who could, as it were, step into a place in her affections alongside the spot he and his family now occupied.

Edgar, while not presuming on Mrs Unston so far as to say so, knew that this was indeed the situation, and he and Rachael racked their brains in wondering how they could find someone who would fill this particular part of the bill. None of the farm staff could do the job, they knew. Either Jeremy Richards, the herdsman or his brother Aaron, the shepherd, would have coped well in terms of man management. But they did not have the breadth of knowledge necessary for other aspects of running a modern farm. Edgar knew one person who would have been perfect – his grandson Ben, who had spent many months at Withymoor, as a boy and young man. But Ben now had his own farm in North Wales, and his wife Aelwen and her family had contributed substantially towards setting him up in it. He could not under any circumstances be asked to throw it up to become a paid employee, even of Griselda Unston, who would have adopted him and his family as she had the other Tophams, including Elspeth.

But as they pondered, the blow struck, and Rachael encountered the third great tragedy of her life. Edgar had a massive heart attack.

He was driving in his Land Rover to meet shepherd Aaron, and help him attend to some of the flock's feet. As he stopped and got out, to open a gate, the seizure struck and he died within seconds. Aaron, two hundred yards distant, saw him fall but thought he had tripped. His dogs, always eager to greet Edgar, dashed up to him and started to whimper. Even from his distance, the young man could see that something bad had happened, from the dogs' behaviour, and he ran to investigate. When he reached Edgar, he quickly became almost certain that there was nothing he or anyone else could do. A big lad, he was able to lift his boss into the vehicle, and drive to Withymoor. Afterwards, he became concerned about whether he should have done so, but was assured by the doctor that nothing else he could have done would have made the slightest difference.

True to the pattern of her life, apart from those few hours at Edenhope when blind anger took over and set in train events over which she had no control, Rachael shrugged off the tsunami of grief that hit her, and just "got on with it." Griselda, although Edgar's loss was a double whammy for her, took on the immediate duty of conveying the news of their father's death to Stephen and Elspeth, and to Aunt Ida. The doctor immediately confirmed the cause of his death and started the rest of the necessary proceedings. But from that point Rachael was in control.

Almost as it had been that other time, she amazed everyone by the way she appeared to hold herself together. They all knew how she had loved Edgar, through forty years of a union besieged by troubles that could have wrecked even a marriage as solidly founded as theirs. They could guess at the joys that came their way nonetheless: Edgar's pleasure and gratitude every time he was brought to realise, as if he didn't know already, what a wonderful, resourceful, capable wife he had found, all those years ago at Eaton; hers as Edgar emerged from the financial morass in which he had been left by his own father, to prove his farming mettle; Stephen's success in education, profession and marriage to a girl they both loved. And Elspeth: also prosperous and almost famous as a poet, despite... but still, she seemed happy enough.

The very next day she broached the subject, with Griselda, of what was to be done about the farm. There need be no immediate panic, they both knew; like a well-oiled machine, it would run on its own for weeks, if necessary, provided there were no unexpected disasters. But Rachael did not want Mrs Unston to think she was taking anything for granted.

"You'll have to have a manager, ma'am. The men (she might have said 'and women,' for there were now two girls among the staff) are very good and know what they're doing, and they certainly don't need someone standing over them, but there are things they don't know about, aren't there?"

"Rachael, you know it's been worrying me for months, with Edgar wanting to retire. I don't feel I want the hassle of finding a new manager, and everything that goes with it. I've got lazy, I suppose. He's been doing it so well – with your help, I know..." and she stopped as her own words brought form to an idea she had already had.

"It's not my business, ma'am, but have you thought about giving up the farm? Renting it out, or even selling it," Rachael asked as Griselda seemed to dry up. "You don't have to worry about me. I'll soon find somewhere to live."

"Rachael, don't think like that. You're not going from here. And what about the other people? If we sold it, it might be bought by somebody who didn't want them, or not many of them. They've lived here all their lives, most of of them. No, I don't want to give it up, my dear. Not yet. And I've got an idea..."

"Yes, ma'am?"

"No, ma'am. I must think about it a little more. But if anyone asks, tell them I mean the farm to carry on, won't you."

Griselda's idea did indeed need thinking about. She wondered if, between them, she and Rachael could manage the farm. That meant Rachael essentially, she knew. She could do little more than she had done with Edgar in charge. But she felt she would enjoy helping his widow, her best friend, take on the challenge. She knew Rachael was well versed in animal husbandry, and guessed she knew her way round grassland and other crop management. There were excellent people among the staff. Young Jeremy Richards the dairyman had been brought up by Edgar, who had thought highly of him; Aaron the shepherd could manage a flock with the best; and there were men among the general workers who knew crop routines well, and who Edgar had often consulted. She had few other commitments. The rest of the estate was now managed by Edward Boulton. Her daughters were both married and living in the south.

Against these positive points were one or two negatives, she had to admit. Her age, for one, and for that matter Rachael's. She was seventy-five and Rachael only ten years younger. Was it realistic to think they could maintain the energy needed to keep running even the well-oiled farm machine that was Edenhope-Withymoor's six hundred-odd acres? In spite of the plus points she had totted up to a persuasive conclusion in favour, she knew there would be unknowns for which neither she nor Rachael would have an immediate answer. She decided the only way forward was to talk to her, without delay. The farm staff and others needed to know what her plans were.

The next day, although it was only 48 hours after Edgar's death, she asked Rachael to go along to Withymoor House. She could not go to the cottage; there were too many others there.

"About the farm," she said. "I know what I'd like to do. I don't want to find another manager, but I don't want to give it up. I'd like you and I to carry on running it for as long as we can. What do you think?"

Rachael smiled. "I'd an idea that was what was going through your mind yesterday, ma'am. It needs some thinking about though, doesn't it?"

"Of course it does. A lot of thinking. But in principle, would you be prepared to do it?"

"You mean, manage it?"

"My idea is that you'd manage the day to day running, and I'd look after the finances, but working with you, of course. Perhaps we'd need a foreman. But essentially you'd be in charge."

"Do you think it would work? I mean, don't you think they'd resent being told what to do by a woman?"

"By some women, p'raps. But not by you, Rachael."

Mrs Unston took the younger woman's non-objection as tacit agreement, and next day she did a tour of the farm, and some of the cottages, asking all the workers to what she called "a conference about the farm." They all attended, and when she told them that Rachael would take on the management, broke into warm applause. So much for fears that they would resent being bossed by a woman. Griselda also hoped, she said, that they would all join her and the families for 'a cup of tea and a bun' after the funeral, which she knew they would all wish to attend.

"My godfeythers, folks," Ted Marchett said afterwards, outside, and with some slight disregard for historical and etymological accuracy: "There was that chap years ago as moaned about 'the monstrous regiment 'o women,' because there was a queen on the throne; but when you see how different it is here now, compared wi' what it was under that bugger she shot, I say bring 'em on."

§

Edgar was greatly missed, but his widow and her employer managed well for a full decade. The two women remained as good friends as ever, had no more than the most minor differences over the running of the farm. Stephen complained that his mother was "doing too much." By then Rachael was 75 and Griselda 85, which might have been thought good grounds for his concern, but the ladies laughed it off. "We'll let you know when I can't add up a few figures or your mother has to be lifted into the Land Rover," Mrs Unston told him.

Griselda's biggest headache was not the farm, or the rest of the estate, but Edenhope House, as it had been for most of the time since her husband's death. Like her employees, she could find no enthusiasm for the place. She certainly could never have lived there. She would have liked to sell it, but found that legal shenanigans a century before, linked to the farmland, would probably have cost as much to unravel as the place was worth. It had already been modernised internally, as much and as well as was possible for such a house, and put it into the hands of a national agent, at a modest rent.

The first tenant, a city financier who took the house only on condition that the whole estate's shooting rights went with it, stayed less than two years. His wife and the staff they brought with them complained that despite Mrs Unston's refurbishment the house was dank and dreary and there was "an atmosphere." Through one of the maids, who wanted a spot of social life and took herself off to Ludstone in search of it, they learned of the tragedy enacted there a few years before. From that point, none of the servants would go into the study.

"I can't go in there, madam," one said to the lady of the house. "It gives me the creeps."

More tenants followed, but none stayed longer than three years, one only three months, the wife in this case, who had not seen it beforehand, reportedly threatening her husband with divorce if he did not find somewhere else immediately, rental agreement or not. One couple, who Marion Richards described to Rachael as "rich nutters," took the house *because* they had heard it was haunted, and wanted to investigate for themselves. They found no ghost, told Mrs Unston that the report of an atmosphere was nonsense, but the house was indeed dreary and they would not stay there beyond the twelve months to which they were committed.

Over the forty years following the fatal incident, the house had a dozen different occupiers, but was empty for at least a third of the period. Maintenance of the gardens was always the estate's responsibility, under letting agreements, and Griselda made sure this was continued even when the house was empty. When Andrew Perkins the gardener left for retirement she engaged another.

§

Farming in Britain was going through many changes while Stephen was climbing the Techmaster ladder and Elspeth making her first forays into the poetry that would eventually make her well known. Low wages, a demand by farmworkers for some of the goodies they saw, or thought they saw, their opposite numbers in the towns and villages increasingly enjoying, the steady encoachment of mechanisation were among the factors fuelling the "drift from the land" that was often a feature of demographic discussion in the post war years. The holding of forty acres that had provided a decent living in 1935 was a millstone round the neck of a family trying to live off it in 1965, unless they could hit on some way of adding to the normal income from milk, pigs and poultry. Diversify, diversify became the in-phrase.

Even large farms like Edenhope/Withymoor, which as Griselda Unston told Edgar around 1950 paid for her own household, her daughters' expensive education and more, were not exempt from change. Between them, the two farms, when he and Rachael came to Edenhope in 1937, employed a score of workers, mostly living in the farms' own cottages. Twenty-five years later the number was down to a dozen. Edgar's twenty per cent of the profits barely kept up with inflation, in cash terms. On his initiative, he and Griselda had discussed giving up the dairy operation – the farm was well capitalised, removing reliance on the monthly milk cheque – and getting rid of the 70 cows to which the herd had grown would have cured headaches like the need for twice a day, 365 days a year milking and finding relief so the cowman could have time off. All stock required a deal of attention but beef cattle and sheep could be left to their own devices at some times and seasons. But, Griselda pointed out, young Jeremy the cowman's heart and soul was in the cows and their calves; and the high wages he earned through them were needed now he and his wife had two teenage children. Her approach in this case reflected her attitude towards anything that affected her people. They must not be hurt, if it could be avoided.

Nevertheless she and Rachael had to cope with increasing financial pressures. No-one was ever sacked, but three of the six cottages at Edenhope and another at Withymoor became vacant as workers retired or left for greener pastures in the years before and after Edgar died. Griselda tried letting them, but the boom in country properties which has so changed so much of rural Britain was not yet under way and their isolated situation made them unattractive to most working people, and she decided they must be sold. They were the first estate properties to go since her father had bought Withymoor nearly half a century before.

TEN

The Odd Couple

Later in her life, Elspeth wondered that she not gone completely off the rails, under the pressure of her monstrous inhibition. Indeed, through her middle years, she had moments, and longer spells, of agonising self-examination. But the other parts of her life won out. She and Lance continued as before. Friends and colleagues thought they were an odd couple, an obvious natural pair, made for each other, as their relatives had thought for years, not married or living together; but friends they remained. She saw much of her poetry published, the critics were kind, and a volume of her work was selling well by poetry standards. She was happy in her work at the library, and had made a number of friends, among colleagues, academic staff and students. Lance appeared to have accepted that theirs was to be a brother and sister type relationship. On one occasion, when they were both going to Paris for a literary event and had to leave for the airport at four o'clock in the morning, he stayed with her, at her suggestion, sleeping in the second of her little house's two bedrooms. And little changed in a decade and a half.

Lance was well thought of at Oxford, without doing anything to set the world on fire. He wrote two books, biographies of less well-known nineteenth century authors, which were accepted by a specialist publisher and enjoyed a good reception and modest sales among the literary cognoscenti. It was one of these that brought the next important development in his life, and, eventually, Elspeth's. Just before his fiftieth birthday, in 1982, he was offered the chair of English literature at an Australian university, Adelaide.

He wanted to accept, for in spite of being apparently absorbed in his studies and his teaching, he knew he would enjoy expanding his horizons. His own parents had died a few years before; Rev Arthur in the philosophical way he had met most of his life's exigencies; Elizabeth his mother less so, for she had never quite come to terms with the knowledge that she was not going to be a grandparent.

But there was Elspeth. He loved her as much as ever, even though he had by then given up any hope that she would become his wife. There were not many days when he did not see her. Almost routinely, they had their evening meal together, sometimes "out," sometimes at her house. The thought of leaving her for the other side the world almost made him decide there and then that he would turn down the Australian offer.

He told her about it the day the call came, before the offer had been confirmed in writing.

"I had a call from Australia today," he said as they drank their coffee after their dinner, through which he had been rather quiet, and she had wondered why.

"Oh, from Peter Carr?" a writer with whom he had been corresponding.

"No, from the vice-chancellor of Adelaide University. They're offering me a chair – English Lit."

"Oh, Lance, that's wonderful. Professor Percival!"

"I don't think I'm going." She looked at him. She knew what he was going to say.

"Unless you'll come with me." She looked at him again. He continued: "I'd like it to be as my wife, my darling. You know that. Same terms. But come anyway. As long as I can have you near..."

"I won't marry you on those terms, Lance, as I told you before. It wouldn't be fair. And the rest of it – it's still the same... I'm so sorry... it's awful..."

They sat and looked at each other, before she said: "But you've got to take that job. For my sake, as well as yours. I'll come to – where is it, Adelaide? – as soon and as often as I can. But you must go. Really, you must."

He was persuaded, as much as anything because he knew there was another issue making it difficult for Elspeth to leave for the other side the world. Her mother's employer and closest friend, Griselda Unston, was gravely ill, probably with only weeks to live. Mrs Unston had been like a godmother to her, closer even than to her own daughters. Her death would leave Rachael, her mother, widowed eleven years before, with a host of lonely problems.

§

Griselda was dying from an inoperable pancreatic cancer. She kept quiet about it for months, except to Rachael, but when she knew her time was down to weeks she also knew there were important matters to settle. Rachael was herself in her mid-seventies, and must not be asked to carry on running the farm on her own. She summoned her daughters.

Ursula and Deborah Unston, although they unwittingly played a key role in much of what transpired at Edenhope from the day of their birth, have not appeared very much on these pages. They were of an age with Elspeth, and while she was at home and at school she saw a little of them, in the holidays, encouraged by her father, and by Griselda. But the twins found they had little in common with her. Their mother had done her best to prevent their father's worst characteristics, especially the domineering and bullying trait, coming out in them, and had largely succeeded. But she came to regret her decision to send them to the Yorkshire boarding school where her revered governess had been educated many decades before. They emerged, not as likenesses of the gentle Miss Hardaker, but with socialite addictions and little love for the life found at Withymoor, the kind of nature or literature that Elspeth loved. Especially poetry. If it did not rhyme or was not funny, poetry it was not, they might have said.

Their welfare had been the driving force behind almost everything Griselda did in their early years, but despite the blood link there seemed to be little in the way of bond through their school days and when they left at the age of nineteen. They soon made it clear they had no intention of settling down to any kind of country life. Griselda shrugged a metaphorical shoulder and allowed them to leave for London at the invitation of their cousins, whose own mother, Jasper Unston's sister, was married to a wealthy city financier, and who could not begin to understand her sister-in-law's attachment to people she would have seen merely as servants, let alone that one was a woman who had murdered her brother. The girls never returned for more than two or three weeks at a time, dutifully expressing pleasure at getting back to peace and quiet but in reality itching for a return to the city.

And before they were 25 they had found city-based boy-friends and married them. Visits to Withymoor became rare, only embarked upon when duty like presenting a grandchild had to be fulfilled; or when Mrs Unston made decisions about changes to her will and felt they must be told in person. It was a situation that might have driven most women to emotional distress, but for years, their mother had reconciled herself to a situation where more love and warmth came from the so-called servants than from her own daughters. Yet she never regretted the stand she had taken forty-odd years before.

Now, still definitely compos mentis, Griselda made no bones about getting down to business with the girls, by this time in their forties and each with two teenage children of her own, away at school.

"This might seem a bit grisly, asking you to talk about carving things up when I'm gone," she told them, in an interview more redolent of a Victorian will-reading than a modern mother's get-together with her daughters. "I've made a will, and you know what's in it. Everything goes to you, all but one or two special items which you won't have to worry about, and apart from the taxes, which I warn you will be substantial, you'll get it without strings. You'll be quite well-off, and I hope you'll use your money responsibly. And that brings me to the most important things I want to say.

"I expect you'll want to sell the farm and most of the estate, all of it perhaps, and I'm not going to try to stop you. You've got different lives, now. But please, consider the effect decisions you make will have on others, especially the men and women who've worked here and contributed to the wealth you're going to have handed to you on a plate. Rachael – Mrs Topham – will have her house under my will, and some money. She's been my best friend as well as my employee, for years, and her husband before her. But it's not just her. They're all my friends. Please, my dears, try to think of them like that, for my sake. They're good people. The salt of the earth."

It was the first time in forty years of devotion to their practical welfare, to trying to make sure they did not lose out to the results of their father's miserable propensities, that Griselda had opened her heart to her daughters so fully. It was not in her nature, bestowed by her mill-owning inheritance and coal-mining parentage, to talk to them of her innermost feelings. She could more easily have talked to Rachael. More than once, she had admitted to herself that she had made mistakes in their upbringing. She should have kept them close to her, educated them through a home-based teacher like her own, much loved Eliza Hardaker, or even through local schools.

But her appeal to them, late as it was, by no means fell on stony ground. The girls were moved, more than she would have thought likely. After she died, a few weeks later, her possessions were indeed sold, almost all of them, but Ursula and Deborah made sure the sales were handled in a way that recognised the needs of farmers, cottage tenants and workers. Jeremy Richards the cowman took a similar job on a big farm in Herefordshire, where dairying on a large scale had been introduced by members of a family from Cheshire. His brother Aaron, well known as an exceptional shepherd, was offered more than one position but chose instead to take over his wife's family's hill farm in Wales, assuring them both of years of hard, poorly-rewarded but ultimately satisfying work which took him to a respected position in his community. The estate's six tenanted farms were all sold to their occupiers, rather below market price, despite the half-hearted objections of the girls' stockbroker husbands. Withymoor Farm itself was sold with its original 250 acres to a wealthy Midlands businessman on much the same basis as it had been purchased 50 years before by Griselda's father: he thought it would be good to be a landowner. The rest of the land managed by the Tophams was offered to adjoining tenants but only about half was sold, and the daughters, in an uncharacteristic spell of sentiment, decided they would keep the rest in their own hands, putting it out for rent through the successor to Edward Boulton the solicitor, and was taken by the Lummas family who had occupied, and now bought, the adjoining Eden Fields Farm.

Edenhope House remained what it had been for best part of a century, ever since the girls' grandfather decided he could make a silken purse out of the more useful pig's ear. More than once, they and their husbands put it on the market, for sale or rent. They were even less successful than Griselda had been. One possible purchaser offered to buy it at site value if he could demolish it and put up the kind of house he wanted, but the local council was adamant in refusing planning permission. In the end, it just stood there, degenerating year by year into the gloomy, inhospitable eyesore witnessed by Stephen on his lonely venture into the past.

§

Lance went to Australia, spent years in the delightful South Australia city as enjoyably as possible without Elspeth nearby, was well received by the down-to-earth but intellectually upbeat university population. She joined him twice a year, and in Oxford's long summer vacation stayed for two months at a time, feted by the local arts community. But she decided against leaving England permanently. Her mother was now on her own after Mrs Unston's death, and Stephen was fully occupied in caring for Susan, suffering from a rare and eventually fatal illness.

Elspeth retired at sixty from her work as a senior Bodleian librarian and went to live with her mother at Withymoor Cottage, which on Griselda's death had become her own property. She did not go to Australia again, partly because Lance was also to retire at the end of his college year, and would return to England, but more important because Rachael, now in her upper eighties, was at last losing some of her vitality and Elspeth felt she needed her support.

The doctor, who had known her and her history for forty years said he could find nothing organically amiss. "I'm afraid she's basically suffering from the disease that catches up with us all, sooner or later – an accumulation of years, and in her case a life full of hard work and stress," he told Elspeth.

Rachael began to feel her days were numbered. As she told the doctor, the energy that had driven her for seven decades seemed to have disappeared. But there was one thing she desperately wanted to do while she was able.

"Love," she said to Elspeth as she lay on her chaisse-longue, watching a man and his dog rounding up sheep in the 30-acre field that had been part of first Edgar's then her own farming responsibility: "I don't think I've got too long with you, and Stephen. It doesn't worry me for myself; I'm not afraid. But there's something I must do before I go."

"Mum, don't talk like that. You're not going to leave us for a long time."

Rachael smiled. "Well, we shall see. Elspeth, you've made me very proud of you. And your father was, too. When you were very young we wondered a little whether you'd cope with the world. We never thought you'd become a famous poet –"

"Mum, I'm not, I'm a very ordinary one," she interrupted.

"Well, whatever you like to call yourself, I know you're a real poet, and a good one, and many thousands, millions p'raps of other people think the same. Don't try and take away the thing that makes me so proud, please, love. It's my gift to the world, as well, you know. You know I don't believe in all that religious stuff. I don't think I'll meet your dad on the other side. But your poetry... it makes us both immortal. It'll be there long after I'm gone. And you, for that matter."

"Oh, Mum..."

"But that isn't what I wanted to say to you now, while it's there in my mind. It's been there for a long time, but it might be gone tomorrow. My mind isn't keeping hold of things like it was, even important things like this."

Elspeth knew what she was going to say, at least what it was about, and wished she wouldn't. But nothing would have made her try to stop Rachael saying it.

"Love, I wish you would try to see your way to marrying Lance. It would make me so happy. And I think it would make you happy. I know it would. And it would put... that awful business... where it belongs... dead and buried..."

Elspeth, who had been sitting on a stool alongside the couch, sank to her knees, her head on her mother's breast.

"Oh, Mum, I'm sorry. I know I shouldn't feel like I do. It's awful. I do love him. I've loved him for forty years. But I just can't..."

Rachael sighed. "Please think about it again, my sweetheart. It's like the albatross in that poem, a burden round my neck, dragging me down. Goodness knows what it must be like for you. Try to cut it free."

Elspeth stayed where she was for a long time. When she rose, she went outside, walked along the lane which led to another and eventually to Edenhope, through a wood that had always been a favourite haunt in childhood and since, whenever she was at Withymoor; over a brook, the inspiration of one of her poems, and up a steep bank from which she could see, beyond a vista of sheep and cattle in green fields, the upper part of the house where her life had been dealt the blow that was marring her mother's last days; and, although he concealed it so wonderfully, was reducing Lance, her dear, dear Lance, to a hanger-on, a cipher, something less than the man he could be. She gazed across at the house, for nearly half an hour. And suddenly, out of nowhere she thought afterwards, came the knowledge of what she must do. And if it did not release her from this ghastly bondage, what she must still do. She went back to Withymoor. Her mother was still on her couch, her eyes red from weeping.

Elspeth knelt in front of her, caught her hands. "Mum, I've decided. I'm going to marry him. I'll cut it free, and bury it. I will, I promise. Whatever it takes."

TWELVE

A Mother Passes

Years before her mother-in-law took on the management of the Edenhope farms, Susan had shrugged off the tribulations of her marriage's early years, never again worried that Stephen might go off the rails; and had no more than the parent's usual concerns about her sons as they navigated the choppy waters of teenage and adolescence. Oliver developed an attachment to a girl at school that had her worried, for she seemed to be a flighty creature with an apparent vacuum in the space between her ears; Edward went through a spell, at more or less the same time, when he wanted to stay out all night and she feared he was mixing with a gang who were into drugs. Oliver's girl however turned out to be nothing like as empty-headed as she first appeared, just not academic, and eventually she and Ollie were happily married after the usual spell of living together when he was studying engineering at university; Edward quite quickly saw the light when one of his friends went to gaol after a stabbing incident.

Her mother had been ill, progressively, for years, and Susan and her sister put in much time helping to look after her, not easy at a distance of nearly a hundred miles, in Susan's case. Relief from that burden came, inevitably, with Mrs Baines' death, and her father giving up their hardly-economic farm and going to live with his other daughter. But soon afterwards Susan herself was hit by the first impact of the disease that had killed her mother – a rare, hereditary, progressive complaint passed down the female line.

At first, it was nothing more than a mild pain in her arms, which the doctor thought was a muscular problem and treated with pain-killing tablets and eventually injections over a period of five years. But through her fifties, the pain and inability to use her limbs spread through most of her body. By her sixtieth birthday walking was difficult and she found it hard to turn the pages of a book. The disease did not affect her mentally, except, inevitably, that she had bouts of depression. She had no need to worry about housework or any kind of chore, for she had a full-time cook-maid and "dailies" as necessary. Stephen's position as head of Techmaster made sure they could have all that kind of thing without hardly having to think about it, although he was never one to throw money about. They still lived in the five-bedroomed house at Alderley, bought when they returned from the USA. They had been able to help Ben, now married with two children, set up in a modest farm in North Wales; and assist Ollie and Madeline to buy a house. Edward had gone off round the world and was currently in Australia, where he looked like staying. None of the boys were the cause of Susan's depressed states. Rather, they helped lift her out of them.

Stephen would have liked to retire at 60, to spend most of his time with Susan, but it would have left Techmaster without a chief on whom he could depend. However, in two years more he had brought an intended successor up to a level where he was confident that with him, Stephen as chairman of the company, the firm would continue its progress in the world of research and development.

He did not know how long he would then have with her, but he determined to make the most of what time there was. She had always been a keen traveller. He bought a soft-top Mercedes car, her choice, had the passenger seat modified so that it was as comfortable for her as possible, and commissioned a specially-designed wheelchair that would fit in the boot. Over the next three years, they expanded their knowledge of Britain until they knew almost every corner, then carried on into other parts of Europe. Although she was often in considerable discomfort, she never wanted to cut short a trip. If there was something she badly wanted to see, but which proved to be inaccessible, she would send him off with instructions and a camera.

During this time, her disease worsened, although not as rapidly as they had both feared. But on their return from a trip to Italy in 1995, she was attacked with pains in parts of her body that had so far escaped. And this time her speech was affected. She could hardly make him understand what she wanted. Rushed to hospital, she was seen by the consultant who had dealt with her all along.

"I'm afraid there's no hope of any improvement," he told Stephen.

"What do you think will happen? Will she just stay like this?"

"We don't know a great deal about this disease, Mr Topham. It's very rare. But I would say not. I think some of the organs are affected now."

"You mean – it'll get worse? She'll die?"

"I'm afraid so. I'm terribly sorry."

Stephen turned away, before asking:"How... long...?

"As I said, we don't know too much about it. But I would say – a week or two, perhaps less."

Stephen managed to thank the consultant for his honesty, and went back to Susan.

She was struggling to say something, and eventually managed it.

"Going to die, darling. Not here, please. Home. Boys."

§

She left him, quietly and peacefully in the end, at three o'clock on a quiet September afternoon, Stephen holding her hand, sensing rather than feeling the life creeping away. Their sons were in a room adjoining. They knew she would be gone soon, and that he must be alone with her at the last.

Ben had to go back to the North Wales farm Stephen had helped him buy and set up, two hundred and fifty acres of mostly hill pasture which he and his wife Aelwen ran alone. Aelwen was a local girl he had met at the Reaseheath farm college. She had to stay to look after the farm and their two young children while he was away with his father. Oliver too had to return to his job with an engineering firm in the Midlands, but his wife Madeline, once thought of as empty headed, stayed to look after Stephen, along with Edward, who would eventually return to Australia where he had a job with a regional daily newspaper and, he revealed, a girl friend he wanted to marry. Stephen liked Madeline, and was sorry that he and Susan had once characterised her as having nothing between her ears. Elspeth and Lance, still in the state that others thought of as perpetual past-times courtship, and which reminded Madeline, she told Oliver, of Aunt Emily and Mr Gentle in *Seven for a Secret;* not that Lance was anything like that poor gentleman, except in being middle-aged. They came for three days, slept in separate bedrooms at Alderley, but also had to get back to their occupations.

By two days after the funeral he was left alone, apart from the daily visits of a cook-housekeeper who lived nearby. He started to put in more time at Techmaster, but felt he was now regarded as superfluous, indeed something of a nuisance. Certainly he was not needed there. The managing director, who he had brought through the ranks, was doing an excellent job, he believed, and the firm was thriving and paying him, as company chairman, a fee that more than sufficed for all his needs even without his income from shares in the concern.

Inevitably, over many months, the agony of his loss receded. But the feeling that never disappeared, grew almost in parallel, was the sense of loneliness that became more intense, week by week and month by month. He started to travel again, visiting parts of the world they had never managed to get to, but, every time he came on something they would both have stood and looked on with awe and wonder, hit with a sledgehammer blow when he could not turn to her and share the feeling. Nearer home, he went weekly to see his mother, now coming to the end of her eighties, becoming frail but still living at Withymoor Cottage, as mentally alert as ever and looking forward to being joined by Elspeth after her retirement; and drove to Edenhope House for the first time in half a century – although he had been no more than two miles away every time he visited Withymoor, the thought of approaching *that* house repelled him. He knew that Susan had done so, with one or other of the boys, driven by a natural desire to have a physical image of the background to the demons she knew still beset her husband and his family. But her deep sensitivity had prevented her from discussing it with him.

He spent time with the boys and their families, and enjoyed it, especially the hard-working weeks on Ben's farm on the edge of

Snowdonia. Even those could not eradicate the loneliness, but it was one of them that led to his life's next developments, as far-reaching as any so far.

§

He was walking up Snowdon, nearly two years after Susan's death. It was something he had never done, despite having spent time at the great mountain's foot, on Ben and Aelwen's farm near Capel Curig. Now, he seized the opportunity while they took the children on a rare excursion to the seaside, after he had completed the few chores he had insisted they leave for him. He drove to Pen-y-pass, from where two frequently used paths, the Miners' Track and the Pyg Track, led to Yr Wyddfa, the summit. He chose the Pyg Track, tougher going but shorter, intending to return by the other route, if not too pressed for daylight time.

Walking quickly, overtaking two or three other groups, he was within half an hour from the summit, he reckoned, when something hit him on his right shoulder, and he was knocked of his feet and head first down a forty-five degree, twenty-foot drop. His head struck a rock and after a flash of blinding pain he knew nothing.

He never remembered the two women scrambling down the scree-strewn slope to him, or being winched up to the helicopter, or its rotors whirring feet from a rock face. Next day, he could only vaguely recall his first return to semi-consciousness, the previous evening, or the shapes which seemed to be doing something, saying he knew not what; or the substance of anything that happened through the night.

Sometime mid-morning, he came to the realisation that he was in a hospital. His head felt as though it was about to split open. He tried to lift a hand to feel what it was, and a separate blast of agony ran down his side. Someone was standing by his bed, and he tried to speak to her – or was it him.

"Something hit me," he said.

"Yes," said the doctor. "But don't worry about that. You're going to be alright. We'll soon have you fixed up."

There were others in the room, two of them familiar. Yes, of course, it was Ben, and Aelwen.

And did he he not know the other one? But before his brain could summon anything more, he was gone again.

"I think that's as far as you're going to get with him for today," the doctor told them. "But I don't think you need to worry. We won't lose him."

Outside, Ben spoke to the woman who had been in the room with them. He said: "We haven't thanked you yet for what you did. You probably saved his life, from what they've told us."

The woman, who seemed to be about sixty, grey-haired, pretty with a face speaking of strong character, said: "It was my daughter, really. She's a doctor and she knew what to do. But the most important thing was that she had a mobile phone and called the mountain rescue people."

Ben asked: "Is she still here? We'd like to talk to her."

"No, she had to get back to her hospital, and there was nothing more she could do for your father."

"But you – are you staying locally?"

"I was going home last night but I decided to stay here. I found an hotel. I shall stay on for a day or two, until we see how he gets on. I've nothing I must get home for – at least, I've a dog and cats and some poultry, but a neighbour's looking after them. I've phoned her and she's alright with them for a few days."

Ben thought for a moment. He had immediately liked the woman, and was confident he was speaking for Aelwen when he asked: "Would you like to come and stay with us? If you wouldn't mind roughing it a bit. It's a farm near Capel Curig, about fifteen miles away..."

Aelwen broke in: "Yes, please do. We'd try to make you comfortable."

The lady said: "Oh, you're so kind. But I mustn't impose on you. I expect you're very busy."

"You wouldn't be imposing. But you'd have to tolerate two boisterous girls, and two dogs. Please come. We'd like to hear what happened, from you. Wouldn't we, darling?"

"Yes," Ben said. "But would you like to tell us your name? Did I hear the doctor call you Mrs Browning?"

"That's right. Alice. Please call me that."

She collected her car, Ben and Aelwen their ten-year-old Land Rover, and she followed them, first to Pen-y-pass where Ben retrieved Stephen's car, then on to the farm, where the children were being looked after by a neighbour's daughter, their baby-sitter on the few occasions they needed one. As they got out, Alice looked carefully at the soft-top Mercedes.

Introductions to baby-sitter, children and border collies over, they sat with tea round the kitchen table, and Alice told them what had happened on Snowdon.

"We were only about fifty yards behind him," she said. "He'd actually overtaken us a little while before, on a broad bit of the path. He was walking very quickly. The bit where it happened, there was a rock face on the top side and the track was quite narrow, only just wide enough for one person. I was in front and just saw him fall down. The rescue man said it looked as though he'd been hit by something, on the head or shoulder. The path did a zig-zag and was going back but still climbing. They thought perhaps a big stone had been dislodged by someone above. Esme climbed down to him and found he was unconscious but his pulse and so on was alright. She phoned the rescue people right away. She checked as well as she could for broken bones and didn't think there were any. I'd got down to her by then and we took a spare jacket out of my rucksack and put it round him, and one of her sweaters under his head."

"How long did you have to stay there?" Aelwen asked.

"Not long. Twenty minutes or so, I should think. The helicopter men were terrific. There were two of them besides the pilot. They winched themselves down and got your father into some kind of a cradle then one of them went back up with him. It was wonderful the way they did it. It was a steep slope, big loose stones under, you had a job to keep your footing, never mind lift a heavy person. And those rotor blades – I don't think they were more than ten feet from the rock."

The others, including the children, had listened attentively. Ben said: "We can only say thank-you to both of you. We'll write to the mountain rescue people, and send a donation."

Aelwen asked: "Is there anyone you'd like to contact, Alice, to let them know what you're doing?"

"No, I've only Esme. I lost my husband five years ago. I'll call her tomorrow, if I may. Or perhaps I could leave a message at her hospital, just to let her know where I am."

"Of course," Ben said.

It was nearly dark by that time, and all that could be done was for Aelwen to give the children something to eat and prepare a meal for themselves. Alice asked if she could go to bed afterwards.

"It's been a bit of a day," she said.

Next morning, Ben had cattle and sheep to inspect and feed, and when he came back for breakfast he found Alice outside, looking attentively at his father's car.

"It *is* a beauty, isn't it," he said.

"It certainly is. And do you know, I think I've seen it before, and your father. I thought he seemed familiar when I saw him on the mountain, and the car confirms it. It's an unusual number, isn't it?"

"Yes, it is. By accident though. It's not personalised. Dad thought those were only for show-offs. He got that car when my mother became ill. Where do you think you've seen it – and him?"

"It was just outside my home, in Shropshire. Last year. He was looking at a big empty house. I thought perhaps he was thinking of buying it..."

Ben looked at her in surprise.

"Whereabouts in Shropshire?"

"Oh, it's a little village – well, a tiny hamlet really – in the hills, about ten miles from Ludstone. Edenhope, it's called..."

Ben stared at her, excitedly. "Alice, you did see him. It must have been him. He lived in that house as a child. I didn't know he'd ever been back, though. He didn't like the place – the house I mean. And then – something awful happened..."

"Yes, I've been told about that. Oh, the poor man – boy I suppose he was then..." She stopped. She thought she ought not to go into it any further. Ben guessed why.

"It's alright," he said. "Water under the bridge, and all that. Do you know my grandmother?"

"No, I've never met her. But I know where she lives, at Withymoor. Frank – my husband – and I used to drive or walk past there sometimes."

"Golly, you're almost an old friend. I used to go and stay there with Gran and Grandad. He managed the farm, you know. I loved going there. I never went into the big house, though. It was usually let. Grandad would never have gone in, anyway. Anyway, let's get some breakfast, and ring the hospital."

"Your wife's already done that. They said he was 'more comfortable.' And you can see him any time you like, this afternoon."

She went with him, in the end, while Aelwen stayed home with the children, both of whom were at home, in the last few days of the summer holiday.

They found him half awake, under the influence of the pain-killers and other drugs. The staff nurse who took them into his small ward said: "Stay as long as you like, Mr Topham, but it would be better if you didn't try to talk too much."

Ben said: "Hello, Dad. How are you feeling?"

"Full of beans. Mountain's a bit worse for wear. You were here last night, weren't you? Bit second-hand then, I expect."

"You were. It's good to see you making progress, though. Aelwen sends her love. She had to stay with the children."

Stephen's bandaged head was immobile, but Ben saw his eyes directed at Alice.

"Dad, this is Mrs Browning. She and her daughter found you on the mountain, and helped you, and sent for the mountain rescue. She's staying with us."

Stephen still looked at her. "Mrs Browning. Were you... here last night? Know I've seen you before."

"And before that, Mr Topham. And my name's Alice."

"Alice. That's a nice name. Stephen."

Ben reached for the only chair in the room, made her sit on it while he went in search of another. Stephen said, the words coming more slowly: "Seem to know you... Alice... can't think how... come back, I expect."

She said: "We're not supposed to talk, but I'll tell you that much. It was at Edenhope. You were looking at the big house, and I was cheeky and stopped to speak to you."

"Course. That pretty lady... walking a dog... asked if I was buying it... didn't think you were cheeky. You're still..." He was going to say she was still a pretty lady but instead said: "Thank you... saved my life, reckon."

"It was my daughter, really. But don't talk any more, Stephen. You mustn't."

Ben returned with a chair. Stephen's hand on his good side was out of the clothes, and he took hold of it. His father looked at Alice again, and closed his eyes.

§

Stephen was in the hospital at Bangor for a fortnight, then was allowed "home" to the care of Ben, Aelwen, and the district nurse; and Alice. She had stayed on at the warm invitation of the family, including the girls, Rachael and Bronwen, only returning to Edenhope for one overnight stay to make new arrangements for her poultry and cat, and bring her dog Khama back with her. She went every day, with either Ben or Aelwen, except once or twice when she stayed with the children. Towards the end, she usually took her own car so she could stay on a little longer than Ben was able. The first day she missed, disappointment showed on Stephen's face, although he quickly hid it. But it did not go unnoticed by Aelwen.

"She's good for him, isn't she?" she asked Ben as they left.

"She certainly is." He looked at her. "You don't suppose...?"

"Oh, I don't know. But I wouldn't be surprised. Wait and see. Would you mind? Or the others?"

"Oh, God, no, if it made him happy. She's alright. Very different from Mum. But alright. Really alright. And he's awfully lonely."

They were not wrong. The fact was that Stephen and Alice had fallen for each other. "Hook, line and sinker," Ben said to Oliver, who came from Manchester to visit. "She'd have climbed into bed with him if she could." Quickly adding: "No, not really," as Oliver's eyebrows threatened to disappear into his hairline.

"Would you mind if they did get together – got married, p'raps?" Ben asked.

"I'm OK with anything that makes Dad happy. I've only met her a couple of times but I certainly like her. What do you think about her – she's lived with you all this time, hasn't she?"

"I think she's a smasher, an absolute smasher. And so does Aelwen. And the kids. They call her 'Nanny Alice.' They'll be upset when she goes."

"What are her – circumstances? Do you know?"

"You mean, brother, is she after Dad's money? A fortune hunter?"

"Well, I wouldn't put it like that. But there are such women, aren't there?"

"I don't think she's rich. But from one or two little things she's let drop, I don't think she's on the breadline. I know she has two pensions, the state one and one from her job, and I'd be surprised if she hasn't got something from her husband's.

"But I'll bet you anything you like, Oll, she's not after Dad's money. Anything you like."

§

Ben and Aelwen were absolutely right. Stephen and Alice had, plainly and simply, fallen in love. Money, houses, even the Mercedes, for which she made no secret of her admiration, did not come into it. Perhaps the seed had been sown at their brief meeting a year before. He had certainly thought, as he drove away, how pleasant she seemed. He would have liked to have talked longer, but her questions already threatened to take him in a direction he did not want to go.

Many young people cannot understand how men and women in their sixties and older can experience such emotions – often as heart wrenching, and as long-lasting, as anything the twenty-year-olds who seem to think they have a monopoly of such feelings can experience. On his part, the prospect of an end to the miserable sense of loneliness that pervaded so many of his days was perhaps a factor.

Be all that as it may, Stephen and Alice very quickly knew that the most enjoyable experience in their lives now was to be together. In the Merc, on walks as soon as he was able, at the mealtable, entertained by her daughter or his sons and daughters-in-law, helping Ben with the sheep, even overcoming Madeline's initial suspicions of anyone supplanting, as she briefly saw it, Susan's place in her father-in-law's life.

As she had told Ben, she knew the essentials of what had happened that terrible weekend when Stephen was a schoolboy. Now he told her how his mother had coped with her prison life, still fulfilled her role as wife and mother, how the wife of the man she had killed had become her best friend, patron and employer. Touched on his own agony because he had sent Elspeth to Jasper Unston's study. And agonised afresh as he spoke of the lasting effect it had on her.

"But she's become quite famous, hasn't she?" Alice asked. "I've read some of her poetry. It's beautiful."

"Yes, I know. But she won't... can't..."

"You mean she won't have anything to do with men? But her poetry – it's full of love..."

"She loves someone, and he loves her. He's a grand chap – university professor. I think he inspires a lot of her poetry. But she won't marry him. Mother says it's because she can't bear the thought of... going to bed with him... I mean..."

"Oh, Stephen... the poor girl..."

They were silent for a few moments, before he asked: "Will *you* marry *me*?"

She took a step away from him, and for a moment, a brief moment, for he knew, just as she did, his heart was in his stomach.

"Need you ask? Stephen, need you ask?"

They had indeed already taken it for granted. But they had to discuss practicalities, one of which was that she must get back to her house at Edenhope and make sure all was well there. The cat and half a dozen hens were being looked after by a neighbour, with whom she had been in telephone contact, but she felt the time had come when she must put in a physical appearance. Stephen went with her, that same afternoon.

They drew up past the gloomy, empty and still unkempt Edenhope House and when they arrived, Stephen had somewhat of a surprise: her house was where he had spent the first of his Shropshire childhood years, although now much extended and improved.

By the time he had been introduced to and spent time with the neighbour, inspected the house and the "livestock," it was nearly dark. Stephen said: "It's a bit late to go to Mother's, tonight. She goes to bed quite early, nowadays. I think it would be better if we went down to the Maestonbury pub. They do good food there and they've got several rooms."

Alice said: "I've got a better idea. Let's stay here. I can find food, one way or another. I'll be welcoming you home, almost."

After a few seconds, she added, almost mischievously: "There's only one bed made up, though."

§

Next morning, at Withymoor, he introduced her to Rachael and Elspeth: "Mum, this is Alice, Mrs Browning. Alice, my mother, and my sister, Elspeth. She's the lady who rescued me on the mountain, as I told you. And I told you where she lives, didn't I? Now I've just discovered it's our old cottage, although you'd hardly recognise it. Isn't that a remarkable coincidence?"

Rachael said: "Well, I never. But I do remember your name as one who bought one of the cottages. I hadn't realised it was that one, though. Well, it is a coincidence – a nice one though."

"Mum, Elspeth, I've something more important to tell you, and I'd better do it right away," Stephen resumed. "Alice and I are going to be married."

Rachael looked at him and smiled: "Now you don't surprise me. You couldn't stop talking about her when you phoned me. Are you happy about it, Alice? Do you want me to give you a list of his faults? But not now, because we've something to tell *you*, haven't we, love?"

"You tell them, Mum."

"Alright. But first, you two. I'm very pleased. I've never met you before, Alice, but I know you'll make him happy. Don't ask me how I know, but I do.

"But our other news is something that has made *me* happy. I can't tell you how happy, and I can't tell you why. It's about Elspeth. She and Lance are going to be married."

"Oh, Sis, wonderful. Absolutely wonderful. When? Soon?"

"In about a month," Elspeth said. "As soon as he's back from Adelaide."

Stephen debated, first with himself, then with Alice, whether to suggest a double wedding. They consulted Rachael, who killed the idea.

"They won't," she said. "The last thing they want is any hint of a 'do.' They mean to go a registry office with just two witnesses." She thought a moment, then added: "I'll tell you what, though. I was going to be one witness. We hadn't decided on the other. Would you like it to be you two?"

"Oh, no, Mrs Topham," Alice protested. "I couldn't allow you to be pushed out."

In the end, they decided all three should attend, subject to Lance's approval.

§

Stephen was in touch with the chief executive at Techmaster, with whom he had always got on well but who seemed lately to be less communicative that usual. That afternoon he had a call from the deputy chief, asking him to get to Manchester urgently, for reasons he could not detail over the mobile phone they were now using.

"It sounds serious," he told Alice. "I'd better get up there tomorrow."

They stayed the night at her house, named "Edenwell" by her and her husband, and he left at eight o'clock next morning. She thought she ought to stay there, after more than a month away, and he reluctantly agreed.

He called at Alderley to tell Julia the housekeeper of recent developments, including his forthcoming marriage, and that he expected to stay there for at least one night.

She said: "Oh, congratulations. I'm so happy for you, Mr Topham. But I'm glad you've come. They've been pestering me to get hold of you, but I didn't have any number. I tried the number for Ben, but it's the old one in the book, isn't it, and there wasn't one for Ollie, or your mother."

"No, they're just on my phone," he said. "Sorry, Jules."

Becoming more concerned, he swallowed the coffee Julia insisted on making, and drove on to Sale, and Techmaster.

Although outwardly all looked the same at the office complex where he had spent most of his working life, he immediately sensed it was far from so. The receptionist who for years had greeted him with a cheery smile and "Good morning, Mr Topham" was not there. Her desk was vacant. He walked on to his own office, maintained for him as company chairman. It was not exactly bare, but there was no computer screen, or telephone, on the desk. He went on to the managing director and chief executive's office, and found it empty. But the deputy, his old cooeague Brian Foster was next door, with another man, a stranger.

"Steve, thank God you've come," Forster said. "We've been trying to get in touch with you."

The other man was a senior police detective. If they had been able to locate Stephen, which of course they would have, sooner or later, he could have been arrested on suspicion of complicity in a fraud which robbed Techmaster of most of its assets, financial and technical, and would leave him a comparatively poor man. No wonder the MD had spoken of "interesting developments." He had disappeared ten days before and was still missing. Stephen's own apparent disappearance linked him in naturally suspicious eyes and minds with the man who, it was well known, had been his close colleague, and whom he had groomed as his successor.

§

Stephen had little difficulty in showing that he had had nothing to do with the fraud, except as a victim. Indeed the firm's own facts and figures had already shown it, the only question lingering in the investigators' minds being over his apparent disappearance. But the effect on his own finances was drastic. The whole of his income from Techmaster – shares, chairman's fee – was gone. It left him with his state pension and a smaller one bought as an annuity from his personal resources: less than £5,000 a year in total.

All this had become clear to him by the end of the day. And as he sat over yet another lonely meal, left by Julia to be warmed in the microwave, facing the prospect of calling Alice as he had promised, the implication of the situation as it must impinge on her emerged as the final blow, the heaviest of all. No way could he marry her now. He sat at the table, longing to hear her voice, even via the phone, but dreading the thought of uttering the words he must.

He was saved from having to make the move. The phone rang. It was her, Alice. "Hello, darling," she said.

"Hello," he answered.

"I wanted to make sure you're alright. It's getting a bit late."

"Yes."

"Stephen, are you alright? You sound terrible. Is something the matter?"

He was silent. She thought he sobbed.

"Stephen, darling, what is it? What's the matter? What's happened?"

After a few moments: "It's the firm. It's gone bust. There's been a fraud. I'm broke... stoney broke... stoney bloody broke..."

Now it was her turn for silence.

"Are you sure, love? Are you sure it's as bad as that?"

"They – the police – were looking for me because they thought I'd something to do with it. That's alright now, they know I didn't. But the money and everything's gone..."

She was quiet again. He kept the phone to his ear, but said nothing.

"I'm coming up," she said.

"You can't... you mustn't... Alice, you mustn't... you must forget about me..."

"Don't talk nonsense, Stephen... Stephen, my love, don't say things like that. Just tell me how to find the house."

She went, that evening, taking the dog Khama with her, apologetically asking Olivia the neighbour to care for the cat and the hens. It was nearly 11 o'clock when she arrived. But oh, how good it was to see him, wipe away his hidden tears, babble away of her love, like a seventeen-year-old, until he smiled, but knew, as if he had not known it before, that for richer for poorer, in sickness and in health were the themes by which they would live, together, for as long as they were on this earth.

§

In fact, as Alice soon divined, jointly they were quite a way from "stoney bloody broke."

They owned two houses, and an income between them that at worst must be labelled "comfortable."

She suggested that one of the houses should be sold, or let, preferably Stephen's because it would bring more money. She did not see any need to use the resulting capital for themselves. It could be salted away and, hopefully enlarged, passed on to Ben, Ollie and Edward eventually. They could live at Edenhope, but sell it if Stephen found he did not like it, and buy something elsewhere. Either way, their home would be her daughter's inheritance.

Stephen thought it all made sense. But first he wanted to stay on at Alderley to help Brian Forster and the remaining Techmaster staff with whatever sorting out or picking up of the pieces was possible. He had never been a fire-eating entrepreneur. From the days when his mother had delighted him with a second-hand Meccano set, his prime interest had been in mechanical science. He had always been pleased with the firm's commercial success, but the technology, some of it extremely advanced, coming from his own and his colleagues' brains had been what turned him on, rather than the money they made. Now though he blamed himself for what had happened, to a degree. If he had been more of an eagle-eyed financier he would have spotted that something was going wrong. Should, have, anyway, he told himself, and was driven into a state of near-depression.

It did not last however. He and Forster found there was sufficient income due in the next few months to enable a nucleus of staff and equipment to be kept on, to service developments already in the field and even to work on new ones. He spent weeks liaising with customers, and gradually re-established a base from which they might move forward. Alice stayed at Alderley, and went with him on his first trips. They talked everything through, and he found she grasped the business side well.

The first expedition kept them away for two weeks, much of it in Germany, Holland and Scandinavia. There was still more to do, and Alice thought they, or at least she, ought to get back to Shropshire and her house at Edenhope. Stephen felt he needed to stay at or near Techmaster, for the time being. Alice left, promising to update Rachael and Elspeth on all that had happened. They had said nothing up to then because they did not want to break the news by phone; and Alice would assure his mother that if Stephen was no longer rich, between them they would be at least comfortably off. Also, he and Brian Forster were beginning to be confident that the firm would carry on, able to employ the best of its researchers and enough back-up staff to enable them to function. He phoned Alice every day with a progress report and for news of his mother and sister, to whom he also gave assurances.

Another fortnight on, Lance returned, almost euphoric, Alice said, at the prospect of at last, at long, long last, being married to Elspeth, with whom she had now established a warm relationship, as with Rachael.

"Oh, Stephen, he's so happy," she told him. "And he's so nice. But why do you think they haven't been married before? I can tell they've loved each other for a long time."

He was quiet for a moment. "It was because of what happened... there... I told you..."

"Yes. I can understand that it would have a terrible effect on her. But to stop her marrying the person she loved... for all those years... oh, what a wicked man he must have been... evil..."

"Yes, darling. Evil. But talk to my mother about it. She'd like you to, I know."

Alice had a long talk to Rachael, that evening. For the first and only time, Rachael told her the grim story of that Saturday half a century before, and how it had left Elspeth in her terrible state of loving denial.

"Yes, my dear," her mother-in-law-to-be said. "It's been one of the saddest things in my life. Goodness knows, how they've loved each other. I've tried to tell her there's nothing to be afraid of, it's part of loving someone. But she…"

"What do you think's happened now then?"

Rachael looked at her.

"If I tell you this, will you keep it to yourself, love? It's only an idea, anyway. Probably wrong."

"Yes, of course I will. But don't tell me if you don't want to."

"No, I want to." She paused.

"I've an idea she thought she could get rid of it by… oh, I don't know… confronting it in some way…

"You know, none of us – Edgar, myself, or her, or Stephen have ever been inside that house since… that day… when it happened…"

"I know. Stephen's told me."

"I think she may have gone there. Made herself go. The key's missing, that Mrs Unston left with me when she died. Something's happened, anyway. She's not frightened any more. She's started writing again… and I think she and Lance are sleeping together…"

FIFTEEN
"Rest in Peace, Edenhope"

Alice

It would be wonderful to be able to say I knew we were going to love each other, that day I came on Stephen looking round Edenhope, fifteen years ago now. Fifteen wonderful years, filled almost entirely with joy, on my part and, he has told me so many times, on his. Only the passing of Rachael, his mother, could be inked in black on the calendar of our happiness. But even that could not mar our hourly, daily, yearly delight in each other's company. But that first time I saw him, I came nearer to falling in love with his beautiful Mercedes car than with its owner. No, that's an immense exaggeration. But I did like it. What does that say about me? It was actually the choice of his first wife, Susan. Obviously a lady of taste and discrimination, in cars and men. Especially men, even if she did have to lick him into shape, for one brief period. Thank you, Susan. Sleep peacefully.

That day at Edenhope, I simply thought he looked a pleasant, rather good-looking man. There was no stirring under the ribs, and as you will know if you have read the first chapter of this book, not under his, either. It was a year later that I fell in love with him, when his head was swathed in a bandage, and he was barely compos mentis. When we've talked about it since, he has said only: "I just knew." And that's how it was with me, I suppose. I admired Frank, and loved him for his gentle, unflappable, hard-working nature; but I don't think he ever engendered that kick in the stomach that came on me that day in the hospital at Bangor, at an age when emotions should have reached Milton's "calm of mind, all passion spent," instead of sending their host spinning round like a giddy schoolgirl.

Stephen felt he should stay up in Cheshire for the time being, to help Brian Forster get the firm back on some kind of track. At the same time, I did not think I should leave my cottage and its "livestock" until some permanent arrangement for their care had been arranged. Also, there was his mother. Rachael and I "got on" from the first time we met. No, more than that. We developed a real affection. She was not completely alone at Withymoor; Elspeth was there between her various engagements and a local lady went in every day to clean and do odd jobs; and she still drove. Stephen came every weekend, and always spent a few hours with his mother, and I made a point of going most days.

I sometimes walked, through the fields and along the farm tracks, to Withymoor; it was about a mile and a half that way and three miles by the road. And it was twice, on those excursions, that I saw Elspeth. The first time, I started my walk through the entrance to the farm buildings and as I rounded them I saw a woman apparently coming from the direction in which I was going, and making for the far end of the house itself. I was intrigued for I had never seen anyone there before. She was about a hundred and fifty yards away when I recognised the tall, willowy figure. She went straight towards a door at the far end of the house, seemed to take a key from her pocket, unlocked the door and went inside. I wondered whether I should follow her but remembered what her mother had told me. That was it. Elspeth was confronting the scene of the awful events that had condemned her to forty years of shunning the embraces of a man she truly loved.

The second time I saw her was two days before she and Lance were to be married. She seemed to have come out of the house and was walking in a direction that would converge on mine. I let her go on until she was out of sight, and followed. We were taking a route that included a path through a small wood. As I entered the spinney, I saw her. She was dancing, a fairylike ballet, and her face was in raptures. I dodged behind a little thicket of hazel, through which I could still see her. She continued her dance for perhaps five minutes, then sank to her knees. I thought at first that she was crying, and indeed she was, for tears were flowing in rivers. But she was laughing as well. She got up, shook her hair, amazingly showing not a trace of grey, picked up the little coat she must have discarded for her sylvan celebration, for that it surely was, and set off, slowly. I emerged from my screen and caught her up.

"Hello, Alice."

"Hello. My, you look happy. Anyone would think you're going to be married."

She laughed, almost as I'd seen her laugh a few minutes before.

"Yes," she said, and looked at me.

"Did you... did you... see...?"

"I saw." And I threw my arm round her, which must have looked odd if there had been anyone to see, for she is a head taller. "I'm so happy, for you, Elspeth."

We walked on. After a few moments she said: "Yes, it's going to be alright." As if she knew that I knew.

§

Next day, Stephen came. We fed the cats and the hens, leaving them plenty of food for we would be away for twenty-four hours, but took Khama with us. She would be fine at Withymoor. As we got into the car, Stephen said: "Can you smell anything?"

"Like what? What kind of smell?"

"I thought I could smell burning, or smoke."

I sniffed, and did indeed detect a slight smell of smoke. He looked all round but could see no signs of fire. I said: "Mrs Egerton (my next door neighbour but one) had a bonfire a day or two ago. It must have been from that."

We drove to Withymoor, where we were staying the night before going to the register office with Lance and Elspeth next day. We made no pretence of keeping up old conventions, and slept together as usual. The happy couple stayed apart, Lance at the Unston Arms at Maestonbury.

At two o'clock next day, they were finally united, in the rather scruffy little register office at Ludstone. We all went back to Withymoor Cottage, for a beautiful if abstemious meal, for the newlyweds were driving on the first leg of a honeymoon trip to the Scottish islands, where neither had ever been. We went back to Eden Cottage, to feed the animals and birds, but returned to Withymoor to sleep, as company for Rachael.

As we went to bed, Stephen went to the window to open it and draw the curtains.

"Darling!" he exclaimed. "There's a fire. Look! Oh, god, I think it's up at Edenhope. I knew I smelt something. I bet it's the straw in that barn."

I was out of bed, scrambling into some clothes, as he dashed downstairs to the phone. He put the receiver down as I reached him.

"They knew about it. The firemen are on their way. Your neighbour called them. But darling it's not the barn! It's the house. The big house!"

He dressed, hastily. "I'm going up there. I think you'd better stay here in case Mother wakes up."

I was about to agree when the door opened and Rachael appeared, in her nightdress.

"Edenhope's on fire," she said. "I can see it. I'm going to get the fire engine."

We told her it had already been done and that Stephen was going there.

"Don't you want to go?" she asked. "It's awfully close to your house."

"Will you be alright?" I asked.

"Of course I will. Ring me and let me know what's happening."

Ten minutes later we neared the first of the six former cottages and stopped behind a police car, almost awestruck by the sight of the conflagration. Flames were leaping above Edenhope House, to more than the building's own height, and sparks were being carried by a strongish breeze towards the gardens opposite. A policeman stopped us.

"You'll have to go back," he said. We explained that our house was at the other end of the six.

"You oughtn't to go," he said. "All this stuff that's coming over is dangerous. They're concentrating on protecting the houses, and the farm buildings. The house itself is too far gone. Thank God there wasn't anyone living there."

Stephen said: "Yes. Thank God." He retreated down the road and called his mother on his mobile. When he came back, I asked him: "Is she alright? Is she upset?"

He did not answer for a few moments. Then he asked: "What do you think she said when I told her it looked as though the house would be destroyed?"

She said: "'And a damn good riddance. P'raps Edenhope can be a happy place now.'"

§

Everything was alright at Eden Cottage, and the other five houses. The firemen had kept them well soaked, and the wind had taken the heat and sparks away from the farm buildings and Mr Lummas's hay and straw in the dutch barn.

In consultation with Rachael, we decided to stay with her until Elspeth and Lance returned when, as had always been the plan, we would be married. In the meantime we tried to decide on permanent plans for ourselves. There was a case to be made for living at Alderley, so Stephen would be near Techmaster. But he had other ideas. He thought he should retire as chairman and hand over to Brian Forster and the new chief executive. And, somewhat to my surprise, he wanted to live in Shropshire again. He was not a native, and had spent most of his life elsewhere, but recently our county had encased him, as it has so many others, in such a feeling of belonging that it was where he felt truly at home. Even more surprisingly, to me, who had yet hardly begun to realise the full horror of those events half a century ago, he started to talk about possibly living permanently at my house. The accepted wisdom about second marriages is that they should locate themselves in a residence new to both partners. Would not the shades of my first marriage lurk behind the walls to threaten our future, I asked him. "I could ask you the same," he said. "And remember, I lived here as well, for a time." And when I asked whether the ghosts of those awful events would not haunt him, so close was their scene, he said: "Not now, I think." I believe he meant because of the fire. In the end we decided to give it a try. We could always move if we wanted to. But we found we never did.

Elspeth and Lance always meant to live at Withymoor Cottage. He was the most unassertive of husbands and sons-in-law, and was supremely happy to share a home with Rachael, who seemed to have developed a new lease of life, and as long as it lasted seemed to glow in the light of the love that enveloped the two. Being near to them was one factor in Stephen's wish to stay at Edenhope. And oh, the happy times we had in both houses, entertaining each other in turn. Discussing literature and music from the Bible to Terry Pratchett, Vivaldi to the Rolling Stones (although only Lance wanted to dwell long on them), persuading Elspeth to read some of her own verse, playing hilarious games of Scrabble. And outside, walking until we knew almost every yard of footpath in a dozen parishes, and beyond.

One downside of living at Edenhope was the state of the big house, or rather, its site, left by the fire. Most of the exterior walls were standing, more or less intact up to roof level, the windows glaring out like ghastly eye sockets. The interior walls, most of which were lath and plaster, and the roof, had gone, apart from one or two charred timbers, leaving a mass of slate on the ground.

After we were married, we decided one or two additions were needed at our house, and we put them in train. Stephen and I did most of the work ourselves, bringing in specialist tradesmen where necessary. It took about a year, and we were coming to the end when Stephen said, one day, that "something ought to be done about that lot over the road. It can't stay like that for ever." Through his mother, he got in touch with the Unston daughters, Ursula and Deborah, who were selling or had sold the estate. They had never been interested in living in Shropshire, and had not been as close to their mother as they should have been, bearing in mind what she had gone through in bringing them into the world. But whether through the pricking of daughterly consciences or because it was the easiest thing to do, they agreed to sell us the house and what had been the gardens at not much more than the sale equivalent of a peppercorn rent.

Turning the site into a two-acre garden became our work, hobby, obsession. We used the stone from the house to build a high wall at its back, constructed by Stephen with me as his labourer, to shield it from the less than beautiful farm buildings. Lance and Elspeth came occasionally to lend such hands as their academic natures allowed; Ben, Ollie, Edward, Esme and their families likewise, to a modest degree; and even Rachael, with the Land Rover she still insisted on using, was enlisted as a "gofer" when we ran into a shortage of urgently-needed sand and cement. She is still there, my mother-in-law, through the roses nurtured by her ashes, and in the middle of them a tablet to her memory. Another is beside it, bearing the name of Griselda Unston, the widow of the vile man she killed, but who became her dearest friend.

Rachael, days before she died, dictated the words she wanted on the plaque. "In memory of Griselda Unston, a dear friend and patron. Widow of Jasper and mother of Ursula and Deborah."

Stephen asked her: "Are you sure you want... that name... on it, Mum?"

"Quite sure," she said. "You can change the order if you want to, and add the dates, but keep those words. Please."

She died, at the age of 96, after we four had been married for five years. She never developed dementia; her brain was as lively in the last months of her life as it had ever been, until the pain-killing drugs of her final weeks took their inevitable toll. She was a wonderful lady. She never again spoke to me of the events of that terrible weekend at Edenhope, but there was not much else I did not learn about her. How she was orphaned at twelve years old, brought up in a charitable home, worked as a servant, met and married Stephen's father and helped him through a period of economic disaster and poverty to become the much respected manager of the Edenhope and Withymoor farms. Stories of her dear friends, Mrs Unston, Miss Johnstone and Aunt Ida. And even from her years in prison; how she tried to still be a loving wife and mother; of other inmates, and even the officers.

I have not quite made up my mind what should be done with that garden, when I go. Stephen and I always told the neighbours to look on it as theirs as well as ours, and some of them have. They put more seats there, and often joined us on fine afternoons. Our families tell me I must do whatever I like with it. Stephen's memorial plaque is already there and I'd like my name to be added, and my ashes added to his. As long as that can be done I don't mind who owns it. I hope it will be looked after, though.

§

Fire officers and police were in no doubt, they told us and said publicly, that the blaze which destroyed Edenhope House had been started deliberately. There had been several points of initial ignition which left no doubt about that, or that the intention was to cause maximum damage. But they never found anyone on whom they could lay the charge of arson. The names of one or two individuals thought to have a grudge against the Unston family were muttered, in various places where such hints are traded, but Stephen did not think any of them held water. And the consensus seemed to be that it didn't matter, anyway. The fire had caused no great loss. Nobody wanted to live there, did they, and then there had been what happened there just after the war.

But now I am going to say something that I have never said or written before, even to Stephen. I could not allow his mind, or the mind of Rachael, or Lance, to be disturbed by the thoughts I have had. Now they, and Elspeth, are all gone, and I have been asked to write this footnote to the often dreary story of that house, I do not feel I can keep it to myself.

Was that fire started by Elspeth, as a way of finally ridding herself of the ghastly incubus that had blighted her life since that Saturday in 1946? That's as far as I can go. I don't mean I positively believe she did it. But I can't be sure she did not. Rachael thought she had the key that had gone missing. And I had seen her actually go into the house, on one occasion, and apparently come from it on another, two days before the fire. Slender evidence on which to base an accusation of arson. I am not doing that, anyway.

So what am I doing? Is that house, that home of so much wrong, even evil, where not a single person, as far as I can see, was allowed to experience happiness of any lasting kind, extending its influence on me, from beyond the grave, as it were? Is it saying, spitefully: "There is a price to pay for thinking you can get rid of me by setting fire to me, or trying to make something beautiful out of me. I will haunt you, put wicked thoughts into your mind."

I almost hear it. But I say: "Rubbish, house. You have already been beaten. You've gone. And since you've gone, and before when no-one wanted to know you, the people you tried to make miserable have known joy such as you and the likes of Jasper Unston could never fathom.

"I don't care whether Elspeth set a torch to you or not. Whoever it was did us all a service. Your walls have hidden their last evil. Rest in peace, Edenhope."

also by

Francis John Simcock

The Lyndford Trilogy:

- Lyndford -

- Angie and Debra -

- December Song -